D0594109

	DATE DUE	

SMITH COLLEGE STORIES

A door opened and in a dead hush the sophomore team trotted
in, two and two, the Suttons leading, bouncing
the big ball before them

SMITH COLLEGE STORIES

TEN STORIES

By
JOSEPHINE DODGE (DASKAM) BACON

ILLUSTRATED

Short Story Index Reprint Series

 BOOKS FOR LIBRARIES PRESS
FREEPORT, NEW YORK

First Published 1900
Reprinted 1969

STANDARD BOOK NUMBER:
8369-3079-7

LIBRARY OF CONGRESS CATALOG CARD NUMBER:
70-94701

*To my Mother, who sent me to college,
I offer these impressions of it.*

J. D. D.

PREFACE

IF these simple tales serve to deepen in the slightest degree the rapidly growing conviction that the college girl is very much like any other girl—that this likeness is, indeed, one of her most striking characteristics—the author will consider their existence abundantly justified.

J. D. D.

CONTENTS

ILLUSTRATIONS

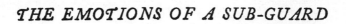

THE EMOTIONS OF A SUB-GUARD

I

THE EMOTIONS OF A SUB-GUARD

THEODORA pushed through the yellow and purple crowd, a sea of flags and ribbons and great paper flowers, caught a glimpse of the red and green river that flowed steadily in at the other door, and felt her heart contract. What a lot of girls! And the freshmen were always beaten—

"Excuse me, but I *can't* move! You'll have to wait," said some one. Theodora realized that she was crowding, and apologized. A tall girl with a purple stick moved by the great line that stretched from the gymnasium to the middle of the campus, and looked keenly at Theodora. "How did you get here?" she asked. "You must go to the end—we're not letting any one slip in at the front. The jam is bad enough as it is."

Theodora blushed. "I'm—I'm on the Sub-team," she murmured, "and I'm late. I—"

"Oh!" said the junior. "Why did you come in here? You go in the other door. Just pass right in here, though," and Theodora, quite crimson with the consciousness of a hundred eyes, pulled her mackintosh about her and slipped in ahead of them all.

Oh, *here's* to Ninety-*yellow*,
And her *praise* we'll ever *tell*—*oh*,
Drink her *down*, drink her *down*, drink her *down*,
down, down!

the line called after her, and her mouth trembled with excitement. She could just hear the other line:

Oh, *here's* to Ninety-*green*,
She's the *finest* ever *seen!*

and then the door slammed and she was upstairs on the big empty floor. A member of the decorating committee nodded at her from the gallery. "Pretty, isn't it?" she called down.

"Beautiful!" said Theodora, earnestly. One half of the gallery—her half—was all trimmed with yellow and purple. Great yellow chrysanthemums flowered on every pillar, and enormous purple shields with yellow numerals lined the wall. Crossed banners and flags filled in the intervals, and from the middle beam depended a great purple butterfly with yellow wings, flapping defiance at a red and green insect of indistinguishable species that decorated the other side. A bevy of ushers in white duck, with *boutonnières* of English violets or single American beauties, took their places and began to pin on crêpe paper sun-

[2]

bonnets of yellow or green, chattering and watching the clock. A tall senior, with a red silk waist and a green scarf across her breast, was arranging a box near the centre of the sophomore side and practising maintaining her balance on it while she waved a red baton. She was the leader of the Glee Club, and she would lead the sophomore songs. Theodora heard a confused scuffle on the stairs, and in a few seconds the galleries were crowded with the rivers of color that poured from the entrance doors. It seemed that they were full now, but she knew that twice as many more would crowd in. She walked quickly to the room at the end of the hall and opened the door. Beneath and all around her was the hum and rumble of countless feet and voices, but in the room all was still. The Subs lounged in the window-seats and tried to act as if it was n't likely to be any affair of theirs: one little yellow-haired girl confided flippantly to her neighbor that she 'd "only accepted the position so as to be able to sit on the platform and be sure of a good place." The Team were sitting on the floor staring at their captain, who was talking earnestly in a low voice— giving directions apparently. The juniors who coached them opened the door and grinned cheerfully. They attached great purple streamers to their shirt-waists, and addressed themselves to the freshmen generally.

"Your songs are great! That 'Alabama Coon' one was awfully good! You make twice the noise that they do!"

The Team brightened up. "I think they're pretty good," the captain said, with an attempt at a conversational tone. "Er—when do we begin?"

"The Subs can go out now," said one of the coaches, opening the door importantly. "Now, girls, remember not to wear yourselves out with kicking and screaming. You're right under the President, and he'll have a fit if you kick against the platform. Miss Kassan says that this *must* be a quiet game! She *will not* have that howling! It's her particular request, she says. Now, go on. And if anything happens to Grace, Julia Wilson takes her place, *and look out for Alison Greer*—she pounds awfully. Keep as still as you can!"

They trotted out and ranged themselves on the platform, and when Theodora got to the point of lifting her eyes from the floor to gaze down at the sophomore Subs across the hall in front of another audience, the freshmen were off in another song. To her excited eyes there were thousands of them, brilliant in purple and yellow, and shouting to be heard of her parents in Pennsylvania. A junior in yellow led them with a great purple stick, and they chanted, to a splendid march tune that made even the members of the Faculty keep time on the platform, their hymn to victory.

Hurrah! hurrah! the yellow is on top!
Hurrah! hurrah! the purple cannot drop!
We are Ninety-yellow and our fame shall never stop,
'Rah, 'rah, 'rah, for the freshmen!

They sang so well and so loud and strong, shouting out the words so plainly and keeping such splendid time, that as the verse and chorus died away audience and sophomores alike clapped them vigorously, much to their delight and pride. Theodora looked up for the first time and saw as in a dream individual faces and clothes. They were packed in the running-gallery till the smallest of babies would have been sorely tried to find a crevice to rest in. A fringe of skirts and boots hung from the edge, where the wearers sat pressed against the bars with their feet hanging over. They blotted out the windows and sat out on the great beams, dangling their banners into space. She could not see the Faculty behind

[5]

her, but she knew they were adorned with rosettes, and that the favored ones carried flowers—the air where she sat was sweet with violets. A group of ushers escorted a small and nervous lady to the platform: on the way she threw back her cape and the sophomores caught sight of the green bow at her throat.

> Oh, *here's* to Susan *Beane*,
> She is *wearing* of the *green*,
> Drink her *down*, drink her *down*, drink her *down*,
> *down, down!*

they sang cheerfully.

Just behind her a tall, commanding woman stalked somewhat consciously, decked with yellow streamers and daffodils. The junior leader consulted a list in her hand, frantically whispered some words to the allies around her box, and the freshmen started up their tribute.

> Oh, *here's* to Kath'rine *Storrs*,
> Aught but *yellow* she *abhors*,
> Drink her *down*, drink her *down*, drink her *down*,
> *down, down!*

Miss Storrs endeavored to convey with her glance, dignity, amusement, toleration of harmless sport, and a repudiation of the personality involved in the song; but it is to be

[6]

doubted if even she was satisfied with the result. Theodora wished she had seen the President come in. She had been told how he walked solemnly across the hall, mounted the platform, unbuttoned his overcoat, and displayed two gorgeous rosettes of the conflicting colors—his official and exclusive privilege. And she had heard from the Team's retreat the thunder of applause that greeted this traditional rite. She wondered whether he cared who won: whether he realized what it was to play against a team that had beaten in its freshman year.

A burst of applause and laughter interrupted her meditations. She felt herself blushing—was it the Team? No: the sophomore Subs were escorting to the middle of the floor a child of five or six dressed in brightest emerald green: a child with a mane of the most remarkable brick-red hair in the world. She wore it in the fashion of Alice in Wonderland, and it grew redder and redder the longer one looked at it. She held a red ribbon of precisely the same shade in her hand, and at the middle of the floor the sophomores suddenly burst away from her and ran quickly to their seats, revealing at the end of the ribbon an enormous and lifelike green frog. The child stood for a moment twisting her little green legs undecidedly, and then, overcome with embarrassment at the appreciation she had evoked, shook her flaming locks over her face, and dragging the frog with her, sometimes on its side, sometimes on its head, fled to the sophomores, who bore her off in triumph.

"They got her in Williamsburgh," said somebody; "they 've been hunting for weeks for a red-haired child, and that frog was from the drug store—oh, my dear, how *perfectly* darling!"

Alone and unabashed the freshman mascot took the floor. He was perhaps four years old and the color of a cake of chocolate. His costume was canary yellow—a perfect little jockey suit, with a purple band on his arm adorned with Ninety-yellow's class numerals. He dragged by a twisted cord of purple and yellow a most startling plum-colored terrier, of a shade that never was on land or sea, with a tendency to trip his master up at every step. In the exact middle of the floor the mascot paused, rolled his eyes till they seemed in danger of leaving their sockets, and then at a shrill whistle from the balcony pulled his yellow cap from his woolly head and made a deep and courtly bow to his patrons. But the storm of applause was more than he had been prepared for, and with a wild look about the hall and a frantic tug at the cord he dragged the purple and protesting animal to a corner of the room, where a grinning elder sister was stationed for his comfort.

Theodora's heart beat high: theirs was the best! Everybody was laughing and exclaiming and questioning; the very sophomores were shrieking at the efforts of the terrier to drag the little darkey out again; one member of the Faculty had laughed himself into something very like hysteria and giggled weakly at every twitch of the idiotic purple legs.

"It was Diamond Dyes," Theodora heard a freshman just above call out excitedly, "and Esther Armstrong thought of it. They dyed him every day for a week—"

The mascot and the dog had trotted up again, and as they ran back and the animal gave a more than ordinarily vicious dart, the poor little boy, yielding suddenly, sat down with exquisite precision on his companion, and with distended eyes wailed aloud for his relative, who disentangled him with difficulty and bore him away, his cap over his ear and his little chocolate hands clutching her neck. In

the comparative silence that followed the gale
of laughter some bustle and conference was
noticed on the sophomore side, and suddenly
the leader rose, lifting her green and red stick,
and the front line of sophomores and seniors
intoned with great distinctness this thrilling
doggerel:

> I never saw a purple pup:
> I never hoped to see one:
> But now my mind is quite made up—
> I'd rather see than be one!

This was received favorably, and the gallery congratulated the *improvisatrice*, while
Theodora wondered if that detracted at all
from the glory of the freshmen! The chattering began again, and she drummed nervously with her heels against the platform,
while the Centre, sitting next her, prophesied
gloomily that Grace Farwell felt awfully blue,
and that Miss Kassan had said they were
really almost too slight as a team—the sophomores were so tall and big. Harriet Foster
had said that she was perfectly certain she'd
sprain her ankle—then who would guard
Martha Sutton? It was all very well for Caroline Wilde to say not to worry about that—
she had n't been able to guard her last year!

She was just like a machine. Her arm went up and the ball went in; that was all there was to it. And Kate was as bad. They might just as well make up their minds—

"Oh, hush!" cried Theodora, her eyes full of nervous tears; "if you can't talk any other way, just keep still!"

"Very well," said the Centre, huffily, and then the chattering died away as Miss Kassan made mysterious marks on the floor, and the coaches took their places with halves of lemon and glasses of water in their hands. A door opened, and in a dead hush the sophomore team trotted in, two and two, the Suttons leading, bouncing the big ball before them. There was such a silence that the thudding feet seemed to echo and ring through the hall, and only when Martha suddenly tossed it behind her at nothing and Kate from some corner walked over and caught it did the red and green burst forth in a long-drawn single shout:
"Ninety-gre-e-e-e-e-n!"

Miss Kassan looked apprehensive, but no *'Rah, 'rah, 'rah!* followed; only,—

Here's to *Sutton M.* and *K.*
And they'll *surely* win the *day,*
Drink 'em *down,* drink 'em *down,* drink 'em *down,*
down, down!

[11]

Theodora set her teeth. "Humph! Will they?" she muttered savagely.

"Here they come!" cried the Centre, and they ran in, the big yellow numerals gleaming effectively against their dark suits, their braids bobbing behind them. Grace Farwell was quite pale, with one little spot of red in each cheek, but Harriet Foster was crimson with excitement, and the thick braids of auburn hair that fell over her breast bumped up and down as she breathed. The thunder of recognition died away, and they tossed the ball about nervously, with an eye on Miss Kassan, who handed a ball to her assistant and took her place on the line to watch fouls.

"All ready!" said the assistant. There was a shuffling about, a confusion in the centre, a concentration of eyes. Harriet Foster took her place by Martha Sutton and sucked in her under lip; Grace lined up with Kate in the centre, clasping and unclasping her hands. Near her stood a tall slim girl with green numerals on her sleeve. Her soft dark hair was coiled lightly into a Greek knot—it seemed that the slightest hasty movement must shake it over her sloping shoulders. It grew into a clean-cut widow's peak low on her smooth white forehead; below straight, fine brows two great, sad, gray eyes, wide apart, wondered at life; her oval face was absolutely colorless and threw out the little scarlet mouth that drooped softly at the corners. Her hands lightly folded before her, she swayed a little and looked dreamily over the heads of the others; she seemed as incongruous as a Madonna at a bull-fight.

"Who is that lovely girl in the middle?" said some one behind Theodora.

"That is a Miss Greer," was the reply. "She is one of the best—"

"Play!" called the assistant, and the big ball flew out of her hands into Kate Sutton's. Kate gave an indescribable twist of her shoulder, the ball rose in the air, passed over an utterly irrelevant scuffle in the centre, and landed in Martha's hands. Martha balanced it a moment and threw it into the exact middle of the basket, while the sophomores howled and pounded and the freshmen looked blankly at one another. They had not been accustomed to such simple and efficacious methods.

"One to nothing!" said the assistant, quietly. "Play!"

Theodora caught her breath. She dared not look at Grace, but she stared hard at Harriet. What was Harriet thinking? Not that she could have done anything—Martha was two inches taller and had the ball tight in her hands two seconds after the assistant had tossed it— Ah, what was that?

The ball had reached the floor and Grace had somehow gotten it. She threw it to Virginia Wheeler, whose hands were just grazing it when something shot like a flash of lightning upon her. She fell back and some one slapped the ball from between her very finger-nails up, up into the air, where Kate caught it, and a few short, sharp, instantaneous passes got it into Martha's relentless hands. When it dropped into the basket Alison Greer was looking beyond the tumult, across the gallery, into the sky—white and unruffled. Theodora winked and tried to think that some one else had swooped down from her place six seconds before.

The sophomores were shouting yet. Some one said: "That's as pretty a piece of team work as you'll often see, is n't it? Those twins have eyes in the backs of their heads."

"Two to nothing—play!" said the assistant.

Theodora did not see the next goal won. Through a mist she stared into the gallery. Her eye caught a face she knew, and she wondered angrily how Miss Carew could smile so nonchalantly—it was her own class! From the plume in her exquisite toque to the tip of her patent leather toe she looked the visiting lady of leisure. The little lace handkerchief dangling from her hand had a green silk monogram in the corner—how dared she wear green? She nodded at a senior, across the game, and fanned herself. The freshmen broke into a roar of delight that ended in a long-drawn *A-a-a-a-h!* There was a scuffle, a little cry, a flash from Alison Greer's corner, and the assistant's "Three to nothing—play!" was drowned in the sophomore shouts.

"You see the freshmen have no chance, really," said some one behind, calmly, and as if it made little matter at best. "They are terribly scared, of course, and they 've never had the training of a big game. The sophomores have been all through this before—they don't mind the crowd. And then, they beat last year, and that gives them a tremendous confidence. They 're so much bigger, too—"

Theodora turned and stared at her. She was very pretty; she had a bunch of violets as big as her head pinned to her dress, and her hands were full of daffodils. That was like the Faculty! To take their flowers and talk that way! "Horrid thing! *Horrid* thing!" she muttered, and the Centre, looking angrily at Miss Greer, assented.

"She's a perfect tiger! Look at her eyes! She knocked Virginia right over — you could n't stop her with a steam-engine — Oh! Oh! *Oh! Ninety-yellow! Rah, rah-a-a-a-ah!*"

Right out of their hands it had slipped, and the two girls slid across the floor, fell, reached out, missed it, and gritted their teeth as the Centres, with a long-practised manœuvre, passed it rapidly from hand to hand to Martha, whose long arm slid it imperturbably into the basket.

"That Guard does n't accomplish much," said somebody.

"Good heavens, how can she? Look at the girl! She lays it in like — like that," was the answer, as the assistant called, "Five to nothing — play!"

Theodora looked up at the purple and yellow gallery. The freshmen stared as if hypnotized at their steady misfortune, their faces flushed, their mouths tremulous: when the players ran to suck the half-lemon or kneeled to tighten their shoes, their class-mates held breath till they returned; when Grace got the ball or Virginia pushed it aside, they started a cheer that faded into a sigh as Alison Greer drove everything before her or Kate sent that

[16]

terrible Sutton throw to her sister. Theodora suddenly started. Just before the ball left Kate, she threw up her left hand with the palm slightly spread, and some instinct moved Theodora to glance at Martha. Her left hand went up instantly as if to throw back a braid, but it waved toward the right, and while Harriet braced herself for a jump the ball flew into the air far off to the right and the instinctive motion toward Martha left the way clear for one of Alison Greer's rushes and sudden, bird-like throws. In a moment Martha had it, and as Harriet bent forward to guard, and the ball toppled unsteadily on the edge of the basket and fell off, in the midst of the hubbub and scuffle some one pushed heavily on Harriet, four hands grasped the ball firmly, somebody called, "Foul, foul!" and as five panting girls hurled themselves against the wall and the assistant tossed up where it fell, to make sure of fair play, Harriet dropped with her foot beneath her and did not get up. Martha put the ball in from an amazing distance, and in the storm of applause no one noticed the freshman Guard, till the cry of, "Six to nothing—play!" found her still sitting there.

The ball was dropped, and they ran up to her. Two doctors hurried out; she half rose, fell back and bit her lip. The freshmen craned out over the gallery, the sophomores shook their heads; "Too bad, too bad!" they murmured. Two freshmen made a chair, lifted Harriet quickly and ran out with her, the doctors followed, and in the dead hush they heard her voice as the door closed.

"I'm so sorry, girls—go right on—don't wait—"

"Plucky girl," said a man's voice. "It's a shame!"

The freshmen looked very blue; the team stood about in groups; the sophomores waited politely at one side. Martha went over to Grace and held her hand out: "I'm terribly sorry," she said earnestly, "it's too bad. They say your Subs are very good, though."

Grace nodded, and ran over to the coaches, who walked aside with her for a moment, talking earnestly. Presently they came over to the platform and the Centre nudged Theodora enviously. "Go on!" she whispered. "Grace wants you!"

Theodora gasped. "Not me—not me!" she objected feebly. "Me—guard—Martha Sutton!"

"Go on!" said somebody, and they pushed her out.

EMOTIONS OF A SUB-GUARD

"Come on, Theodora—hurry up, now!"

The people seemed to swim before her; for one dreadful moment she longed for her home as she had never longed before. Her knees shook and the clapping of the class sounded far away. With her eyes on the floor she moved out; halfway to the centre Virginia Wheeler stepped to meet her and put her arm over Theodora's shoulder.

"Don't be scared, Theo," she said, "don't be scared, but help us out—heaven knows we need it!"

"Watch Martha—don't take your eyes off her!" whispered the coach as she handed the lemon to the new Guard.

As in a dream Theodora passed to the lower basket. Martha patted her on the shoulder. "Hello!" she said in a bluff, friendly way, and then the assistant called, "Six to nothing, play!" and threw the ball. It dropped in the middle, and there was a terrible scrimmage for at least four minutes, while the people swayed and sighed and clapped and screamed, for the freshmen were getting terribly excited and rapidly losing their self-control, as it became evident that their team was struggling desperately and making one of the longest fights on record for the ball they were determined to have. It was almost in the basket, it tottered on the edge, it fell, and Kate Sutton caught it—how, no one knew, for it was nowhere near her. The freshmen were shrieking with rage, the sophomores clapping with triumph. Every eye in the hall was fixed on Kate Sutton—every eye but Theodora's.

She watched Martha, and saw above her head that long brown hand wave ever so slightly to the left as she tossed her hair back. She braced herself, and just as Martha made a dash to the right, Theodora let her go and flew to the left. She went too far, but even as Martha dashed up behind her and put up her hands, Theodora jumped, caught the ball with her left hand and with her right hit it a ringing blow that sent it straight over to the other basket. It hit Alison Greer's head as she rushed toward it, and while she was raising her hand Grace Farwell snatched it from her shoulder, glanced desperately at the Home, who had lost them two balls, and bounded across, throwing the ball before her. The roar of delight from the freshmen was literally deafening, and as Grace put it into the basket it seemed to Theodora that the roof would surely drop.

"Six to one and the first half's up," said somebody, and Theodora was pushed along with the Team—*her* team—into the sanctum of their rest. But as they neared the door, the applause became a song, and before she quite understood what the verse was, it rang out above her head:

> Here's to *Theodora Root*,
> She's our *dandy* substi*toot*,
> Drink her *down*, drink her *down*, drink her *down*,
> *down*, *down!*

Any one who has never been a subject of song to some hundreds of young women cannot perhaps understand why the mention of one's name in flattering doggerel should be so distinctly and immediately affecting. But any one who has had that experience knows the little contraction of the heart, the sudden hot tightening of the eyelids, the confused, excited desire to be worthy of all that trust and admiration. It is to be doubted if Theodora ever again felt so ideally, impersonally devoted to any cause, so pathetically eager to "make them proud of her."

In the little room the Team dropped on the floor and panted. The coaches bustled in with water, shook the hand of the new Guard and told her to lie flat and not talk. A strong odor of spirits filled the room, and Theodora, turning her head languidly—for she felt very tired all at once—saw that one of the juniors was rubbing somebody with whiskey. Grace was nursing an elbow and excitedly asking everybody to sit on Alison Greer: "She works her elbow right *into* you! She runs you right down—"

"There, there!" said one of the juniors, "never mind, never mind, Gracie! She's a slugger, if you like, but you've got to beat her! Don't be afraid of her."

"It's no good," said the Home that had missed two balls, "we're too—"

"That's enough of that," interrupted the coach who was fanning Virginia Wheeler. "You're playing finely, girls. Now all you've got to do is to make up your five goals. Don't you see how low you've kept it down? You did some fine centre work. Last year it was eight to something the first half. You tried to put it in standing right under the basket, Mary—stand off and take your time."

They trotted out to the music of the sophomore prize song. It was a legacy from the seniors, who had themselves inherited it. It leaped out at them—a mocking, dancing, derisive little tune to which everybody kept time.

It was repeated indefinitely, and at every

repetition it went faster and more furious, and strangers who had not heard it laughed louder and louder.

Grace smiled grimly. The Team remembered her words just before the door opened.

" Girls, it is n't likely that we 'll win, *but we can give 'em something to beat!* "

And as the ball went back and forth and could not get free of the centre, the sophomores realized that they had "something to beat." The freshmen had somehow lost their fear; they smiled up at their friends and grinned cheerfully at their losses, which is far better than to try to look unconscious. A little bow-legged girl with a large nose and red knuckles accomplished wonders in the centre, and won them their second basket by stooping abruptly and rolling the ball straight between Kate Sutton's feet to Grace, who sat upon it and threw it so hard at Alison Greer that it bounded out of her hands and was promptly caught by Virginia Wheeler and put into the basket. This feat of Grace's was due entirely to her having quite lost her head, but it passed as the most daring of manœuvres, and received such wild applause that Miss Kassan very nearly stopped the game.

" What *shall* I do ? This is terrible. I never

heard such noise as the freshmen are making!"
she mourned, with an apprehensive glance at
the platform. At that moment the ball soared
high, fell, was sent up again, and caught by a
phenomenal leap on the part of the little bow-
legged girl, who got it into the basket before
the Home knew what was happening. The
war broke out again, and Miss Kassan beheld
two members of the Faculty pounding with
their canes on the platform.

"Did you see her jump? George! That was
a good one! Did you see that, Robbins?"

But Robbins was standing up in his interest
and cheering under his breath as Martha Sutton snatched a ball clearly intended for some
one else, quietly put it in the basket, and smiled
politely at her enthusiastic friends.

"Lord! What a Fullback she'd make!" he
muttered, as Alison charged down into the
centre. The lavender shadows under her eyes
were deep violet now; her mouth was pressed
to a scarlet line; her eyes were fixed on the
ball like gray stars. People seemed to melt
away before her: she never turned to right or
left.

Theodora saw nothing, heard nothing but
the slap of hands on the ball, the quick breaths
that slipped past her cheek. She knew that the

[24]

score was nine to five now; a little later it was nine to six. She caught the eye of the girl in the toque: she was standing now, her cheeks very red, and the little lace handkerchief was torn to shreds in her hands.

"Does she really care?" thought Theodora, as she jumped and twisted and doubled. Back on the senior side sat Susan Jackson, her eyes wide, her lips parted; Cornelia Burt was breathing on her hands and chafing them softly. "Nine to seven—play!" called the assistant.

Harriet sat near the fireplace, her bandaged foot on a bench before her, her hands twisting and untwisting in her lap.

> *Here's* to Harriet *Foster*,
>   And we're *sorry* that we *lost* her,
> Drink her *down*, drink her *down*, drink her *down*,
>   *down, down!*

sang the freshmen. Would Harriet have done better? Would she have—Ah!

"Ten to seven—play!"

And they were so near, too! They *were* playing well—Grace and Virginia were great —they could have done something if that stupid Home—Oh!

Theodora leaped, missed the ball, but

danced up in front of Martha and warded off
the girl who slipped in to help her. Martha
uttered an impatient exclamation and scowled.
The freshmen howled and kicked against the
gallery, and as the freshman Home woke out
of an apparent lethargy and put the ball in
neatly Theodora clapped and cheered with
the rest.

"Ten to eight—play!"

There was a scuffle, a fall, and a hot discussion. Two girls grasped the ball, and the
captains hesitated. Miss Kassan ran up, and
in the little lull Theodora heard from the
platform:

"Oh, give it to the freshmen! They deserve it!"

"No, Miss Greer had it!"

"She knocked the girl off it, if that's
what—" A rebellious howl from the yellow
gallery as Miss Greer bore off the ball, and
a man's voice:

"Oh, nonsense! If you don't want 'em to
howl, don't let 'em play! The idea—to get
'em all worked up and then say: 'No, young
ladies, control yourselves!' How idiotic! I
don't blame 'em—I'd howl myself—Jiminy
crickets! *Look* at that girl! Good work! *Good
work!*"

EMOTIONS OF A SUB-GUARD

"Eleven to eight—play!"

"Good old Suttie! Good girl! Ninety-gre-e-e-en!"

Theodora's mouth was dry, and she ran to the coach for a lemon. The junior's hand shook, and her voice was husky from shouting.

"It's grand—it's grand!" she said quickly. "Martha's mad as a hatter! See her braid!"

Martha had twisted her pale brown pigtail tightly round her neck, and was calling with little indistinct noises to her sister. Adah Levy was talking to herself steadily and whispering, "*Hurry now, hurry now, hurry now!*" as she doubled and bent and worried the freshman Home out of her senses. Grace Farwell was everywhere at once, and was still only when she fell backwards with a bang that sickened the visiting mothers, and brought the freshmen's hearts into their mouths. A great gasp travelled up the gallery, and the doctor left her seat, but before she reached the players Grace was up, tossed her head, blinked rapidly, and with an unsteady little smile took her place by Alison Greer. And then the applause that had gone before was mild in comparison with the thunder from both galleries, and Miss Kassan looked at her watch uneasily and moved forward.

Now everybody was standing up, and the men were pushing forward, and only the gasps and bursts of applause and little cries of disappointment disturbed the stillness — the steady roar had stopped.

Theodora knew nothing, saw nothing: she only played. Her back ached, and her throat was dry; Martha's elbow moved like the piston of a steam-engine; her arm, when Theodora pressed against it, was like a stiff bar; she towered above her Guard. It was only a question of a few, few minutes—*could* they make it "eleven to nine"?

She must have asked the question, for Martha gasped, "No, you won't!" at her, and her heart sank as Miss Kassan moved closer. The ball neared their basket; the little bow-legged girl ducked under Alison's nose and emerged with it from a chaos of swaying Centres, tossed it to Grace, who dashed to the basket—

"*Time's up!*"

The freshmen shrieked, the Team yelled to its captain: "Put it in! put it in!" The sophomore Guards had not heard Miss Kassan, and Grace poised the ball. A yell from the freshmen—and she deliberately dropped it.

EMOTIONS OF A SUB–GUARD

"Time's up," she said, with a little break in her voice, and as Miss Kassan hurried forward to stop the play she gave her the ball. Through the tumult a bass voice was heard: "I say, you know, that was pretty decent! I'm not sure I'd have done that myself!"

And as the assistant and Miss Kassan retired to compare fouls, and the noise grew louder and louder, the freshman team, withdrawn near the platform, heard a young professor, not so many years distant from his own alma mater, enthusiastically assuring any one who cared to hear, that "That girl was a dead game sport, now!"

For a moment the feeling against Grace had been bitter—the basket was so near! But as the sophomores were openly commending her, and as Miss Kassan was heard to say that the Team had played in splendid form and had given a fine example of "the self-control that the game was supposed to teach," they thought better of their captain with every minute.

"Eleven to eight, in favor of Ninety-green —fouls even!" said Miss Kassan, and the storm broke from the gallery. But before it reached the floor, almost, Martha was energetically beating time, and above the miscel-

laneous babble rose the strong, steady cheer
of the sophomores:

'Rah, 'rah, 'rah!
'Rah, 'rah, 'rah!
'Rah, 'rah, 'rah!—Ninety-ye-e-e-e-llow!

"Quick, girls! quick!" cried Grace, for
Miss Kassan was running toward them with
determination in her eye.

'Rah, 'rah, 'rah!
'Rah, 'rah, 'rah!
'Rah, 'rah, 'rah!—Ninety-gre-e-e-e-n!

Then it was all a wild, confused tumult.
Theodora had no distinct impressions; people kissed her and shook her hand, and Kathie
Sewall carried Grace off to a swarm of girls
who devoured her, but not before Martha,
breathless from a rapid ride around the floor
on the unsteady shoulders of her loyal team,
had solemnly extended her hot brown hand
to the freshman captain and said, with sin-
cere respect, "That was as good a freshman
game as ever was played, Miss Farwell—
we're mighty proud of ourselves! Your centre work was simply great! And—and of
course we know that that last goal was—was
practically yours!"

Theodora had expected to feel so ashamed

and sad—and somehow she was so proud and happy ! The sophomores last year had locked themselves in for one hour and—expressed their feelings; but the freshmen could only realize that theirs was the closest score known for years, and that they had made it against the best team the college had ever seen; that Martha had said that in fifteen minutes more, at the rate they were playing, nobody knew what might have happened; that Miss Kassan had said that except in the matter of noise she had been very proud of them; and that Professor Robbins had called their captain a Dead Game Sport !

It would not have been etiquette to carry Grace about the hall, but they managed to convey to her their feelings, which were far from perfunctory, and in their enthusiasm they went so far as to obey the Council's earnest request that the decorations should remain untouched. They cheered Theodora and Virginia and Harriet and the bow-legged girl till you would have supposed them victorious; and when Harriet told Grace, with a little gulp, that it was all up with her, for her mother had said that a second sprained ankle meant no more basket-ball, the little sympathetic crowd brightened, and all eyes turned to Theodora, who breathed hard and tried to seem not to notice. Could it be? Would she ever run out bouncing the ball in that waiting hush? . . .

They were out of the Gym now, and only the ushers' bonnets, the green and yellow flowers that the Council had *not* controlled, the crumpled, printed sheets of basket-ball songs, and the little mascots posing for their pictures on the campus made the day different from any other.

"Come and lie down," said somebody, regarding Theodora with a marked respect. "You'll want to get rested before the dinner, you know."

And as Theodora stared at her and half turned to run after Grace, whom Kathie Sewall was quietly leading off, the girl—she was in the house with her—held her back.

"I'd let Grace alone, if I were you," she said. "She's pretty well used up; she hurt her elbow quite badly, but she wouldn't say anything, and Dr. Leach says she'll have to keep perfectly quiet if she wants to be at the dinner—wants to! the idea! But she said *of course* you were to come. They say they're going to take some of the Gym decorations down.—What! Why, the idea! *Of course* you 'll go ! You 're sure to make the Team, anyhow, for that matter ! I tell you, Theodora, we 're proud of you ! It was n't any joke to step in there and guard Martha Sutton with a score of six to nothing !"

Theodora paused at the steps, her mackintosh half off, her hair tangled about her crimson cheeks, her sleeve dusty from that last mad slide.

"No," she said, with a wave of reminiscence of that sick shaking of her knees, that shrinking from a million critical eyes. "No, it was n't any joke—not in the least !"

And she climbed up the stairs to a burst of applause from the freshmen in the house and the shrill cry of her room-mate:

"Come on, Theo ! I 've got a bath-tub for you !"

A CASE OF INTERFERENCE

II

A CASE OF INTERFERENCE

"WHAT I want to know," said the chairman of the committee, wearily, "is just this. Are we going to give the *Lady of Lyons*, or are we not? I have a music lesson at four and a tea at five, and while your sprightly and interesting conversation is ever pleasing to me—"

"Oh, Neal, don't! Think of something for us! Don't you want us to give it?"

"I think it's too love-making. And no one up here makes love. The girls will howl at that garden scene. You must get something where they can be funny."

"But, Neal, dear, *you* can make beautiful love!"

"Certainly I can, but I can't make it alone, can I? And Margaret Ellis is a stick—a perfect stick. But then, have it! I see you're bent on it. Only I tell you one thing—it will take more rehearsing than the girls will want to give. And I shan't do one word of it publicly till I think that we have rehearsed enough together. So that's all I've got to say till Wednesday, and I *must* go!"

The door opened—shut; and before the

[37]

committee had time for comment or criticism, their chairman had departed.

"Neal's a trifle cross," suggested Patsy, mildly. "Something's the matter with her," said Julia Leslie. "She got a note from Miss Henderson this afternoon, and I think she's going to see her now. Oh, I have n't the vaguest idea — What? No, I know it's not about her work. Neal's all straight with that department. Well, I think I'll go over to the Gym and hunt out a suit. Who has the key to the property box now?"

The little group dissolved rapidly and No. 18 resumed its wonted quiet. "There's nothing like having a society girl for a room-mate, is there, Patsy?" said the resident Sutton twin, opening the door. She and her sister were distinguishable by their room-mates alone, and they had been separated with a view to preventing embarrassing confusion, as they were incredibly alike. "Could n't I make the Alpha on the strength of having vacated this hearth and home eighteen times by actual count for its old committees?"

"I've put you up five times, Kate, love, but they think your hair's too straight. Could n't you curl it?"

Kate sniffed scornfully. "I've always known

[38]

that the literary societies had some such system of selection," she said to the bureau. "Now, in an idle moment of relaxation, the secret is out ! Patsy, I *scorn* the Alpha, and the Phi Kappa likewise."

"I scorn the Phi Kappa myself, theoretically," said Patsy.

"Do you think they 'll take in that queer junior, you know, that looks so tall till you get close to her, and then it 's the way she walks ?"

"Dear child, your vivid description somehow fails to bring her to my mind."

"Why don't you want her in Alpha ? But be careful you don't wait too long ! You 're both leaving me till late in the year, you know, and then, ten to one, the other one gets me !"

"A little violet beside a mossy stone is a poor comparison, Katharine, but at the moment I think of no other. I am glad you grasp the situation so clearly, though."

"But, truly, I wonder why they don't take that girl—is n't her name Hastings ?—into Phi Kappa ? She writes awfully well, they say, and I guess she recites well enough."

The other Sutton twin sauntered in, and appearing as usual to grasp the entire conversation from the beginning, rolled her sister off the couch, filled her vacant place, and entered the discussion.

"But, my dear child, you know she won't make either society! She's too indifferent— she does n't care enough. And she's off the campus, and she does n't go out anywhere, and she is always alone, and that speaks for itself—"

"Oh, I'm tired of talking about her! Stop it, Kate, and get some crackers, that's a dear! Or I'll get them myself," and Patsy was in the hall.

Kate shook her head wisely at the bureau. "Something's in the air," she said softly. "Patsy is bothered. So is Neal. And there are plenty of crackers on the window-seat!"

Miss Margaret Sewall Pattison sauntered slowly down the stairs. For one whose heart was set on crackers she seemed strangely indifferent to the hungry girls standing about the pantry with fountain pens and lecture books and racquets and hammocks under their arms. She walked by them and out of the door, stood a moment irresolutely on the porch, and then, as she caught sight of Cornelia Burt coming out of the dormitory just beyond, she hurried out to meet her.

"Busy this hour, Neal?" she said.

A CASE OF INTERFERENCE

"No," said Cornelia, briefly. "Where shall we go?"

"We can go to the property box and get some clothes," said Patsy, "and talk it over there."

In the cellar of the gymnasium it was cool and dim. The beams rose high above their heads, and a musty smell of tarlatan and muslin and cheese-cloth filled the air. Patsy sat on an old flower-stand, and pushed Cornelia down on a Greek altar that lay on its side with a faded smilax wreath still clinging to it.

"What did she say to you, Neal?" she asked.

Neal looked at the floor. "She was lovely, but I did n't half appreciate it. I was so bothered and—vexed. Pat, I did n't know the Faculty ever did this sort of thing, did you?"

"I don't believe they often do," said Patsy. "Did she read that thing to you, too?"

"Yes. Patsy, that's a remarkable thing. Do you know, when I went there I thought she was going to call me down for taking off the Faculty in that last Open Alpha. The girls say she hates that sort of thing. You know she always says just what she thinks. And she said, 'I want to read you a little story, Miss Burt, that happened to come into my hands, and that has haunted me since.'"

"How do you suppose *she* got hold of it?" queried Patsy.

"I don't know, I'm sure. I certainly shouldn't pick her out to exhibit *my* themes to!—I never saw them together."

"I think I saw them walking once—well, go on!"

"'For the *Monthly*?' said I.

"'No,' said she. 'I think the author would not consent to its publication.' And then she read it to me. Pat, if that girl has suffered as much as that, I don't see how she stays here."

"She's too proud to do anything else," said Patsy. "Go on."

"Then Miss Henderson said: 'I needn't tell you the value of this thing from a literary point of view, Miss Burt.'

"'No,' said I, 'you needn't.'

"'Very well,' said she; 'then I'll tell you something else. Every word of it is true.'

"'I'm sorry,' said I."

"Oh, Neal! I cried when she read it to me! I blubbered like a baby. And she was so nice about it. But I hated her, almost, for disturbing me so."

"Precisely. So I said: 'And what have you read this to me for, Miss Henderson?' And then she told me that the girl in the story was

A CASE OF INTERFERENCE

Winifred Hastings. She has always lived with older people and been a great pet and sort of prodigy, you know, and was expected to do great things here, and found herself lonely, and was proud and did n't make friends, and got farther away from the college instead of nearer to it, and all that. And I said, 'I suppose she's not the only one, Miss Henderson.' And she looked at me so queerly. 'Mephistopheles said that,' said she."

"Oh! Neal! How could you? I — why are you so cold and—"

"Unsympathetic? I don't know. We all have the defects of our qualities, I suppose. Miss Henderson was quite still for a moment, looking at me. I felt like a fly on a pin. 'Why do you try so hard to be cruel, Miss Burt?' said she, finally. 'I think you have an immense capacity for suffering and for sympathy. Is it because you are afraid to give way to it?' And I said, 'Exactly so, Miss Henderson. I never go to the door when the tramps come.'

"'Neither did I, once,' said she, 'but I found it was a singularly useless plan. You 've got to, some time, Miss Burt.'

"'That 's what I 've always been afraid of, but I 'm putting it off as long as I can,' said I.

"And then she told me that this was the

first time that she had done anything of this kind for a long while. 'I don't believe in helping people to their places, as a rule,' she said. 'They usually get what they deserve, I fancy. But this is a peculiar case. You suppose she is not the only one, Miss Burt? I hope there are very few like her. I have never known of a girl of her ability to lose everything that she has lost. There are girls who are queer and erratic and somewhat solitary and perhaps discontented, but they get into a prominence of their own and you call it a "divine discontent," and make them geniuses, and they get a good deal out of it, after all. There are girls who are queer and quick-tempered, but good students, and devoted to a few warm friends, and their general unpopularity doesn't trouble them particularly. There are the social leaders, who don't particularly suffer if they don't get into a society, who are popular everywhere, and get the good time they came for. But Winifred Hastings has somehow missed all these. She got started wrong, and she's gone from bad to worse. She is not solitary by nature, and yet she is more alone than the girls who like solitude, even. She is not naturally reserved, and yet she is considered more so than almost any girl in college. I believe her to have great executive ability. I consider her one of the distinctly literary girls in her class, —and if there is anything in essentially "bad luck," I do honestly believe that she is the victim of it. Her characteristics are so balanced and opposed to each other that she can't help herself, and she does things that make her seem what she is not. Her real self is in this story. You can see the pathos of that!'"

Neal drew a long breath. "Did she say that to you?" she concluded.

"No, not exactly. She told me that she was speaking to me as one of the social influences of the college. I felt like a cross between Madame de Staël and Ward McAllister, you know. And then she spoke of the power we have, the girls like me, and how a little help —oh, Neal! it *does* mean a good deal, though! I can't make people take this girl up, all alone! The girls are n't—"

"They are! They 're the merest sheep! If you do it, they 'll all follow you. That is, if she 's really worth anything. Of course, they are n't fools."

"She sat on me awfully, though, Neal! I said, 'I suppose you think we ought to have her in Alpha, Miss Henderson.' She gave me a look that simply withered me. 'My dear

Miss Pattison,' said she, in that twenty-mile-away tone, 'I am not in the habit of suggesting candidates for either of the societies: I must have made myself far from clear to you.' And I apologized. But it's what she meant, all the same!"

"Of course it is. Well, I suppose she's right. It isn't everybody would have dared to do that much. I respect her for it myself. You are to launch her socially, I am to—"

"Neal Burt, I think you ought to be ashamed! Didn't Miss Henderson tell you how Winifred Hastings admired you?"

"Yes. She said that I was the only girl in the college whose friendship—Oh, dear! I wish she had gone to Vassar, that girl! Heavens! It's half-past three! I must go this minute. Well, Patsy, we're honored, in a way. I don't think Miss Henderson would talk to every one as she has to us, do you?"

"No," said Patsy, gravely, "I don't. You know, Neal, just as I was going, she said, 'Of course you realize, Miss Pattison, that only you and I and Miss Burt have seen this story?' 'I understand,' said I. 'Perhaps I have done this because I understand Miss Hastings better than she thinks,' she said. 'I—I was a little like her, myself, once, Miss Pattison!'"

A CASE OF INTERFERENCE

"Yes," said Neal, "she told me that."

"I don't see why Miss Henderson doesn't take her up herself, if she understands her so terribly well," scowled Patsy. "She looks just like the kind of girl to be devoted to one person and all that, you know. Miss Henderson could go for walks with her and—"

"Too much sense!" said Neal, briefly. "She wants to get her in with the girls. That sort of thing would kill her with the girls, and she knows it."

"Oh, bother! Look at B. Kitts—she's a great friend of Miss Henderson's, and look at yourself!"

"Not at all," Neal returned decidedly. "Biscuits was in with your set long before she got to know Miss Henderson, and I knew Marion Hunter at home before she came up here. It's all very well to chum with the Faculty if you're in with the girls, too, but otherwise—as my friend Claude says, Nay, nay, Pauline! Besides, Miss Henderson doesn't go in for that sort of thing anyhow—she's too clever."

"Oh, well, I suppose it *is* best for us to do it. I guess she's right enough," said Patsy, rising as she spoke, "and I suppose we can do it as well as anybody, for that matter."

They mounted the stone steps and came out into a light that dazzled them. "There she is!" said Patsy softly, as a tall girl, plainly dressed, walked quickly by them. Her face was strangely set, her mouth almost hard, her eyes looked at them with an expression that would have been defiant but for something that softened them as they met Neal's. She bowed to her, hardly noticing Patsy's "Good afternoon, Miss Hastings!" and hurried off to the back campus. Behind were two freshmen loaded with pillows. "Is n't that Miss Hastings?" said one.

"Yes. She's going to leave college."

"Oh! Well, we can lose her better than some others I could mention," said the prettier and better dressed of the two. Then, catching sight of Patsy and Neal, she stopped and blushed a little. "Did—did you get my note, Miss Burt? Will you come?" she asked prettily. Neal smiled.

"Why, yes, I shall be pleased—at four on Saturday, I think you said?" And then as the two moved on she added, "I heard you say something about Miss Hastings: is it true she's going to leave?"

"Yes," said the other freshman, importantly. "Immediately, she told Mrs. White.

I'm in the house with her. I think she said next week. She's disappointed in college, I guess. Well, I should think she would be. She—"

"I trust the college has given her no reason to be," said Neal, gravely. "I sometimes think her attitude—if that should happen to be her attitude—somewhat justifiable." And before the freshman could recover, Miss Burt and her friend were halfway across the campus.

Patsy sighed with admiration. "Oh, Cornelia, how I reverence you!" she said. "I couldn't do that to save my soul. No. Once I tried it, and the freshman laughed at me. I slunk away—positively slunk."

But Neal did not laugh. "I can't see what to do," she half whispered, as if to herself. "Next week—next week! Why then, why then, it's all over with her. She's thrown up the sponge!"

Patsy peered into Cornelia's face and caught her breath. "Why, Neal, do you care? Do you really care?" she said. Neal looked at her defiantly through wet lashes. "Yes, I do care. I think it's horrible. To have her beaten like this!—I have to go now. Be sure to come to Alpha to-night!"

"When Cornelia leaves, she leaves sudden,"

said Kate Sutton, from the window. "Coming up?"

Patsy stamped slowly up the two flights, and rummaged in a very mussy window-box for a silk waist. Her room-mate listened for some expression of grief or joy to give the tone to conversation, but none came; so she began on her own account.

"Martha says," indicating her twin, who was polishing the silver things with alcohol and a preparation fondly believed by her to be whiting, but which incessant use had reduced to a dirty gritty gum, "Martha says she knows who's going in to-night."

"Oh, indeed?"

"Yes. She says it's Eleanor Huntington and Leila Droch. She knows for certain."

"Great penetration she has — they've never been mentioned," returned the senior, absent-mindedly, grabbing under the chiffonier for missing hair-pins.

A shriek of triumph from the twins brought her to her knees.

"Aha! I told you they weren't in it! Perhaps you'll believe me again! Perhaps I can't find out a thing or two!"

The twins shook hands delightedly, and Patsy, irritated at her slip, grabbed again for the hair-pins, incidentally discovering a silver shoe-horn and a fountain pen.

"Very clever you are—very," she remarked coldly. "Quite unusual, and so young, too. No wonder your parents are worried!"

This was a bitter cut, for the twins were industriously engaged in living down the report that the Registrar had in their freshman year received a note from Mrs. Sutton imploring her to curb if necessary their passion for study, which invariably brought on nervous headaches. This was peculiarly interesting to their friends, who had never remarked any undue application on their part and were, of course, proportionately eager to caution them against it. They squirmed visibly now and changed their tone abruptly.

"They say that Frances Wilde was terribly disappointed about making Alpha—she'd much rather have got Phi Kappa," said Kate, with a mixture of malice and humility.

Patsy was silent. Martha grinned and took up the conversation.

"But her heart would have been broken if she had n't gotten in this year," she returned amiably.

Patsy turned and glared at them, one arm in the silk waist.

"What utter nonsense!" she broke out. "As if it made any matter, one way or the other! As if it made two cents' worth of difference! You know perfectly well that it's no test at all—making a society. Look at the girls who are in! It's a farce, as Neal says—" She stopped and scowled at them defiantly. The twins gasped. This from a society girl to them, as yet unelect! Even for a conversation with the Sutton twins, with whom, owing to their own contagious example, truth was bound to fly out sooner or later, this was unusual. It was odd enough to discuss the societies at all with perfectly eligible sophomores who might reasonably expect to enter one or another sometime and who were nevertheless yet uncalled; but the twins discussed everything with everybody, utterly regardless of etiquette, tradition, or propriety, and their upper-class room-mates had long ago given up any ideas of reserve and discipline they might have held.

Martha gasped but promptly replied. "That's all very well for Cornelia Burt," she said, with the famous Sutton grin. "Anybody who made the Alpha in the first five and was known well enough to have been especially wanted in Phi Kappa and even begged to refuse—"

A CASE OF INTERFERENCE

"How did you know that, Martha Sutton?"

"Oh! how did I? The President confided it to me one day when he was calling. As I say, Neal Burt and you can afford to talk; you can say it's a bore and all that and make fun of the meetings—"

"I don't!"

"You do! I heard you growling about it to Neal. And Bertha Kitts said she'd about as soon conduct a class prayer-meeting as Phi— Oh, not to me, naturally, but I know the girl who heard the girl she said it to! Heard her tell about it, I mean.

"It's all very well for you, but you'd feel differently if you were out! It's just like being a junior usher. There are plenty of spooks in, but there aren't many bright girls out. Everybody knows that lots of the society girls are pushed in by their friends and pulled in for heaven knows what—certainly not brains! But, just the same, you know well enough that you can count on one hand all the girls in the college that you'd think ought to be in and aren't. You don't know anything about it, for you were sure of it and everybody knew it, but the ones that aren't, they're the ones that worry! Why, I know sophomores to-day that will cry all night if they don't get their notes and their flowers and their front seat in chapel Monday!"

"Oh, nonsense!"

"Oh, nonsense, indeed! Won't they, Katie?"

"Sure!" returned her sister, placidly.

"I guess Alison Greer will cry all right, if she's not in!"

Patsy bit her lip and tapped her foot nervously. Then she shrugged her shoulders and opened the door, turning to remark, "You don't seem to be wasted away, either of you!"

"Oh, we! We're all right!" replied Martha, comfortably. "We never expected it sophomore year, anyhow. Nothing proddy about us, you know. Too many clever girls in the sophomore class, you see. But we expect to amble in next year, we do. And violets from you. And supper at Boyden's. Oh, yes! Don't you worry about us, Miss Pattison, we're all right!"

Miss Pattison sighed: sighs usually ended one's conversations with the twins, for nothing else so well expressed one's attitude.

"It's a pity you're so shrinking," she contented herself with observing. "I'm afraid you'll never come forward sufficiently to be known well by either society!" And she went down to get her mail.

A CASE OF INTERFERENCE

II

THERE was a full meeting of the Alpha that Saturday night. The vice-president was lobbying energetically in behalf of a sophomore friend who would prove the crown and glory of the society, if all her upper-class patroness said of her could possibly be true. There was but one place open for the rest of the term, for the society had grown unusually that year, and some conservative seniors had pressed hard on the old tradition that sixty was a suitable and necessary limit, and put a motion through to that effect, and every possible junior had been elected long ago. So the vice-president was distinctly hopeful. Amid the buzz and clamor of fifty-odd voices, the president slapped the table sharply. "*Will* the meeting please come to order!" she cried. A little rustle, and the handsome secretary arose. "The regular meeting of the Alpha Society was held—" and the report went on.

"Are there any objections to this report?" asked the president, briskly. "Yes. It's far too long," muttered Suzanne Endicott, flippantly. The president looked at her reproachfully, and added, "If not, we will proceed to the election of new members—I mean the new member. As you probably know, there is but

one place left, according to the recent amend-
ment, and I think that we will vote as usual
on the three that are before us, and elect the
one having the most affirmative ballots. Are
there any objections to this method?" There
were none. The vice-president glanced ap-
pealingly at the girl she was not quite sure of
and smiled encouragingly at the sophomore
she had successfully intimidated. The secretary rose again. "The names to be voted on
this evening are Alison Greer, '9–, Katharine Sutton, '9–, Marion Dustin, '9–," she
announced. "I may add that Miss Sutton has
the highest marks from the society, and that
if we don't take her this time there is very
little doubt that Phi Kappa Psi will. They'll
be afraid to risk another meeting."

"That's true," said somebody, as the buzz-
ing began again. "We're carrying this point
a little too far. I declare, it's harder to decide
on the people that aren't prods than anybody
would imagine. We know we want 'em sometime, but we put it off so long—"

"Kate Sutton's awfully bright! I think she
should have been here before. I've been
trembling for fear we'd lose her by waiting
so long—"

"Still, Marion is *such* a dear, and it's pretty

[56]

A CASE OF INTERFERENCE

late for a girl that's been known so well for so long, without getting in, it seems to me," said the vice-president, skilfully. "Why did n't she get in before if she was so bright?"

"And there's Martha, too. They're just alike. I think Martha's a little brighter, if anything. Shall we have to take 'em both?"

"No. The girls all say to give her to Phi Kappa, and tell 'em apart by the pins!"

"Like babies!"

"How silly!"

"To be perfectly frank, Miss Leslie, I must say I don't think so. Alison is an awfully dear girl, and all that, but I hardly think she represents the element we hope to get into Alpha. I 'm sorry to say so, but—"

"The voting has begun," said the president. "Will you hurry, please?"

"Miss President," said Cornelia Burt, rising abruptly, "may I speak to the society before the voting?"

"Certainly, Miss Burt," said the president. There was an instant hush, and the girls stood clustered about the ballot-table in their pretty, light dresses—a charming sight, Neal thought vaguely, as she hunted for the words to say.

"I know perfectly well that what I am about

to propose is quite unconstitutional," she began, and to her own ears her voice seemed far
off. How many there were, and how surprised
and attentive they looked! They were no fools,
as she had said. They represented the cleverest element in the college, on the whole, and
they had, naturally enough, their own designs
and inclinations—why should they be turned
from them in a moment?

"I know that no girl is eligible for voting
upon until she has been read two meetings
before, and been properly put up for membership, and all that," said Neal, quietly, with
her eyes fixed on Patsy's, who tried to evade
them. Poor Patsy. She wanted Kate to get the
society in her sophomore year! "But I am
in possession of certain facts that seem to me
to warrant the breaking through the constitution, if such a thing can ever be done."

The silence had become intense. An omi-
nous look of surprise deepened on the girls'
faces, and the president looked doubtfully at
the secretary.

"I think I am quite justified in believing
that I have not the reputation of a sentimental
person," said Cornelia. She had herself well
in hand, now. The opposition that she felt
nerved her to her customary self-possession.

A CASE OF INTERFERENCE

A little grin swept around the room. She was, apparently, quite justified.

"I have been in the Alpha as long as any one here," said Neal, quietly still, "and in all this time I have never proposed any one for membership in it. I have voted whenever I knew anything about the person in question, and I have never blackballed but once. I think I may say I have done my share of work for the society——"

There was a unanimous murmur of deep and unqualified assent. "You have done more than your share," said the president, promptly.

"I mention these things," said Neal, "in order that you may see that I recognize the need of some apology for what I am about to propose. I want to propose the name of Winifred Hastings to-night, and have her voted on with the rest. If it is a possible thing, I want her elected. That she would be elected without any doubt, I am certain, if only I could put the facts of the case properly before you. That she must be elected, now, to-night, is absolutely necessary, for by another meeting she will have left the college—left it for the lack of just such recognition as membership in the society will give her."

Cornelia Burt was a born orator. Never

was she so happy as when she felt an audience, however small, given over to her, eyes and ears, for the moment. She stood straight as a reed, and looked easily over their faces, holding by very force of personality their attention. She spoke without the slightest hesitation, yet perfectly simply and after no set form. Insensibly the girls around her felt conviction in her very presence: they agreed with her against their will, while she was speaking.

"Before I go any farther, I want to tell you that Miss Hastings is no friend of mine," said Neal. "I hardly know her. Only lately I have learned the circumstances that led me to take this step. I feel that I must do this thing. I feel that we are letting go from the college a girl whose failure in life, if she fails, will be in our hands. We can elect these others later: Winifred Hastings leaves the college next week. And, speaking as editor of the college paper, I must say that she carries with her some of the best literary material in the college. You ask me why we have never seen it—I tell you, because she is a girl who needs encouragement, and she has never had it. She can do her best only when it is called for. Some of you may think you know her—may

think that she is proud and solitary and disagreeable: she is not. *This* is the real girl!"

And, stepping farther into the circle, Cornelia, by an effort of memory she has never
equalled since, told them, with the simplest
eloquence, the pathetic story of Winifred
Hastings' life, as she had written it. She did
not comment—she only related. Her keen
literary appreciation had caught the most effective parts, and she had the dramatic sense
to which every successful speaker owes so
much. Under her touch the haughty, solitary
figure of a scarcely known girl melted away
before them, and they saw a baffled, eager,
hungry soul that had fought desperately, and
was going silently away—beaten.

Cornelia Burt had made speeches before,
and she made them afterward, to larger and
more excited college audiences, but she never
held so many hearts in her hand as she did
that night. She was not a particularly unself-
ish girl, but no one who heard her then ever
called her egotistic afterward. Her whole nature was thrown with all its force into this
fight—for it was a fight.

Perhaps there is nowhere an audience less
sentimental and more critical than a group of
clever college girls. They see clearly for the

most part, and, like all clever youth, somewhat cruelly. They object to being ruled by any but their chosen, and however they admired her, Cornelia was not their chosen leader. It was not because her speech was able, but because it was so evident that she believed herself only the means of preventing a calamity that she was striving with all her soul to avert, that she impressed them so deeply.

For she did impress them. When she ended, it was very quiet in the room. "I have broken a confidence in telling this," she said. "The girl herself would rather die than have you know it, I'm sure, and now—I feel afraid. It has been a bold stroke; if I have lost, I shall never forgive myself. But oh! I *cannot* have her go!"

She sat down quickly and stared into her lap. The spell of her voice was gone, the girls looked at each other, and a tall, keen-eyed girl with glasses got up. "I wish to say," she said, "that while Miss Burt's story is terribly convincing, still this may be a little exaggerated, and, at any rate, think of the precedent! If this should be done very often—"

"But it won't be!" cried some one with a somewhat husky voice, and Patsy rudely interrupted the speaker. Dear Patsy! She crushed her handkerchief in her hand and said good-by to Kate: she would have liked to put her pin in Kate's shirt-waist, and now —now Phi Kappa would get her! When Patsy spoke, it was with the voice of eleven, for she carried at least ten of the leading set in the Alpha with her.

"I think we are all very glad to realize that there won't be many such cases—most people have compensations—we ought to be willing to break the constitution again for such a thing, anyhow—and, Miss President, I move that Miss Hastings be voted upon by acclamation!"

"I second the motion," said the vice-president, quickly.

"It is moved and seconded that Miss Hastings be voted upon by acclamation," said the president. "All in favor—"

"Miss Hastings has yet to be proposed," said some one, after the vote.

The president looked at Cornelia.

"I propose Winifred Hastings, '9–, as a member of the Alpha Society," said Cornelia, with flaming cheeks and downcast eyes. She dared not look at them. Were they going to punish her? She heard the motion announced, she heard the name put up.

"All in favor please signify by rising," said the president, and only when the Alpha rose in a body did Cornelia lift her eyes.

They were all looking at her, and she stepped a little back.

"I cannot thank you," she said, so low that they leaned forward to hear. "It was no affair of mine, as I said. But—I think you—we—shall never regret this election." And then they applauded so loudly that the freshmen on the campus could not forbear peeping under the blinds to see what they were doing. They saw only the president, however, as she stepped back to the table and said with an air of relief—for, after all, emotion is very wearing—"We will now proceed to the literary programme of the evening!"

"But Neal, dear," said Patsy, as they settled themselves to listen, "do you think she'll stay? (Oh, Neal! I'm so proud of you!)"

"Shut up, Patsy!" said Neal, rudely. Then, as she thought of what Miss Henderson had told her of Winifred Hastings: "You are the only girl whose friendship"—she blushed. Then, assuming a bored expression, she looked at the girl who was reading. "I fear there's no doubt she will!" said Cornelia Burt.

MISS BIDDLE OF BRYN MAWR

III

MISS BIDDLE OF BRYN MAWR

"I WOULDN'T have minded so much," explained Katherine, dolefully, and not without the suspicion of a sob, "if it was n't that I 'd asked Miss Hartwell and Miss Ackley! I shall die of embarrassment—I shall! Oh! why could n't Henrietta Biddle have waited a week before she went to Europe?"

Her room-mate, Miss Grace Farwell, sank despairingly on the pile of red floor-cushions under the window. "Oh, Kitten! you did n't ask them? Not really?" she gasped, staring incredulously at the tangled head that peered over the screen behind which Katherine was splashily conducting her toilet operations.

"But I did! I think they 're simply grand, especially Miss Hartwell, and I 'll never have any chance of meeting her, I suppose, and I thought this was a beautiful one. So I met her yesterday on the campus and I walked up to her—I was horribly scared, but I don't think I showed it—and, said I, 'Oh, Miss Hartwell, you don't know me, of course, but I 'm Miss Sewall, '9–, and I know Henrietta Biddle of Bryn Mawr, and she 's coming to see me for two or three days, and I 'm going to make a little tea for her—very informal—and I've heard her speak of you and Miss Ackley as about the only girls she knew here, and I'd love to have you meet her again!'"

Miss Farwell laughed hysterically. "And did she accept?" she inquired.

Katherine wiped her face for the third time excitedly. "Oh, yes! She was as sweet as peaches and cream! 'I shall be charmed to meet Miss Biddle again, and in your room, Miss Sewall,' she said, 'and shall I bring Miss Ackley?' Oh, Grace, she's lovely! She is the most—"

"Yes, I've no doubt," interrupted Miss Farwell, cynically; "all the handsome seniors are. But what are you going to say to her to-day?"

Katherine buried her yellow head in the towel. "I don't know! Oh, Grace! I don't know," she mourned. "And they say the freshmen are getting so uppish, anyway, and if we carry it off well, and just make a joke of it, they'll think we're awfully f-f-fresh!" Here words failed her, and she leaned heavily on the screen, which, as it was old and probably resented having been sold third-hand at a second-hand price, collapsed weakly, dragging with it the Bodenhausen Madonna, a silver rack of photographs, and a Gibson Girl drawn in very black ink on a very white ground.

"And if we are apologetic and meek," continued Miss Farwell, easily, apparently undisturbed by the confusion consequent to the downfall of a piece of furniture known to be somewhat erratic, "they'll laugh at us or be bored. We shall be known as the freshmen who invited seniors and Faculty and townpeople to meet—nobody at all! A pretty reputation!"

"But, Grace, we couldn't help it! Such things will happen!" Katherine was pinning the Gibson Girl to the wall, in bold defiance of the matron's known views on that subject.

"Yes, of course. But they mustn't happen to freshmen!" her room-mate returned sententiously. "How many Faculty did you ask?"

"I asked Miss Parker, because she fitted Henrietta for college, at Archer Hall, and I asked Miss Williams, because she knows Henrietta's mother—Oh! Miss Williams will freeze me to death when she comes here and sees just us!—and I asked Miss Dodge, because she knows a lot of Bryn Mawr people. Then Mrs. Patton on Elm Street was a school friend of Mrs. Biddle's, and—oh! Grace, I *can't* manage them alone! Let's tell them not to come!"

"And what shall we do with the sandwiches? And the little cakes? And the lemons that I sliced? And the tea-cups and spoons I borrowed? And that pint of extra thick cream?" Miss Farwell checked off these interesting items on her fingers, and kicked the floor-cushions to point the question.

"Oh! I don't know! Isn't there any chance—"

"No, goosey, there isn't. See here!" Grace pulled down a letter with a special delivery stamp from the desk above her head, and read with emphasis:

D EAR *Kitten,*—*Just a line to say that Aunt Mary has sent for me at three days' notice to go to Paris with her for a year. It's now or never, you know, and I've left the college, and will come back to graduate with '9–. So sorry I can't see you before I go. Had looked forward to a very interesting time, renewing my own freshman days, and all that. Please send my blue cloth suit right on to Philadelphia C. O. D. when it comes to you. I hope you hadn't gotten anything up for me.* With much love,

Henrietta Biddle.

Bryn Mawr, March 5.

"I don't think there's much chance, my dear."

"No," said Katherine, sadly, and with a final pat administered to the screen, which still wobbled unsteadily. "No, I suppose there is n't. And it 's eleven o'clock. They 'll be here at four! Oh! and I asked that pretty junior, Miss Pratt, you know. Henrietta knew her sister. She was in '8–."

"Ah," returned Miss Farwell, with a suspicious sweetness, "why did n't you ask a few more, Katherine, dear? What with the list we made out together and these last extra ones—"

"But I thought there was n't any use having the largest double room in the house, if we could n't have a decent-sized party in it! And think of all those darling, thin little sandwiches!—Oh well, we might just as well be sensible and carry the thing through, Gracie! But I am just as afraid as I can be: I tell you that. And Miss Williams will freeze me stiff." The yellow hair was snugly braided and wound around by now, and a neat though worried maiden sat on the couch and punched the Harvard pillow reflectively.

"Never mind her, Kitten, but just go ahead. You know Caroline Wilde said it was all right to ask her if she was Miss Biddle's mother's friend, and there was n't time to take her all around, and you know how nice Miss Parker

[71]

was about it. We can't help it, as you say, and we'll go and get the flowers as we meant to. Have you anything this hour?"

With her room-mate to back her, to quote the young lady herself, Miss Sewall felt equal to almost any social function. Terrifying as her position appeared—and strangely enough, the seniors appalled her far more than the Faculty—there was yet a certain excitement in the situation. What should she say to them? Would they be kind about it, or would they all turn around and go home? Would they think—

"Oh, nonsense!" interrupted Grace the practical, as these doubts were thrust upon her. "If they're ladies, as I suppose they are, of course they'll stay and make it just as pleasant for us as they can. They'll see how it is. Think what we'd do, ourselves, you know!"

They went down the single long street, with the shops on either side, a red-capped, golf-caped pair of friends, like nine hundred other girls, yet different from them all. And they chattered of Livy and little cakes and Trigonometry and pleated shirt-waists and basket-ball and Fortnightly Themes like all the others, but in their little way they were very social heroines, setting their teeth to carry by

[72]

storm a position that many an older woman would have found doubtful.

They stopped at a little bakery, well down the street, to order some rolls for the girl across the hall from them, who had planned to breakfast in luxury and alone on chocolate and grape-fruit the next morning. "Miss Carter, 24 Washburn," said Grace, carelessly, when Katherine whispered, "Look at her! Isn't that funny? Why, Grace, just see her!"

"See who—whom, I mean? (only I hate to say 'whom.') Who is it, Kitten?"

Katherine was staring at the clerk, a tall, handsome girl, with masses of heavy black hair and an erect figure. As she went down to the back of the shop again, Katherine's eyes followed her closely.

"It's that girl that used to be in the Candy Kitchen—don't you remember? I told you then that she looked so much like my friend Miss Biddle. And then the Candy Kitchen failed and I suppose she came here. And she's just Henrietta's height, too. You know Henrietta stands very straight and frowns a little, and so did this girl when you gave Alice's number and she said, 'Thirty-four or twenty-four?' Isn't it funny that we should see her now?— Oh, dear! If only she *were* Henrietta!"

[73]

Grace stared at the case of domestic bread and breathed quickly. "Does she really look like her, Kitten?" she said.

"Oh yes, indeed. It's quite striking. Henrietta's quite a type, you know—nothing unusual, only very dark and tall and all that. Of course there are differences, though."

"What differences?" said Grace, still looking intently at the domestic bread.

"Oh, Henrietta's eyes are brown, and this girl's are black. And Henrietta hasn't any dimple, and her hands are prettier. And Henrietta's waist isn't so small, and she hasn't nearly so much hair, I should say. But then, I haven't seen her for a year, and probably there's a greater difference than I think."

"How long is it since those seniors and the Faculty saw Henrietta?" said Grace, staring now at a row of layer chocolate-cakes.

Her room-mate started. "Why — why, Grace, what do you mean? It's two years, Henrietta wrote, I think. And Miss Parker and Miss Williams haven't seen her for much longer than that. But—but—you don't mean anything, Grace?"

Grace faced her suddenly. "Yes," she said, "I do. You may think that because I just go right along with this thing, I don't care at all.

But I do. I 'm awfully scared. I hate to think of that Miss Ackley lifting her eyebrows — the way she will! And Miss Hartwell said once when somebody asked if she knew Judge Farwell's daughter, 'Oh, dear me — I suppose so! And everybody else in her class — theoretically! But practically I rarely observe them!' Ugh! She 'll observe me to-day, I hope!"

"Yes, dear, I suppose she will. And me too. But—"

"Oh, yes! But if nobody knows how Miss Biddle looks, and she was going to stay at the hotel, anyway, and it would only be for two hours, and everything would be so simple —"

Katherine's cheeks grew very red and her breath came fast. "But would we dare? Would she be willing? Would it be—"

"Oh, my dear, it 's only a courtesy! And everybody will think it 's all right, and the thing will go beautifully, and Miss Biddle, if she has any sense of humor—"

"Yes, indeed! Henrietta would only be amused — oh, so amused! And it would be such a heavenly relief after all the worry. We could send her off on the next train — Henrietta, you know — and dress makes such a difference in a girl!"

"And I think she would if we asked her

just as a favor—it would n't be a question of money! Oh, Katherine! I could cry for joy if she would!"

"She'd like to, if she has any fun in her—it would be a game with some point to it! And will you ask her, or shall I?"

They were half in joke and half in earnest: it was a real crisis to them. They were only freshmen, and they had invited the seniors and the Faculty. And two of the most prominent seniors! Whom they had n't known at all! They had a sense of humor, but they were proud, too, and they had a woman's horror of an unsuccessful social function. They felt that they were doomed to endless joking at the hands of the whole college, and this apprehension, though probably exaggerated, nerved them to their *coup d'état*.

Grace walked down the shop. "I will ask her," she said.

Katherine stood with her back turned and tried not to hear. Suppose the girl should be insulted? Suppose she should be afraid? Now that there was a faint hope of success, she realized how frightened and discouraged she had been. For it would be a success, she saw that. Nobody would have had Miss Biddle to talk with for more than a few minutes anyhow, they had asked such a crowd. And yet she would have been the centre of the whole affair.

"Katherine," said a voice behind her, "let me introduce Miss Brooks, who has consented to help us!"

Katherine held out her hands to the girl. "Oh, thank you! *thank* you!" she said.

The girl laughed. "I think it's queer," she said, "but if you are in such a fix, I'd just as lief help you as not. Only I shall give you away — I shan't know what to say."

Grace glanced at Katherine. Then she proved her right to all the praise she afterward accepted from her grateful room-mate. "That will be very easy," she said sweetly. "Miss Biddle, whom you will — will represent, speaks very rarely: she's not at all talkative!"

Katherine gasped. "Oh, no!" she said eagerly, "she's very statuesque, you know, and keeps very still and straight, and just looks in your eyes and makes you think she's talking. She says 'Really?' and 'Fancy, now!' and 'I expect you're very jolly here,' and then she smiles. You could do that."

"Yes, I could do that," said the girl.

"Can you come to the hotel right after dinner?" said Grace, competently, "and we'll cram you for an hour or so on Miss Biddle's affairs."

The girl laughed. "Why, yes," she said, "I guess I can get off."

So they left her smiling at them from the domestic bread, and at two o'clock they carried Miss Henrietta Biddle's dress-suit case to the hotel and took Miss Brooks to her room. And they sat her on a sofa and told her what they knew of her alma mater and her relatives and her character generally. And she amazed them by a very comprehensive grasp of the whole affair and an aptitude for mimicry that would have gotten her a star part in the senior dramatics. With a few corrections she spoke very good English, and "as she'd only have to answer questions, anyhow, she needn't talk long at a time," they told each other.

She put up her heavy hair in a twisted crown on her head, and they put the blue cloth gown on her, and covered the place in the front, where it didn't fit, with a beautiful fichu that Henrietta had apparently been led of Providence to tuck in the dress-suit case. And she rode up in a carriage with them, very much excited, but with a beautiful color and glowing eyes, and a smile that brought out the dimple that Henrietta never had.

They showed her the room and the sandwiches and the tea, and they got into their clothes, not speaking, except when a great box with three bunches of English violets was left at their door with Grace's card. Then Katherine said, "You dear thing!" And Miss Brooks smiled as they pinned hers on and said softly, "Fancy, now!"

And then they were n't afraid for her any more.

When the pretty Miss Pratt came, a little after four, with Miss Williams, she smiled with pleasure at the room, all flowers and tea and well-dressed girls, with a tall, handsome brunette in a blue gown with a beautiful lace bib smiling gently on a crowd of worshippers, and saying little soft sentences that meant anything that was polite and self-possessed.

Close by her was her friend Miss Sewall, of the freshman class, who sweetly answered half the questions about Bryn Mawr that Miss Biddle could n't find time to answer, and steered people away who insisted on talking with her too long. Miss Farwell, also of the freshman class, assisted her room-mate in receiving, and passed many kinds of pleasant food, laughing a great deal at what everybody said and chatting amicably and unabashed with the two seniors of honor, who openly raved over Miss Biddle of Bryn Mawr.

As soon as Katherine had said, " May I present Miss Hartwell—Miss Ackley ? " they took their stand by the stately stranger and talked to her as much as was consistent with propriety.

"Isn't she perfectly charming !" they said to Miss Parker, and "Yes, indeed," replied that lady, "I should have known Netta anywhere. She is just what I had thought she would be !"

And Miss Williams, far from freezing the pretty hostess, patted her shoulder kindly. "Henrietta is quite worth coming to see," she said with her best and most exquisite manner. "I have heard of the Bryn Mawr style, and now I am convinced. I wish all our girls had such dignity—such a feeling for the right word !"

And they had the grace to blush. They knew who had taught Henrietta Biddle Brooks that right word !

At six o'clock Miss Biddle had to take the Philadelphia express. She had only stopped over for the tea. And so the girls of the house could not admire her over the supper-table. But they probably appreciated her more. For after all, as they decided in talking her over later, it wasn't so much what she said, as the way she looked when she said it !

But only a dress-suit case marked H. L. B. took the Philadelphia express that night, and a tall, red-cheeked girl in a mussy checked suit left the hotel with a bunch of violets in her hand and a reminiscent smile on her lips.

"We simply can't thank you; we have n't any words. You 've helped us give the nicest party two freshmen ever gave, if it is any pleasure to you to know that," said Katherine. "And now you 're only not to speak of it."

"Oh, no! I shan't speak of it," said the girl. "You need n't be afraid. Nobody that I 'd tell would believe me, very much, anyhow. I 'm glad I could help you, and I had a lovely time—lovely!"

She smiled at them: the slow, sweet smile of Henrietta Biddle, late of Bryn Mawr. "You College ladies are certainly queer—but you 're smart!" said Miss Brooks of the bakery.

BISCUITS EX MACHINA

IV

BISCUITS EX MACHINA

B. S. KITTS—this was the signature she had affixed in a neat clerical backhand to all her written papers since the beginning of freshman year; and she had of course been called Biscuits as soon as she had found her own particular little set of girls and settled down to that peculiar form of intimacy which living in barracks, however advantageously organized, necessitates. She had a sallow irregular face, fine brown eyes surrounded with tiny wrinkles, a taste for Thackeray, and a keen sense of humor. It was the last which was subsequently responsible for this story about her.

She was quite unnoticed for two or three years, which is a very good thing for a girl. During that time she quietly took soundings and laid in material, presumably, for those satiric characterizations which were the terror of her undergraduate enemies and the concealed discomfort of those in high places. During her junior year she began to be considered terribly clever, and though she was never what is known as a Prominent Senior, she had her little triumphs here and there, and in the matter of written papers she was a source of great comfort to those whom custom compels to demand such tributes.

She was the kind of girl who, though well known in her own class, is quite unobserved of the lower classes, and this, if it deprived her of the admirations and attentions bestowed on the prominent, saved her the many worries and wearinesses incident to trying to please everybody at once—the business of the over-popular. She had a great deal of time, which may seem absurd, but which is really quite possible if one keeps positively off committees, is neither musical nor athletic, and shuns courses involving laboratory work. It is of great assistance also in this connection to elect English Literature copiously, when one has read most of the works in question and can send home for the reference books, thus saving an immense amount of fruitless loitering about crowded libraries.

Biscuits employed the time thus gained in a fashion apparently purposeless. She loafed about and observed, with *Vanity Fair* under one arm and an apple in the other hand. She was never the subject or the object of a violent friendship; she was one of five or six clever girls who hung together consistently after sophomore year, bickering amicably and in-

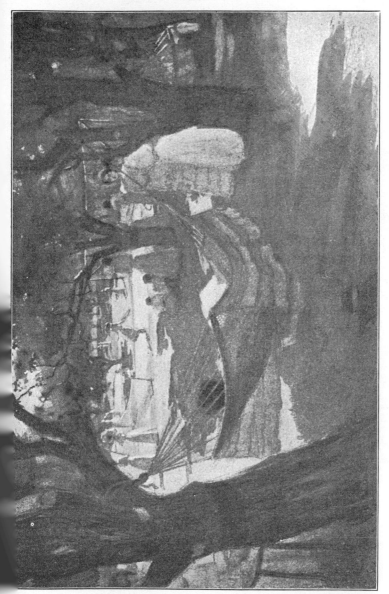

She had a great deal of time. . . . She loafed about and observed

dulging in mutual contumely when together, defending one another promptly when apart. The house president spoke of them bitterly as blasé and critical; the lady-in-charge remarked suspiciously the unusual chance which invariably seated them together at the end of the table at the regular drawing for seats; the collector for missions found them sceptical and inclined to ribaldry if pushed too far; but the Phi Kappa banked heavily on their united efforts, and more than usually idiotic class meetings meekly bowed to what they themselves scornfully referred to afterward as "their ordinary horse-sense."

One of the members of this little group was Martha Augusta Williams. Sometimes she retired from it and devoted herself to solitude, barely replying to questions and obscurely intimating that to *ennui* such as hers the prattle of the immature and inexperienced could hardly be supposed even by themselves to be endurable; sometimes she returned to it with the air of one willing to impart to such a body the mellow cynicism of a tolerant if fatigued *femme du monde*. In the intervals of her retirement she wrote furiously at long-due themes, which took the form of Richard Harding Davis stories--she did them very well—or modern and morbid verses of a nature to disturb the more conservative of those who heard them. At any expression of disturbance Martha would elaborately suppress a three-volume smile and murmur something about "meat for babes;" a performance which delighted her friends—especially Biscuits—beyond measure. Her shelves bristled with yellow French novels, and on her bureau a great ivory skull with a Japanese paper snake carelessly twined through it impressed stray freshmen tremendously. She cut classes elaborately and let her work drop ostentatiously in the middle of the term, appearing at mid-years with ringed eyes and an air of toleration strained to the breaking point. She slept till nine and wandered lazily to coffee and toast at Boyden's an hour later, at least three times a week, with an air that would have done credit to one of Ouida's noblemen.

And yet, in spite of all this, Martha was not happy. The disapproval of the lady-in-charge, the suspicions of the freshmen, the periodical discussions with members of the Faculty, who "regretted to be obliged to mark," etc., "when they realized perfectly that she was capable," etc.,—all these alleviated her trouble a little, but the facts remained that her own particu-

lar set would never treat her seriously, and
that her name was Martha Augusta Williams.
Fancy feeling such feelings, and thinking such
thoughts, and bearing the name of Martha
Augusta Williams! It is, to say the least, dis-
piriting. And nobody had ever called her anything else. Harriet Williams was called, indifferently, Billie and Willie and Sillie. Martha
Underhill took her choice of Mattie, Nancy,
and Sister. A girl whose name was Anna Augusta Something had been hailed as Gustavus
Adolphus from her freshman year on; but
below *her* most daring flights of fiction must
ever appear those three ordinary, not to say
stodgy, names. That alone would have soured
a temper not too inclined to regard life with
favor.

Martha might have lived down the name,
but she was assured that never while Bertha
Kitts remained alive would she be able to appear really wickedly interesting. For Biscuits
would tell the Story. Tell it with variations
and lights and shades and explanations adapted
to the audience. And it never seemed to pall.
Yet it was simple—horribly simple.

Martha had invited a select body of sophomores to go with her to the palm-reader's.
There were two clever ones, who vastly ad-

mired her Richard Harding Davis tales, two curious ones, who openly begged for her opinions and thrilled at her epigrams on Love and Life and Experience, and, in an evil hour, the Sutton twins, whom she admitted into the occasion partly to impress them, and partly so that if anything really fascinating should come to light, Kate Sutton could impart it to her room-mate, Patsy Pattison.

When they were assembled in the palm-reader's parlor, Martha gravely motioned the others to go before her, and they took their innocent turns before the little velvet cushion. The Twins were admirably struck off in a few phrases, to the delight of their friends, and the palm-reader's reputation firmly established. In the case of one of the curious girls, peculiar and private events were hinted at that greatly impressed her, for "how *could* she have known *that*, girls?" The clever girls were comforted with fame and large "scribbler's crosses," also wealthy marriages and social careers, but they looked enviously at Martha, nevertheless, and she smiled maternally on them, as was right. There remained only the other quiet little girl, and she modestly suggested waiting till another day, "so there'll be lots of time for yours, Miss Williams;" but Martha smiled kindly and waved her to the seat, suggesting that hers might not be a long session, with an amused glance at the empty, little pink palm.

The palm-reader turned and twisted and patted and asked her age, and finally announced that it was a remarkable hand. The dying interest revived, and even Martha's eyebrows went up with amazement as the seer spoke darkly of immense influence; tact to the nth degree; unusual amount of experience, or at the least, "intuitional discoveries;" two great artistic means of expression; previous affairs of the heart, and an inborn capacity for ruling the destinies of others—marked resemblance to the hands of Cleopatra and Sara Bernhardt. It was hands like that that moved the world, she said. The sophomores regarded their friend with interest and awe, noted that she blushed deeply at portions of the revelation, recollected her Sunday afternoon improvisations at the piano and her request for a more advanced course in harmony, and attached a hitherto unfelt importance to her heavy mails.

Martha may have regretted her politeness, but she smothered her surprise, sank, with an abstracted air, upon the chair before the cush-

ion, and with a face from which all emotion
had been withdrawn and eyes which defied
any wildest revelation to disturb their settled
ennui, awaited the event. The palm-reader
glanced at the back of the slim hand, noted
the face, touched the finger tips.

"How old are you, please?" she asked.
Martha wearily announced that she was
twenty-one. She was conscious of its being
a terribly ordinary age. The palm-reader
nodded. "Ah!" she said easily. "Well, come
to me again in a year or two. I can't really
tell much now."

Martha gasped at her. "You can't *tell*
much!"

The palm-reader took her hand again.
"There's nothing much to tell!" she explained. "The hand isn't really developed
yet—it's the opposite from the last young
lady's, you might say."

She became conscious of a cold silence
through the room, and added a few details.
"There's a good general ability; no particular
line of talent, I should say; orderly, regular
habits; a very kind heart; I can't see any
events in particular; you've led a very quiet
life, I should say; fond of reading; I shouldn't
say you'd met many people or travelled

much"—she scrutinized the hand more closely—"you'll probably develop a strong religious feeling—"

She stopped and smiled deprecatingly. "It is really impossible to say very much," she said, "just now. It's what we call an immature hand!"

For months after that Martha woke in the night and tried to forget the nightmare of a terrible figure that led her to an amphitheatre of grinning enemies, and leered at her: *It's what we call an Immature Hand!* She could have suppressed the others, but the Sutton twins were beyond earthly and human suppression. It seemed to her that she never met them or passed them in a corridor without hearing their jovial assurance: "Oh, Martha Williams is all right! Why, the idea! She's as kind a girl as ever lived—she's nothing like that story. Gracious, no! She's never been to Paris—she lives in Portland. Why, her father's a Sunday School Superintendent! Oh, bother! She's as good as Alberta May, every bit! She has a strong religious—" and somebody passed on, assured—heavens, perhaps admiring her character! At such times Martha would read furiously in her French novels or regard the skull pensively or sit up all night, which annoyed her room-mate and the lady-in-charge. Her room-mate was an absolutely unimportant person, and does not come into the story at all.

It is now time to revert to the Twins. When they appeared in the house, two solemn-eyed, pigtailed imps from Buffalo, they were packed away together in a double room on the third floor, and except for their amazing resemblance, were absolutely unnoted. The matron uneasily fancied a certain undue disturbance on the third floor, the evening of their arrival, but on going to that level she found all as still as the grave, and immediately went back downstairs. It is only due to her, however, to say that she never again made such an error. From that time on any abnormal quiet in the house was to her as the trumpet to the war-horse; and she mounted unerringly to the all-too-certain scene of action. Their plans for the first year were rather crude, though astonishingly effective at the time. It was they who invented the paper bag of water dropped from the fourth floor to burst far below, and waken the house with the most ghastly hollow explosion; it was they who let a pair of scissors down two flights to tap against the pane of an unfortunate enemy in the senior class, and send her into convulsions of nervous and, as they said, guilty fear. It was they who stuck new caramels to their door-knob, and oblivious to the matron's admonitions of the hour, waited till in exasperation she seized the knob, when they met her disgust with soap and apologies; it was they who left the gas brightly burning and the door temptingly ajar at 10.15, so that the long-suffering woman pounced upon them with just recrimination, only to find her stored-up wrath directed against two night-gowned figures bowed over their little white beds, as it were two Infant Samuels. It is doubtful if a devotional exercise ever before or since has roused such mingled feelings in the bosom of the chance spectator.

It was they who beyond a shadow of doubt won the basket-ball game for the freshmen— an unprecedented victory— by their marvellous intuition of each other's intentions and their manner of being everywhere at once and playing into each other's hands with an uncanny certainty. This gave them position and weight among their mates, which they duly appreciated. They were the recognized jesters of the class, and their merry, homely faces were sure of answering grins wherever they appeared.

When they returned sophomore year more alike than ever, with happy plans for the best double room on the second floor, they were met by quite another kind of grin: its owner, Mrs. Harrow, would have perhaps described it as firm and pleasant—the Twins referred to it bitterly as hypocritical and disgusting.

"No, Martha, no. It's no use to coax me —I can't have it. I cannot go through another such year. If you wish to remain in the house, you must separate. You can have No. 10 with Alberta Bunting, and Kate can go in with Margaret—she says she is perfectly willing, rather than give up the room, and Helen is not coming back till next year. Now, I don't want to have to argue about it; I think you are better apart."

No one ever accused Mrs. Harrow of tact. Her placid firmness was almost the most exasperating thing about her. Her decisions, if apparently somewhat feather-beddish, ranked, nevertheless, with those of the Medes and Persians, and the Twins walked haughtily away—beaten but defiant.

Of course it never occurred to them to leave the house, and Kate, after a time, grew quite contented, for Miss Pattison was eminently pleasant and tactful, kept the room in beautiful order, and spent a great deal of time in the Dewey with her sister, an instructor in the college, and her great friend Cornelia Burt, who was off the campus. This left the room to the Twins, who were almost as much together as of yore. But Martha was in quite another case. In her the insult of a dictated separation rankled continually, and her hitherto mild contempt for Mrs. Harrow deepened into a positively appalling enmity. Circumstances unfortunately assisted her feeling, for beyond a doubt Alberta May Bunting was not adapted to her new room-mate.

She was a wholesome, kindly creature, with high principles and no particular waist-line. She drank a great deal of milk, and was a source of great relief to her teachers, her recitations being practically perfect. From her sophomore year she had been wildly, if solidly, addicted to zoölogy, and to her, after hours spent in the successful chase of the doomed insect, the grasshopper was literally a burden, for she slew him by the basketful. She rendered the surrounding territory frogless in her zeal for laboratory practice, and in her senior year it was rumored that stray cats fled at her approach: "She'll cut me up in my sleep," said Martha, gloomily, "and soak me in formaline in the bath-tub—the idiot!"

For, although the "h'Arrow-that-flyeth-by-day-and-the-terror-that-walketh-by-night," as Martha Williams, in a burst of inspiration, had named her, could not, of course, have known it, Sutton M., as she was most commonly called, loathed and despised bugs, reptiles, and crawling and dismembered things generally, more than aught else beside. She regarded an interest in such things as an indication of mild insanity, and as a characteristic of Alberta May's such a predilection assumed the proportions of a malignant insult.

"It's bad enough to have her drink milk like a cow, and eat graham crackers like a—like a *steam-engine*," she confided to her sympathetic sister, "and smell like a whole biological laboratory, and glower at me, and bobble her head like a China image whenever I open my mouth, and call me Mottha, which I despise, and say, 'Why, the *idea*! Why, Mottha, the *idea*! What *do* you *mean*, Mottha?' without putting little bottles of Things all around, and my having to upset them. My gym suit made me sick to put on for a week because I upset some nasty little claws all pickled in something per cent. alcohol on the sleeve, and I kept thinking the legs were walking on me—ugh! they were leggy claws!"

The h'Arrow-that-flyeth-by-day had fondly hoped that Alberta would "do Martha Sutton a world of good," because of her exemplary, regular habits and her calm, sensible nature, but this consummation, though devoutly to be wished, was fated never to be witnessed. Every one heard the wails and gibes of Sutton M., but to few or none were the woes of Alberta May made known. But that she must have had them, her attitude at the time of the crisis conclusively proved.

The Twins, in the course of their mysterious loitering, overheard a somewhat sentimental discussion between Evelyn Lyon and an extremely stiff and correct young man from Amherst, as to whether chivalry and openly expressed devotion to the fair were not disappearing from the earth. "Men like shirtwaists and golf-shoes," Evelyn had been heard to murmur, with a glance at her fluffy chiffon and bronze slippers, and the senior had protested that they did not, and that emotion, if controlled, was as deep as in the balcony-serenade days. "In fact," said he, finally, " Estabrook and I will serenade you Wednesday night."

"You would never dare," said Evelyn, with a glance at his eye-glasses and collar, which for height and circumference might have been a cuff. "You'd be afraid the girls would laugh." The senior looked nettled. "Expect us at ten on Wednesday next," said he. "It won't necessarily be the Glee and Banjo Club, you understand, but it will be a real, old-fashioned serenade." Then, as Evelyn smiled maliciously, he added, "Only you must appear at the casement, and throw flowers, you know —that's what they did." Evelyn frowned, but agreed. "At the end of the song, I will," she said, with visions of the night-watchman hasting to the scene.

The Twins were unaccountably strolling about as the senior left the house, and wondered with great distinctness and repetition why on earth Evelyn should say she'd be in 14 at the front when of course she'd be in the East corner on the first floor. "She has some game up," shrieked Martha, and Kate called back, "Of course she has—some one will be awfully left, that's all!"

The senior listened, grinned, muttered that women told everything they knew, and went his way. On next Wednesday night, the entire house being congregated in the hall near

BISCUITS EX MACHINA

No. 14, where Evelyn, not to be found wanting in case they *should* get through a verse, was
sorting carnations, a husky burst of song en-
livened the East corner, a mandolin and a
guitar having raced through a confused prel-
ude under the spur of a youth hopping with
nervousness and sputtering as he punched
the mandolin-player: "Hang it all, Pete, get
along, get along! He 'll be here in a minute
—whoop it up, can't you?"

A muffled baritone began, standing so close
to the window with a light in it that its owner
could have touched the sill with his shoulder:

> Last night the nightingale waked me,
> Last night when all was —

The shade went up, the window followed,
and the eyes of the musicians beheld, below
an audience of house-maids, the only people
at present on that side of the house, an enormous woman, with gray hair in curling-kids,
and a blanket-wrapper which added to her
size, grasping a lamp in her hand and regarding them with a mingling of amazement, irritation, and authority that caused their blood
to curdle and their voices to cease. Pattering
feet, a lantern turned on them, and a voice:
"'Ere, 'ere, what you doing? H'all h'off the

campus after ten—get along, now!" completed their confusion, and they left, with an attempt at dignity and a slowness which they had occasion to curse; for as they passed the front of the house, from out of the air above their heads, apparently, two sweet and boyish voices, a first and second soprano, lifted up to the fresh October sky an ancient and beautiful hymn:

> Some*times* a *light* sur*pri*ses
> The *Chris*tian *while* he *sings*,
> It *is*—

A window banged forcibly, and the minstrels stood upon no order but fled to their carriage and rattled out of town.

Evelyn Lyon, with set teeth and artistically loosened hair, rushed down the hall behind Martha Sutton, who made the room she was aiming for, slammed the door, realized that the key was lost, and dragged the first piece of furniture that came to hand against it. This was Alberta May's desk, and upon it were the collected results of her vacation work at Wood's Holl. Six jars upset under the impact of Evelyn's weight, a dozen mounted cross-sections jingled in the dark, a pint bottle of ink soaked a thick and beautifully illustrated note-book; and as the Terror-that-walketh-by-night

[102]

headed Evelyn to her door and mounted a flight to quell the rising tumult, Sutton M., with a hysterical sob, for she was tingling with a delicious excitement, huddled the desk back into the corner, hoped none of the bugs were around the floor, and dropped into bed, wondering how ever Alberta May could sleep through such a night.

And now—though perhaps you may have imagined that there was never going to be any story—now we are coming to it, and though it is short, all the characters appear. Alberta May, with an ugly brick-red flush, told Sutton M. that she need never speak to her again, for no answer would be forthcoming, and that she must have her things out of the room before night. Martha was really horribly frightened, and begged to be allowed to copy the note-book and hire some one to make the slides and re-pickle the scattered Things; but Alberta May merely shook her head, replied that she accepted apologies but could not speak again, and kept her word, for she never noticed Martha from then till the 22d of June.

The h'Arrow-that-flyeth-by-day gave Martha an address that reduced her to a pulp, and having sent the Twins off to cry in each other's arms till dinner-time and got the doctor for

Evelyn, who had sprained her ankle in the rush, she sat down to a cup of tea and council.

To her entered Biscuits, and they talked of odds and ends till Mrs. Harrow had grown a little calm. The girls in the house accused Biscuits of a hypocritical and unnatural interest in the h'Arrow: Biscuits denied this, alleging that she was merely ordinarily courteous and saw no occasion for treating her like a dog, which somewhat strong language was addressed with intention to a few of her friends who certainly did not display any undue consideration in their manner to the lady in question. She was wont to add calmly that she saw no sense in having those in authority hate you when a little politeness would so easily prevent it. And many times had she successfully interceded for the offender and gained seats for guests and obtained the parlor for dancing purposes on nights not mentioned in the bond. On these accounts she made an unusually fine house president in her senior year, and though as a sophomore she had been but suspiciously regarded by that officer, she made as firm a bond as is perhaps possible between powers so hostile as those with which she struggled.

BISCUITS EX MACHINA

To-day she listened sympathetically as Mrs. Harrow held forth, concluding with,—

"Now, Bertha, something *must* be done. I hate dreadfully to make a change, so early in the year, too, but Alberta is decided, and says that she will leave the house to-morrow unless Martha leaves to-night. And Alberta is perfectly justified : nobody could be expected to put up with it. I don't know whom to put her with: she certainly can't be trusted with her friends, and I can't feel that I have any right to put her anywhere else. I hate to have to admit that I can't manage them—Miss Roberts insists that they 're fine girls and will outgrow it all, and I have great respect for her opinion, and yet—think of that disgraceful performance last night ! It would have done credit to a boarding-school ! I was so disgusted—"

"Yes, indeed, and I 've talked to them, Mrs. Harrow, and told them just how the house feels about it, but don't you think that it was rather boarding-schoolish in Evelyn ? She started it all, you know."

"Oh, well, of course. Evelyn should n't have—but then she is a good, quiet girl, and —Oh, not that I would excuse her ! "

"Certainly not," said Biscuits, briskly. This

was good management on her part, for Evelyn
had one friend in the house to the Twins' ten,
though a favorite with Mrs. Harrow.

"Now, Mrs. Harrow, I 've got an idea, and
truly, I think it would work," she added per-
suasively. When she had unfolded the idea, the
lady-in-charge could hardly believe her ears.

"Why, Bertha Kitts, you must be crazy!
Nothing could induce me to think of it for
a moment—nothing! It would be the worst
possible influence!"

Biscuits argued gently. Her three years of
consistent good sense and politeness stood in
her favor, and though Mrs. Harrow had no
sense of humor whatever, she was enabled to
perceive a certain poetic justice in the plan set
before her.

"You know, Mrs. Harrow," she concluded,
"that at bottom they're both nice girls! They're
awfully irritating at times, and of course you
feel that they 've both occasioned a great deal
of trouble; but they 're both honorable, and
I 'm sure it will be all right: truly, I 'd be
willing to take the responsibility—if I can get
them to consent to it!"

"Very well," said Mrs. Harrow, unwillingly,
"you know them both better than I do, Bertha,
of course, and it certainly could n't be any

worse than it is! But at the first outbreak I shall take the matter into my own hands, and act very severely, if necessary!"

Biscuits went directly upstairs and sought out Martha Williams, who lounged on the couch with Loti in her hand and a bag of chocolate peppermints in her lap. Her roommate, observing that Biscuits glanced at the clock as she entered, murmured something about getting a History note-book and obligingly disappeared.

"That's a good harmless creature," observed Biscuits, approvingly.

"Yes, she's in very good training," the creature's room-mate returned. "Have a peppermint?"

"Pity *she* can't room with Alberta May," said Biscuits, lightly; "*she'd* give her no trouble!"

"Lord, no!" Martha agreed; "she wouldn't trouble a fly!"

Biscuits wandered about the room and absent-mindedly picked up a sheaf of papers.

"Themes back?" she inquired. Martha nodded.

"'Me see 'em?" Martha shrugged her shoulders in a manner to be envied of the Continent.

Biscuits opened at a poem that caught her eye, and read it. Martha's eyes were apparently fixed on *Madame Chrysanthème*, but they wandered occasionally to Biscuits' face as she read. The poem was called, —

THE LIFTING VEIL

Do you love me now?
Ah, your mouth is cold!
Yet you taught me how —
Are we growing old?

Did you love me then?
Ah, your eyes are wet!
If the memory's sweet,
Why will you forget?

Could you love me still?
Hush! you shall not say!
Love is not of will —
Shall I go away?

Dare you love me now?
Let me burn my ships!
I, myself, am not so sure —
Am I worth your lips?

"Um — ah — yes," said Biscuits, "sounds something like Browning, does n't it?"

Martha looked only politely interested.

"Do you think so?" she said impersonally.

BISCUITS EX MACHINA

"Yes. I like that line about the ships," added Biscuits, tentatively; "it—er—seems to—er—*imply* so much!"

Martha looked enigmatically at the skull. "Does it?" she asked.

Biscuits caught a glimpse of a long, hastily written story, and gasped.

"Why, Martha, did you really hand *that* in?" she demanded.

"Certainly I did," said Martha; "why not?"

"Because it's really shocking, you know," Biscuits replied. "What *did* she say?"

Martha hesitated, but a twinkle slipped into her eye and she smiled as she replied. "Look and see," she said.

Biscuits turned to the last page, passing many an underlined word or phrase by the way, and read in crimson ink at the bottom: *Mallock has done this better: you are getting very careless in your use of relatives.* At which Biscuits smiled wisely and reassured herself of an announcement she had made in the middle of her junior year to the effect that even among the Faculty one ran across occasional evidences of real intelligence.

"Martha," she said abruptly, "I meant what I said about Mary and Alberta—they'd make a very good pair."

"And Miss Sutton and I—" returned Martha, sardonically.

"Precisely," said Biscuits, "Miss Sutton and you. Oh, I know nobody has the slightest right to ask it of you and we all supposed you would n't, but at the same time I thought I 'd just lay it before you. I firmly believe, Martha, that you are the only person in this house capable of managing Martha Sutton!"

"I?" And *Madame Chrysanthème* dropped to the floor.

"Yes, you. Now, Martha, just look at it: you know that the girl is a perfect child—you know that she means well enough, and in her way she has a keen sense of humor. Now you are much more mature than the average girl up here and you take—er—broader views of things than most of them. You would n't be so shocked at the things Suttie does; you could, very gradually, you know, convey to her that her ideas of humor were just a little crude, you know, and that would strike her far more than the lectures that Alberta used to read her by the hour."

"Oh! Alberta!" Martha gasped. "Alberta was enough to drive *anybody* to drink!"

"Just so. Well, as I told Mrs. Harrow, you were the one, but of course no one had the least right to press it. And of course, in your last year, and all that, and naturally you have n't any special interest in her, and it 's all right if you won't."

Martha scowled for a moment and appeared to be reviewing her own past life, rapidly and impartially.

"It would be a good thing to have her kept out of the halls, at least," she announced, at last, irrelevantly.

"That 's what I told Mrs. Harrow," said Biscuits, eagerly. "You see, Alberta *bored* her so, Martha. She 's a clever child and she likes clever people. She needs tact, and Alberta has n't the tact of a hen. Only, you see, Mrs. Harrow felt that in a great many ways the example—"

Martha rose and confronted her guest. " I hope you understand, Biscuits, that if I ever *did* go into the kindergarten business I should know how to conduct myself properly. I have never for one moment tried to fit everybody to my own standards : I appreciate perfectly that things are—er—relative, and that what may be perfectly safe for me is not necessarily so for others."

Biscuits coughed and said that she had always known that, and it was for just that reason that she had hesitated to ask Martha to give up her ways and habits : habits which if harmless to the unprejudiced observer were a trifle irregular, viewed from the strictest standpoint of a college house.

"There's no particular reason why you should," she concluded, "and perhaps, anyhow, as Mrs. Harrow says—"

"Perhaps what?" snapped Martha.

"Oh, nothing! Only she doesn't believe you could do it, and of course she perfectly loathes having to make a change this way—she says it's a terrible precedent—and—"

"See here, Biscuits," said Martha, solemnly, "never mind about my habits. I suppose," magnificently, "it won't hurt me to get to bed at ten, once in a way, and it's only till June, anyhow. She *is* a bright enough child, and as you say, she needs tact. If it keeps the house quiet and saves you dinging at 'em all the time, I can do it, I suppose. I might try studying for a change before mid-years, too."

Biscuits got up to go. "I appreciate this very much, Martha," she said gravely. "I know what it means to you, but I really think you'll do her a lot of good—I mean," at a sudden pucker of Martha's brows, "I mean, of course, that a person to whom her badness does n't seem so very terrible will be a revelation to her."

"Oh, yes!" said Martha.

Biscuits waylaid Sutton M. on the stairs after dinner and suggested a conversation in her own cosey little single room. Sutton M. accompanied her, suspiciously.

"Now, what do you think you 're going to do?" she inquired bitterly, as Biscuits offered a shiny apple and tipped *Henry Esmond* off the Morris chair. "Going to put me with some spook or other, I suppose—I 'll leave the house first. I 've had enough of that!"

"No, you won't, either," Biscuits replied. "You 'll be as good as Kate is, and not make me curse the day I was elected house president. Now, Suttie, I 'm going to tell you something that must not go beyond this room— beyond this room," she repeated impressively.

"Not Kate? I have to tell Kate," said Sutton M., but with an air of deepest interest. Outsiders rarely confided in the Twins.

"Well, Kate then, but nobody else. Promise?"

Sutton M. nodded.

"I 'm going to do what might be greatly criticised, Suttie, I 'm going to tell you that I think it would be a very good thing for

Martha Williams if you would quietly go in
and room with her and let Mary come in with
Alberta. Now, I 've done no beating about the
bush—I 've told you out straight and plain.
What do you say?"

"I say it's a fool arrangement, and that I
won't have a thing to do with it," said Sutton
M., promptly.

"All right," returned Biscuits, calmly,
"that's all. Is that apple green? I don't
mind it, but it makes some people sick."

"You know perfectly well Martha's the last
girl in the world—we'd fight night and day."

"I know she's one of the brightest girls in
the college, and that she's getting low in her
work, and it's a shame, too," said Biscuits.

"Would I make her higher?"

Sutton M. tried to be sarcastic, but she
showed in her manner the effect of the confidence.

"Yes, you would," said Biscuits. "Mary
Winter's just spoiling her. She's a perfect non-
entity, and she studies like a grammar-school
girl—it just disgusts Martha. And Mary admires her so that Martha just rides over her
and gets to despise good regular studying because Mary does it so childishly. If some one
could be with her who was bright and jolly

and liked fun and had a sense of humor and
did good work, too, for you two do study
well—I 'll give you that credit—it would be
the making of her. And Mary 's such an idiot.
She shows that Martha shocks her so much
that Martha just keeps it up to horrify her—"

"I know," said Sutton M., wisely, "like
those cigarettes—Martha never really liked
them."

"Exactly," Biscuits agreed, though with an
effort, for the Twins certainly knew far too
much. "The moment I told Martha that it
was n't in the least a question of morals with
us but entirely a matter of good taste—that
we did n't think she was wicked at all but that
it was very bad for the house, and that when
we were all represented in the *Police Gazette*
as trotting over the campus with cigarettes in
our mouths, the college would get all the credit
and she would n't get any—why, she stopped
right away. And considering how it irritated her
I think she was very nice and sensible about
it."

"But just because Kate and I studied, Martha would n't, would she?"

"Yes, I think she would. She 'd feel that
it was an example to you if she did n't. And
she 's so bright. It 's a shame she should flunk

as she does. She knows we all know she could get any marks she chose, so she does n't care."

Sutton M. looked thoughtful. "I think her stories are fine," she remarked. "And I suppose I 'd have to go with some spook, if I don't," she added gloomily.

"Mrs. Harrow feels bad enough about the change," Biscuits interposed, "and she said she 'd act very severely next time. I persuaded her that you 'd—that is, I did n't persuade her, I 'm afraid. Of course, she feels that if you *should* by any chance drag Martha into your kiddish nonsense, why—she does n't like Martha any too well, you know, and—"

"Biscuits," interrupted Sutton M., hastily, "if I *should* go in with Martha, and I must say I should think *anybody* 'd be welcome to her after that stick of a Mary Winter, I would n't drag her into a thing—truly, I would n't. I 'd be careful! Kate says that Patsy says she 's lots of fun and awfully jolly and nice when you know her," she added.

Biscuits assented warmly. "And you understand, Suttie," she continued, "that it 's not everybody I 'd speak to in this way or that Martha would have. Martha's rather particular: she understands that Alberta May is a little trying, good and kind as she is. But I realize what a good thing it would be for Martha to be with somebody who would n't be so shocked whenever she said anything to that skull."

"Oh, that skull!" said Sutton M., with a wave of her brown hand. She looked up and caught Biscuits' eye with the sharp, uncompromisingly literal Sutton twinkle. "Biscuits," she demanded, "did anybody ever know of anything really *bad* that Martha ever did—ever?"

"Never," said Biscuits, promptly.

Sutton M. chuckled: "That 's what we always thought," she said, and added: "Well, I 'll try it, and," very solemnly, "you can trust me, Biscuits—I promise you."

When Biscuits went back to Martha's room she missed the skull, and beheld on the newly dusted bookshelves a decorous row of historical works and an assortment of German classics. This gratified her, for it was with the German department that Martha's erratic methods of study most obviously clashed. Martha was detaching from the wall a pleasing engraving representing a long white lady with her head hanging off from a couch, on which she somewhat obtrusively reclined, an unwholesome demon perching upon her chest and a ghastly white horse peeping at her between gloomy curtains. This cheerful effect was entitled "The Nightmare," and as it left the wall, Martha fell upon an enlargement in colored chalk of one of Mr. Beardsley's most vivid conceptions, and laid them away together.

"Why, Martha!" she exclaimed, "this is really too much—there's no reason why you should take your things down!"

Martha smiled tolerantly. "Oh, it makes no matter to me," she said indifferently. "I know the Loti by heart, anyhow, and though none of these things affect me in the slightest way—I really can't see anything in them one way or the other—still I frankly refuse to take any responsibility. If the child should happen to feel that the skull, for instance—"

Biscuits grinned. "It's one less thing to dust, anyway," she remarked, and left Martha to her work of reconstruction.

She wandered in, one evening, two or three weeks later, to get a German dictionary, and beheld with a pardonable pride the Twins gabbling their irregular verbs in whispers by the lamp, while Martha, stretched on the couch beneath the gas, communed with Schiller and the dictionary. The Twins gave her one swift ineffable glance, kicked each other under the table, and bent their eyes upon their grammars: Martha nodded to her, indicated the Twins with one of her three-volume smiles, and drawled as she handed her the dictionary, "In the words of Mr. Dooley and the Cubans, 'Pa-pa has lost his job, and all is now happiness and a cottage-organ'!"

THE EDUCATION OF ELIZABETH

V

THE EDUCATION OF ELIZABETH

I

FROM MISS ELIZABETH STOCKTON
TO MISS CAROLYN SAWYER

Lowell, Mass., Sept. 10, 189–.

MY DEAREST CAROL: The thing we have both wished so much has happened! Papa has finally consented to let me go to college! It has taken a long time and a *great deal* of persuasion, and Mamma never cared *anything* about it, you know, herself. But I laid it before her in a way that I really am ashamed of! I never thought I'd do anything like it! But I *had* to, it seemed to me. I told her that she had often spoken of what a mistake Mrs. Hall made in letting Marjory come out so soon, and that I should *certainly* be unwilling to stay at Mrs. Meade's another year. I'm doing advanced work now, and I'm *terribly* bored. The girls all seem so very young, somehow! And I said that I couldn't come out till I was twenty-two, if I went to college. I teased so that she gave way, but we had a *terrible* siege with Papa. He is the *dearest* man in the world, but just a little *tiny* bit prejudiced, you know. He wants me to finish at Mrs. Meade's and then go abroad for a year or two. He wants me to do something with my music. But I told him of the *fine* Music School there was at Smith, and how much *harder* I should work there, *naturally*. He talked a good deal about the art advantages and travel and French—you know what I think about the *terrible narrowness* of a boarding-school education! It is *shameful*, that an intellectual girl of this century should be tied down to *French* and *Music!* And how can the scrappy little bit of gallery sight-seeing that I should do *possibly* equal four years of earnest, intelligent, *regular* college work? He said something about marriage—oh, dear! It is *horrible* that one should have to think of that! I told him, with a great deal of dignity and rather coldly, I'm afraid, that *my* life would be, I hoped, *something more* than the mere *evanescent glitter* of a *social butterfly!* I think it really impressed him. He said, "Oh, very well—very well!" So I'm coming, dearest, and you must write me all about what books I'd better get and just what I'd better know of the college customs. I'm *so* glad you're on the campus. You know Uncle Wendell knows the President very well indeed—he was in college with him—and, somehow or other,

THE EDUCATION OF ELIZABETH

I 've got a room in the Lawrence, though we did n't expect it so soon! I feel inspired already when I think of the chapel and the big Science Building and that *beautiful* library! I 've laid out a course of work that Miss Beverly—that 's the literature teacher—thinks very ambitious, but I am afraid she does n't realize the intention of a *college*, which is a little different, I suppose, from a *boarding-school* (!) I have planned to take sixteen hours for the four years. I must say I think it 's rather absurd to limit a girl to that who *really* is *perfectly* able to do more. Perhaps you could see the Register—if that 's what it is—and tell him I could just as well take eighteen, and then I could do that other Literature. I must go to try on something—really, it 's very hard to convince Mamma that Smith is n't a *summer resort*! Good-by, dearest, we shall have such *beautiful* times together—I 'm sure you 'll be as excited as I am. We shall *for once* see as much of each other as we want to—I wish I could study with you! I 'm coming up on the 8.20 Wednesday morning.

Devotedly yours,
ELIZABETH.

SMITH COLLEGE STORIES

II

From Miss Carolyn Sawyer to Miss Elizabeth Stockton

Lake Forest, Ill., Sept. 17, 189–

DEAR BESS: I 'm very glad you 're coming up—it 's the only place in the world. I 'm not going to be able to meet you—I 'm coming back late this year—Mrs. Harte is going to give our crowd a house-party at Lakemere. Is n't that gay? I met Arnold Ritch this summer. He knows you, he said. I never heard you speak of him. He 's perfectly *smooth*—his tennis is all right, too. For heaven's sake, don't try to take sixteen hours—on the campus, too! It will break you all up. You 'll get on the Glee Club, probably—bring up your songs, by the way—and you 'll want to be on the Team. Have you got that blue organdie? You 'll want something about like that, pretty soon. If you can help it, don't get one of those Bagdad things for your couch. I 'm deadly sick of mine. Get that portière thing you used to have on the big chair at home. It 's more individual. We 're getting up a little dance for the 26th. If you know any man you could have up, you can come—it will be a good chance to meet some of the upper-class girls.

We may not be able to have it, though. Don't tell Kate Saunders about this, please. She'd ask Lockwood over from Amherst, and I've promised Jessie Holden to ask him for her. We shall probably have Sue for class president this year—I'm glad of it, too. There will be a decent set of ushers. I suppose you'll want me for your senior for the sophomore-senior thing. I'll keep that if you wish. I shall get up by the 24th. I'm in the Morris. Don't forget your songs.

Yours in haste,

C. P. S.

III

FROM MRS. HENRY STOCKTON
TO MRS. JOHN SAWYER

Lowell, Mass., Sept. 23, 189–.

DEAR ELLA: In spite of great uncertainty on my part and actual unwillingness on her father's, Lizzie has started for Smith. It seems a large undertaking, for four years, and I must say I would rather have left her at Mrs. Meade's. But her heart is set on it, and it is very hard to deny her. She argues so, too; really, the child has great ability, I think. She fairly convinced me. It has always seemed to me that a girl with good social surround-

[127]

ings, a good home library, and an intellectual
home atmosphere does very well with four
years at so good a school as Mrs. Meade's,
and a little travel afterwards. Lizzie has quite
a little musical talent, too, and I should have
liked her to devote more attention to that.
Very frankly, I cannot say that I have been
able to see any improvement in Carrie since
she went away. I suppose it will wear off, but
when I saw her this summer she had a manner
that I did not like so well as her very pleasant air three—no, two—years ago. It seemed
a curious mixture of youth and decision, that
had, however, no maturity in it. Katharine
Saunders, too, seems to me so utterly irresponsible for a young woman of twenty-one,
and yet so almost arrogant. I expected she
would know a great deal, as she studied Greek
before she went, but she told me that she always skipped the Latin and Greek quotations
in books ! She seems to be studying nothing
but French and Literature and History; her
father could perfectly well have taught her all
that, and was anxious to, but she would hear
nothing of it. She wanted the college life, she
said. Ah, well, I suppose the world has moved
on since we read Livy at Miss Hopkins' ! I
picked up a Virgil of Lizzie's yesterday and

was astonished to find how it all came back. We felt very learned, then, but now it is nothing.

I hope Carrie will be good to my little girl and help her perhaps with her lessons—not that I fear Lizzie will need very much help! Miss Beverly assures me that she has never trained a finer mind. Her essay on Jane Austen was highly praised by Dr. Strong, the rector of St. Mary's. Of course, dear Ella, you won't resent my criticism of Carrie—I should never dream of it with any one but an old and valued friend, and I shall gladly receive the same from you. But Lizzie has always been all that I could wish her.

Yours with love,
SARAH B. STOCKTON.

IV

FROM MR. WILLIAM B. STOCKTON
TO MISS ELIZABETH STOCKTON

Boston, Mass., Oct. 16, 189–.

MY DEAR NIECE: Your mother advises me of your having just entered Smith Academy. I had imagined that your previous schooling would have been sufficient, but doubtless your parents know best. Your mother seems a little alarmed as to your success, but I have reassured her. I trust the Stockton blood. Whatever your surroundings may be, you can never, I am sure, set yourself a higher model than your mother. I have never known her to lack the right word or action under any circumstances, and if you can learn that in your schooling, your friends and relatives will be more than satisfied.

I enclose my cheque for fifty dollars ($50), in case you should have any special demand on your purse not met by your regular allowance. I remember many such in my own schooldays. Wishing you success in your new life, I remain,

Your affectionate uncle,

WILLIAM B. STOCKTON.

v

FROM MISS ELIZABETH CRAIGIE
TO MISS ELIZABETH STOCKTON

New Haven, Conn., Oct. 21, 189–.

MY DEAR ELIZABETH: Sarah tells me that you are going to college. I am sure I don't see why, but if you do, I suppose that is enough. Children are not what they used to be. It seems to me that four years at Mrs. Meade's should have been enough; neither your Aunt Hannah nor I ever went to college, though

THE EDUCATION OF ELIZABETH

to be sure Hannah wanted to go to Mt. Holyoke Seminary once. I have never heard any one intimate that either of us was not sufficiently educated: I wonder that you could for one instant imagine such a thing! Not that I have any reason to suppose you ever did. However, that is neither here nor there. Your Aunt Hannah and I were intending to give you Mother's high shell-comb and her garnet set for Christmas. If you would prefer them now for any reason, you may have them. The comb is being polished and looks magnificent. An absurd thing to give a girl of your age, from my point of view. However, your Aunt Hannah thinks it best. I trust you will be very careful of your diet. It seemed to me that your complexion was not what it should have been when you came on this summer. I am convinced that it is nothing but the miscellaneous eating of cake and other sweets and over-education. There has been a young girl here from some college—I think it is Wellesley—and her complexion is disgraceful. Your Aunt Hannah and I never set up for beauties, but we had complexions of milk and roses, if I do say it. Hannah thinks that the garnets are unsuitable for you, but that is absurd. Mother was no older than you when she wore them, and looked very well, too, I have no doubt. I send you by express a box of Katy's doughnuts, the kind you like, very rich, and a chocolate cake. Also some salad and a loaf cake, Mrs. Harding's rule. I trust you will take sufficient exercise, and don't let your hands grow rough this winter. Nothing shows a lady so much as her hands. Would you like the garnets reset, or as Mother wore them? They are quite the style now, I understand. Hoping you will do well in your studies and keep well, I am,

Yours lovingly,

AUNT LIZZIE.

VI

FROM MISS ELIZABETH STOCKTON TO MR. ARNOLD RITCH, JR.

Lawrence House, Northampton, Mass.,
Nov. 1, 189-.

MY DEAR ARNOLD: It is only fair to you to tell you that it can never be. No, never! When I—if I did (which I can hardly believe)—allowed you to think anything else, I was a mere child. Life looks very different to me, now. It is quite useless to ask me—I must say that I am surprised that you have spoken to Papa. Nor do I feel called upon to give my reasons. I shall always be a very, very good friend to you, however, and very, very much interested in you.

In the first place, I am, or at least you are, far too young. The American woman of to-day is younger than her grandmother. I mean, of course, younger than her grandmother is now. That is, than she was then. Also I doubt if I could ever love you as you think you do. Love me, I mean. I am not a man's woman. I much prefer women. Really, Arnold, it is very strange how men bore me now that I have known certain women. Women are so much more interesting, so much more fascinating, so much more exciting! This will probably seem strange to you, but the modern woman I am sure is rapidly getting not to need men at all! I have never seen so many beautiful red-haired girls before. One sits in front of me in chapel, and the light makes an aureole of glory about her head. I wrote a theme about it that is going to be in the *Monthly* for November.

I hope that you won't feel that our dear old friendship of so many years is in any way changed. I shall never forget certain things —

I am enjoying my work very much, though it is easier than I had thought it would be, and the life is different in many ways. If I did not think that Miss Sawyer had probably invited you, I should be very glad to have you come up for the Christmas concert, but I suppose it is useless to ask you. I had no idea you were so fond of tennis!

Your friend always,
ELIZABETH WOLFE STOCKTON.

VII

FROM MR. HENRY STOCKTON
TO MISS ELIZABETH STOCKTON

Lowell, Mass., Nov. 1, 189–.

MY DEAR ELIZABETH: Yours received and read with my usual attention and interest. I am glad that your college life continues to be pleasant, and that you have found so many friends. I was much interested, too, in the photograph of Miss Hunter. I find the blue prints are more common than I had supposed, for I had imagined that they were something quite new. It is certainly very accommodating in your teachers to allow themselves to be so generally photographed. Your mother seemed much pleased with Miss Hunter, and glad that you were in the house with her and liked her so much. I was surprised to see her so young in appearance. I had very foolishly imagined the typical old style "school-marm," I suppose. But it seems that she was graduated only a few years ago, herself.

Now, my dear Elizabeth, I am going to speak to you very seriously. I trust that you will take it in good part and remember that nothing can be more to my interest than the real happiness and well-being of my daughter. The tone of your letters to both your mother and me has seemed for some weeks unsatisfactory. I mean that we have found in them a nervous, strained tone that troubles me exceedingly. I cannot see why you should close with such expressions as this (I copy verbatim): "Too tired to write more;" "All used up—lots of Latin to do—can only find time for a note;" "Tired to death because I'm not sleeping quite as well as usual, just now;" et cetera, et cetera.

I have been to see Mrs. Meade, and she assures me that your preparation was more than adequate: that your first year should prove very easy for you, *in Latin especially.* Now what does this mean? You left us well and strong, considering that you have always been a delicate girl. It was for that reason, as you know, that I particularly opposed your going to college.

But there is more. Mrs. Allen's daughter,
Harriet, has been at home for some days to
attend her sister's wedding. Your mother and
I naturally seized the opportunity of inquiring after you, and after some questioning from
us she admitted that you were not looking very
well. She said that you seemed tired and were
"going it a little too hard, perhaps." That
seemed to me a remarkable expression to ap-
ply to a young girl! My endeavors to find out
exactly what it meant resulted in nothing more
explicit than that "Bess was trying to do too
much."

Now, my dear girl, while we are naturally
only too pleased that you should be striving
to stand well in your classes, do not, I beg of
you, imagine for one moment that any intellectual advancement you may win can compen-
sate us or you for the loss of your health. You
remember Cousin Will, who carried off six hon-
ors at Harvard and came home a nervous in-
valid. I fear that the Stockton temperament
cannot stand the strain of too continued mental application.

I must stop now, to attend to some business matters, and I will add only this. Do not
fail to remember my definite conditions, which
have not altered since September. If you are

not perfectly well at the Christmas holidays, you must remain with us. This may seem severe, but I am convinced, your mother also, that we shall be acting entirely for your good.

Yours aff.,
FATHER.

VIII
FROM MR. ARNOLD RITCH, SR., TO MISS MARION HUNTER

New York, N. Y., Nov. 4, 189–.

MY DEAR MISS HUNTER: You may remember meeting, five years ago, in Paris, in the Louvre, an old American, who had the great pleasure of rendering you a trifling assistance in a somewhat embarrassing situation, and who had the further pleasure of crossing on the *Etruria* with you a month later. I was that man, and I remember that you said that if ever there should happen to be an occasion for it, you would be only too happy to return your imaginary debt.

If you really meant it, the occasion, strangely enough, has come. I know well enough from my lifelong friend, Richard Benton, whose family you have so often visited, that you are an extremely busy young woman, and I will state my case briefly. I never make half-confidences,

[137]

and I rely implicitly on your discretion in the following clear statement. My only nephew and namesake, incidentally heir, has been for some time practically engaged to Miss Elizabeth Stockton, the daughter of an old friend. The engagement has been entirely satisfactory to all parties concerned, and was actually on the eve of announcement, when the young lady abruptly departed for Smith College.

My nephew is, though only twenty-four, unusually mature and thoroughly settled : he was deeply in love with the young lady and assures me that his sentiments were returned. She now quietly refuses him, and greatly to her parents' dissatisfaction announces that she intends remaining the four years and "graduating with her class," which seems a strong point with her.

Her father and I would gladly leave the affair to work itself out quietly, were it not for an unfortunate occurrence. Ritch, Jr. has been offered an extremely good opening in a Paris banking-house, which he must accept, if at all, immediately, and for six years. He is extremely broken up over the whole affair, and says that unless Elizabeth returns to her old relations with him, he will go. This will be in three weeks.

THE EDUCATION OF ELIZABETH

I am not so young as I was, and I cannot leave America again. I can only say that if the boy goes, my interest in life goes, to a great extent, with him. He does not mean to be selfish, but young people, you know, are harder than they think, and feel deeply and, for the moment, irrevocably. He says that he is certain that this is merely a fad on Miss Stockton's part, and that if he could see her for two weeks he would prove it. I should like to have him try.

This is my favor, Miss Hunter. Elizabeth respects and admires you more than any of her teachers. She quotes you frequently and seems influenced by you. Arnold has made me promise that I will not ask her parents to bring her home and that I will not write her. I will not. But can you do anything? It is rather absurd to ask you to conspire against your college, to give up one of your pupils: but you have a great many, and remember that I have but one nephew! It is all rather a comedy, but a sad one for me, if there is no change within three weeks, I assure you. They are only two headstrong children, but they can cause more than one heartache if they keep up their obstinacy. Elizabeth has forbidden Arnold to come to Northampton on the score of her work, and wild horses could not drag him there.

I offer no suggestion, I ask nothing definitely, I merely wonder if you meant what you said on the *Etruria*, and if your woman's wit, that must have managed so many young idiots, can manage these?

Yours faithfully,
ARNOLD M. RITCH.

IX
FROM MISS MARION HUNTER TO MRS. HENRY STOCKTON

Northampton, Mass., Nov. 7, 189-.

MY DEAR MRS. STOCKTON: As you have certainly not forgotten that I assured you in the early fall of my interest, professionally and personally, in your daughter, you will need no further explanation, nor be at all alarmed, when I tell you that Elizabeth is a little overworked of late. In the house with her as I am, I see that she is trying to carry a little too much of our unfortunately famous "social life" in connection with her studies, where she is unwilling to lose a high grade. She entered so well prepared that she has nothing to fear from a short absence, and as she tells me that she does not sleep well at all of late, she will

THE EDUCATION OF ELIZABETH

have no difficulty in getting an honorable furlough. Two weeks or so of rest and freedom from strain will set her up perfectly, I have no doubt, and she can return with perfect safety to her work, which is, I repeat, quite satisfactory.

Yours very cordially,

MARION HUNTER.

X

FROM MRS. HENRY STOCKTON
TO MISS ELIZABETH STOCKTON

(*Telegram*)

Lowell, Mass., Nov. 8.

Come home immediately will arrange with college and explain myself.

MOTHER.

XI

FROM MISS MARION HUNTER
TO MISS CONSTANCE JACKSON

Northampton, Mass., Nov. 10, 189–.

DEAR CON: I'm afraid it will be impossible for me to accept your seductive invitation for Thanksgiving. We're pulling the girls up a little sharply this year, and it would hardly do for me to come back late. But it *would* be good to hear a little music once more!

It was rather odd that you should have men-

tioned that idiotic affair of mine in Paris—
the hero of it has just written me a long letter
apropos of his nephew, who wants to marry
that little Miss Stockton, whose Harvard
cousin you knew so well. That portly squire
of dames is actually simple and straightfor-
ward enough to suggest that I precipitate the
damsel into the expectant arms of his nephew
and heir-apparent—he is used to getting his
own way, certainly, and he writes a rather attractive letter. I owe him much (as you know)
and if Elizabeth, who is a dear little thing and
far too nice for the crowd she's getting in
with—you knew Carol Sawyer, didn't you?
—has such a weak-kneed interest in college
as to be turned out of the way by a sight of
the destined young gentleman, I fancy she
would not have remained long with us in any
case. She's a pretty creature and had cunning
ways—I shall miss her in the house. For I
don't believe she'll come back; she's not at
all strong, and her parents are much worried
about her health. It is more than probable
that the Home will prove her sphere.

Personally, I don't mind stating that I
would it were mine. When I consider how my
days are spent ——

You might not believe it, but they grow

stupider and stupider. Perhaps I've been at it a bit too long, but I never saw such papers as these freshmen give one.

And they have begun singing four hymns in succession on Sunday morning! It's very hard—why they should select *Abide with Me* and *Lead, Kindly Light* for morning exercises and wail them both through to the bitter end every Sunday in the year is one of the local mysteries.

I must get at my papers, they cover everything. Remember me to Mr. Jackson; it was very kind of him to suggest it, but I must wait till Christmas for the Opera, I'm afraid. If I should not come back next year—and it is more than possible that I shan't—I may be in Boston. I hope in that case you won't have gone away.

Yours always,
M. I. HUNTER.

XII

FROM MISS ELIZABETH STOCKTON
TO MISS CAROLYN SAWYER

Lowell, Nov. 20.

CAROL DEAR: I am writing in a great hurry, as I have an engagement at four, to tell you that I have decided not to return to-day, as I intended. Will you get the key of 32 from Mrs. Driscoll, as Kitty goes home over Sunday, so it will be locked, and get out my mink collarette and my silver toilet things and my blanket wrapper, and I think there is twenty dollars in my handkerchief case. I am extremely disturbed and confused—when one is really responsible for anything one feels very much disturbed. Of course, I don't believe a word of it—it's all folly and nonsense —but still, six years is a long time. Of course, you don't know at all what I mean, dear, and I'm not sure I do either. I forgot to say that I'm probably not coming back to college this year. Mamma feels very worried about my health—you know I didn't sleep very well nights, and I used to dream about Livy. Anyway, she and Papa are going abroad early in the spring, and really, Carol, a college education isn't everything. If I were going to teach, you know, it would be different, but you see I was almost finished at Mrs. Meade's —I was taking advanced work—and it isn't as if I had had only the college preparation. Then, if we go abroad, I must do something with my French. You know there was simply *no* chance to practise conversation in such a large class, and I was forgetting it, which Ar-

nold thinks would be a pity. He speaks very
fine French himself. Then, you see, there'll
be all the galleries and everything and the
Sistine Madonna and the cathedrals—they're
so educative—everybody admits that. It's
hardly to be supposed that Geometry and Livy
are really going to be as broadening to me as
a year of travel with Papa and Mamma, is it?
And though I never said anything to you
about it, I really have felt for some time that
there was something a little narrow about the
college. They seem to think it is about all
there is of life, you know, with the funny little dances and the teas and all that. Even that
dear Miss Hunter is really *un peu gâtée* with
it all—she thinks, I believe, that a college
education is all there is for anybody. She told
Mamma that I wasn't well—she wanted me
to keep my high grade. Oh! Carol! there are
better things than grades! Life is a very much
bigger thing than the campus even! I think,
dear, that one really ought to consider very
frankly just what we intend to do with our
lives—if we are going to marry, we ought to
try to make ourselves cultivated and broad-
minded, and in every way worthy to be—Oh,
Carol, dearest, I'm terribly happy! It isn't
settled, of course: I am utterly amazed that

they all seem to think it is, but it is n't. Only probably if I still feel as I do now, when we get back, I shall ask you, dear, what we promised each other—to be my brides-maid—the first one! I 'm thinking of asking Sally and Grace and Eleanor—all our old set at Mrs. Meade's, you know. I think that pink, with a deep rose for hats and sashes, would look awfully well on all of you, don't you! It seems a long time since I was in Northampton: the girls seem very young and terribly serious over queer little lessons—or else trying to play they 're interested in each other. Arnold says he thinks the attitude of so many women is bound to be unhealthy, and even in some cases a little morbid. I think he is quite right, don't you? After all, girls need some one besides themselves. I always thought that Mabel Towne was very bad for Katharine. Will you send, too, my Shelley and my selections from Keats? The way I neglected my reading—real reading, you know—oh! *c'était affreux!* I 'm learning the loveliest song—Arnold is very fond of it:

Ninon, Ninon, que fais-tu de la vie?
L'heure s'enfuit, le jour succède au jour.
  Rose ce soir, demain flétrie—
Comment vis-tu, toi qui n'as pas d'amour?

I'm going out now for a walk. I'm sure you'll like Arnold — I think you said you met him. He does n't remember you. Remember me to all the juniors I met, and if you see Ethel Henderson, tell her I'll write to her when I get time. Excuse this pointed pen — I'm learning to use it. Arnold hates a stub.

Yours always,

BETTY.

A FAMILY AFFAIR

VI
A FAMILY AFFAIR

THERE are Jacksons and Jacksons. As everybody knows, many, possibly most, of those who bear that title might as well have been called Jones or Robinson; on the other hand, I am told that certain Massachusetts families of that name will, on solicitation, admit it to be their belief that Eve was a Cabot and Adam a Jackson. Without asserting that she was personally convinced of this great fact, it is necessary to state that Susan was of the last-named variety of Jackson. She was distinctly democratic, however, and rather strong-willed, and for both of these reasons she came to college. It did not entirely please the family: neither of her sisters had gone, and her brothers in particular were against it. It is probable that she would have been decoyed from her plan had it not been that her cousin, Constance Quincy Jackson, had been for a year one of the young assistants who dash like meteors through the catalogue and disappear mysteriously, just as astronomers have begun to place them, into the obscurity whence they came.

Constance, like Susan, had been persistent, and was studying at Oxford before the family had quite made up its mind how to regard her; later, she frequented other and American institutions of learning and bore off formidable degrees therefrom, and at about that time it was decided that she was remarkably brilliant, and that her much commended thesis on the Essential Somethingness of Something or Other was quite properly to be ranked with her great-grandfather's dissertation on the Immortality of the Soul.

She would do very well; she could be relied on; and entrusted to her and further armed with letters of introduction to the social magnates of the vicinity—which, I regret to say, she neglected to present till her sophomore year—Susan began her career. Of the eminent success of this career, it is not the purpose of this story to treat. Beginning as freshman vice-president, she immediately identified herself with the leading set of her class, and in her sophomore year was already one of the prominent students in the college. She was one of Phi Kappa's earliest acquisitions, and belonged to three or four lesser societies, social and semi-educational; she had been on the freshman Team; she was twice a member of the Council; in her senior year she was literary editor of the *Monthly* and class president, besides taking a prominent part in Dramatics. She fulfilled all these duties most acceptably, taking at the same time a very high rank in her classes: in one department, indeed, her work was pronounced practically perfect by a somewhat exigent professor. And in addition, she was well born, well bred, and well dressed, and considered by her most enthusiastic admirers the handsomest girl in the college, though this was by no means the universal opinion.

You might imagine that Miss Jackson was therefore intolerably conceited, but in this you would err. She took no particular credit to herself for her standard of work; she had a keen mind, and had been taught to concentrate it, and her grandfather, her father, and two uncles had successively led their classes at Harvard. It seemed perfectly natural to her to be told that she was the one young woman on whose shoulders a golf cape looked really dignified and graceful—had not her grandmother and her great-aunt been famed for their "camel's-hair-shawl shoulders"? A somewhat commanding manner and a very keen-sighted social policy had given her a prominence that she was conscious of having done nothing to discredit; and as she had been quite accus-

tomed to see those about her in positions
of authority, and had learned to lay just the
proper amount of emphasis on adverse criticism, she steered her way with a signal success
on the perilous sea of popularity. Her idea of
the four years had been to do everything there
was to be done as well as any one could do it,
and she was not a person accustomed to consider failure.

I mentioned at the beginning of this story
the two classes of Jacksons. Emphatically of
the former and unimportant variety was Elaine
Susan Jackson of Troy, New York. Mr. Jackson kept a confectionery shop and ice cream
parlor, going to his business early in the morning and returning late in the evening. This he
did because he was a quiet-loving man, and
his home was a noisy one. Mrs. Jackson was
a managing, dictatorial woman, with an unexpected sentimental vein which she nour-
ished on love-stories and exhausted there.
From these books she had culled the names
of her daughters—Elaine, Veronica, and Doris;
but prudence impelled her to add to these the
names of her husband's three sisters—a triumph of maternal foresight over æsthetic taste
—and they stood in the family Bible, Elaine
Susan, Veronica Sarah, and Doris Hannah.

A FAMILY AFFAIR

Mr. Jackson was not a sentimentalist himself, and read nothing but the paper, sitting placidly behind the peanut-brittle and chocolate mice, and relapsing sometimes into absolute idleness for hours together, deep in contemplation, perhaps, possibly dozing— nobody ever knew. At such times he regarded the entrance of customers as an unwelcome intrusion and was accustomed to hurry them, if juvenile, into undue precipitance of choice. From this even quiet he emerged seldom but effectively: when Veronica entertained the unattractive young men she called "the boys," later than eleven o'clock, when Doris went to the theatre more than twice a week, or when they had purchased garments of a nature more than usually unsuitable and pronounced. Then Mr. Jackson spoke, and after domestic whirlwinds and fires the still voice of an otherwise doubtful head of the family became the voice of authority.

Elaine gave him no trouble of this sort. She did not care for young men, and she never went to the theatre. Her clothes, when she had any choice in the matter, were of the plainest, and she had never teased her father for candy since she began to read, which was at a very early age. *I Say No, or the Love-letter*

Answered, was her first consciously studied book, and between ten and fifteen she devoured more novels than most people get into a lifetime. Incidentally she read poetry —she got books of it for prizes at school— and one afternoon she sandwiched the *Golden Treasury* between two detective stories. She did not care for her mother's friends, gossiping, vulgar women, and she loathed her sisters'. She had a sharp tongue, and as parental discipline was of the slightest, she criticised them all impartially with the result that she was cordially disliked by everybody she knew —a feeling she returned with interest. She found two or three ardent friends at school and was very happy with them for a time, but she was terribly exacting, and demanded an allegiance so intense and unquestioning that one by one they drifted away into other groups and left her.

In her second year at the high school they read the *Idylls of the King*, and she discovered her name and saw in one shame-filled second the idiotic bad taste of it—Elaine Susan! She imagined the lily maid of Astolat behind her father's counter and became so abased in her own mind that the school found her more haughty and disagreeable than ever. From that moment she signed her name E. Susan Jackson and requested to be called Susan. This met the approval of the teachers, and as the schoolgirls did not hold much conversation with her, the change was not a difficult one.

By the time she had been three years in the high school she was considered by every one the most brilliant student there, and the principal suggested college to her. This had never occurred to her. Though they had never lacked for necessities, Mr. Jackson's business was not conducted in a manner to lead to marked financial success, and though he said little about his affairs, it was evident to them all that matters were slowly but surely running down hill. Doris and Veronica were eager to leave school and spend a term at the Business College, some friends of theirs having done this with great success and found positions as typewriters, but their father insisted on their staying at school for two years at least. It would be time enough to leave, he said, when they had to. It was significant of the unconscious attitude of the family that there had never been any question of the oldest daughter's leaving school: Elaine had always been real bright, her mother said, and as long as books was all she took any interest in, she might as well get what she could—she presumed she'd teach.

But this acquiescent spirit changed immediately when she learned that her husband had told Elaine he would send her to college for two years anyway, and as much longer as he could afford. It seemed to Mrs. Jackson a ridiculous and unwarranted expense, particularly as he had refused to allow the term at the Business College partly on the financial score. She lectured, argued, scolded; but he was firm.

"I told her she should, and she shall," he repeated quietly. "She says she thinks she can help along after a while, and you need n't worry about her paying it back—she will, all right, if she can. I guess she's the best of the lot of us; she's worth the other two put together. You let Lainey alone, Hattie, she's all right!"

This was during her last year at school, and as she had on her own responsibility taken the classical course there, finding a fascination in the idea of Greek, she accomplished the preparation very easily.

Her mother, bowing to the inevitable, began to plume herself on her daughter "who was fitting herself to go to Smith's College," and rose many degrees in the social scale because of her. But their ideas of the necessary preparations differed so materially, that after prolonged and jarring hostilities marked by much temper on both sides, the final crash came, and after a battle royal Elaine took what money was forthcoming and conducted her affairs unchallenged from that moment. It was a relief to be freed from the wearisome squabbles, but she cried herself to sleep the night before she left—she did not perfectly know why. Later she told herself that it was because she had so little reason to cry when she left home for the first time.

She went to the train alone, because the girls were at school and her father at his business. She said good-by to her mother on the porch, with the constraint that had grown to characterize her attitude towards them all, but her mother was suddenly seized with a spasm of sentiment, and kissing her wildly, bewailed the necessity that drove her firstborn from her to strangers. Later the girl found it sadly characteristic of her life, that absurd scene on the porch; with her heart hungry and miserable for the love and confidence she had never known, she endured agonies of shame and irritation at the demonstration that came too late. She went away, outwardly cold, with tight-pressed lips; her mother read *Cometh up as a Flower*, and wept hysterically that Fate should have cursed her with such an unfeeling, moody child.

It is hard to determine just what incident convinced Susan—for she dropped the initial on her registration—that life had not changed for her because she was to live it in Northampton, and that she must be alone there, as she had been in Troy. Just before she left college she decided that she had known it immediately: that from the moment when she plunged into the chattering, bustling crowd in the Main Hall, where everybody knew somebody and most people knew all the others, a vague prevision of her four years' loneliness came to her: a pathetic certainty that she could not, even with the effort she was too proud to make, become in any reality a part of that sparkling, absorbed, unconscious current of life that rushed by her.

Sometimes she dated her disillusionment— for she had had her dreams: she knew them only by the pathetic disappointment of the obstinate awakening—from the day that she saw her namesake laughing in the midst of a jolly group of girls to whom she was presenting her father and her aunt. They were handsome, well-dressed people with a distinct air, and they were tolerantly amused at Sue in her new environment and showed it in a kindly, courteous way that was much appreciated. As Susan passed the group there was a great laugh, and she heard Sue's voice above the rest.

"Truly, Papa, I thought you'd finished! You know, whenever I interrupted, Papa used to make me sit absolutely still for a quarter of an hour afterward—it's not so long ago he stopped, either!"

Her father laughed, and patted her shoulder, and Susan went on out of hearing. It was only a flash; but she saw the gracious, well-ordered household, the handsome, dignified people, the atmosphere of generations of good breeding and scholarship, as clearly as if she had visited them, and her heart swelled with angry regret and a sickening certainty that all the cleverness in the world could not make up for the youth she had been cheated out of. She thought of the bickering, squabbling family table in Troy and tried to imagine her father teaching Doris and Veronica not to interrupt: her cheeks burned.

In class Sue was often near her; she knew that she was recognized chiefly by the fact that *she* was Susan Jackson, too. On the first day, when the instructor had called "Miss Jackson" and they had both answered, "Miss Susan Jackson," when they still replied together, and finally "Miss Susan Revere Jackson," when the matter was cleared up, Sue had looked at her with interest, and after the class made some little joking remark. If the other had answered in the same spirit, nobody knows whether this story need have been written. But Susan had heard Cornelia Burt ask: "Is she related at all, Sue?" and heard Sue's answer, "Oh, dear, no! From Troy, I believe."

Now Sue meant absolutely nothing but what she said, but her namesake read into the words a scorn that was not there—either in intention or fact. Her heart was sore with a hot, vague jealousy: this girl, no longer there than she, had stepped so easily into a place prepared, apparently, for her; she knew everybody, went everywhere; admired by her own class and made much of by the upper-class girls, she was already well known in the college. She was a part of it all—Susan only watched it. And because of this and because she admired her tremendously and envied her with all the force of a passionate, repressed nature, the poor child answered her little remark with a curtness that was almost insolent, and the manner of an offended duchess. Sue flushed a little, lifted her brows, threw a swift glance at Cornelia, and walked away with her. Susan heard them laughing in the hall, and bit her lip.

She could not know that Sue had described her in a letter to her father as "a queer, haughty thing, but terribly clever. Nobody seems to know her—I imagine she's terribly bored up here. I said some footless thing or other to her the other day, and she turned me down, as Betty says. Did you meet Dr. Twitchell? He was stopping with the Winthrops. . . ."

Susan used to wonder afterwards if it would all have been different had she been on the campus. I know that most college people will say that it would, and it is certain that campus life was the best thing in the world for Martha Williams: nobody knows with what self-conscious egotism she might have been spoiled if her friends and foes had not conspired to laugh it out of her. But, on the other hand, those who have watched the victims of that reasonless, pitiless boycotting that only women can accomplish so lightly—so unconsciously, do you think?—know the ghastly loneliness of the one who, in the very centre of the most crowded campus house, is more solitary than the veriest island castaway.

There is no doubt that Susan needed a great deal of discipline. She had been for so many years superior to her surroundings, so long not only the cleverest but the finest-grained, most aristocratic of all those she saw about her, that although she had perfectly appreciated the fact that she would probably no longer be in that relative position, she had not estimated the difficulty of the necessary adjustment, and it is only fair to those who gave her her hardest lessons of calm neglect to state at once that her manner was a trifle irritating.

To begin with, she had made herself unpleasantly conspicuous at the time of their first freshman class-meeting by rising after half an hour of unventilated and tumultuous altercation, and leaving the room. Now it is not the custom of popular freshmen to leave their first class-meeting in this manner—not as if one were faint or demanded at recitation, but as merely intolerably bored and not a little contemptuous; and the scrambling, squabbling class regarded her accordingly. Susan Revere Jackson was bored, too—unspeakably bored; but she sat indefatigably in her chair in the front row, applauded nominations, discussed the presumably parliamentary features of the occasion, smiled and agreed, differed at proper intervals, and left the room vice-president. It is hard to know just how much enthusiasm Sue really felt: Susan, to whom she soon became the visible expression of all the triumph and ease and distilled essence of the successful college girl, used to wonder, later, as older than Susan have wondered, how much of her college life was ingenuous and how much a perfectly conscious attitude. For long before she left, Susan realized that she had greatly misjudged a large proportion of the girls, whom the event proved more practically wise than she, and that they who fill the rôle of "fine, all 'round girl" with the greatest success are often perfectly competent to fill others, widely different.

This she did not understand at first, and as a result of her ignorance she included them all in her general condemnation: she found them immature, boisterous, inclined to be silly; or narrow-minded and dogmatic when they were less flippant. She was somewhat exacting, as has been said before, and the solemn, ponderous attitude of the occasional girl who wallows before the abstract Higher Education, and lectures the Faculty gravely on their failure to conduct her to its most eminent peaks during the freshman year, appealed as strongly to her sense of humor as if she had not herself been sadly disappointed in the somewhat restricted curriculum offered her at that period.

This was through no fault whatever of the college, but because the girl had absolutely no practical basis of expectation and knew no more of the thousand implications of college life than she did of normal girlhood with its loves and disciplines and confidences, its tremendous little social experiences, its quaint emotions, and indispensable hypocrisies. Her vague conception of college life was modelled on *The Princess:* she imagined graceful, gracious women, enamoured of a musical, poetic, higher knowledge, deliciously rapt at the wonderful oratory of some priestess of a cult yet unknown to her: a woman beautiful and passionate, who should understand her vaguest dreams and sympathize with her strangest sorrows as no one she had yet known or seen could do. She found a crowd of jostling, chattering schoolgirls, unformed, unpoised; many of them vulgar, many stupid, many ill-bred; overflowing a damp, cold hall that smelled of wet, washed floors; reciting, in a very average fashion, perfectly concrete and ordinary lessons from text-books only too familiar, to business-like, middle-aged women, rather plain than otherwise, with a practical grasp of the matter in hand and a marked preference for regular attendance on the part of freshmen.

It was characteristic of her that what cut deepest in all the disillusionment was not the loss of the hope, but the shamed perception of the folly of it, the realization of the depth of practical ignorance it implied, the perfectly conscious pathos of a life so empty of real experience of the world as to make such naïve visions possible. She did the required work and kept her thoughts about it to herself, but the effect of what she secretly felt to have been a provincial and ridiculous mistake showed itself in her manner ; and the occasional hauteur of her namesake, who had inherited a very effective stare of her own, was diffidence itself compared with the reserved disdain that covered her own smarting sensitiveness.

Girls who had tumbled about with their kind from babyhood, who had found at home, at church, at school a varied if simple social training, resented her formality and could not see that pure shyness of them, pure wonder at their rough-and-ready ease of manner, their amazing power of adjustment, their quick grasp of the situation and each other, lay at the root of her jealous dignity.

So she called them "Miss," and they thought her affected; she waited for invitations that she should have taken for granted, and they thought her haughty; she made no advance in a place where only the very favored are sought out and most must earn even the humblest recognition with honest toil and assiduous advertisement, and they quietly let her alone. She was not on the campus, and as the girls in the small boarding-house with her were industrious and ordinary to the last degree and became very early impressed with her realization of this fact, she saw little of them, and her one opportunity of getting the campus gossip, which is the college gossip, grew smaller and smaller. She took solitary walks, thereby confirming the impression that she preferred to be alone—for who need be alone among a thousand girls unless she wishes it?

On such a walk, late in the fall, she stood for some time on one of the hills that rise above the town proper, looking for the hundredth time at the mountains, outlined that afternoon against the dying light of a brassy, green sky. The trees were bare and black about her; the lights in the comfortable houses were flushing up the windows with a happy evening red; belated children were hurrying home; and now and then groups of girls, fresh-cheeked from their quick walk, swung by, in haste for supper and their evening engagements. Over her heart, hungry and misunderstood, there poured a sudden flood of passionate longing for one hour of unconscious happy comradeship with homes and girls like these; one hour of some one else's—anybody else's—life; one taste of dependence on another than herself. It fell into rhythm and fascinating phrases while she gave herself up to the mood, and she made a poem of it that night. In two days she was famous, for High Authority publicly placed the poem above anything yet done in the college; it was seized by the *Monthly*, and copied widely in the various college publications; to the editorial board and the Faculty who did not have other reason for knowing her, she became "the girl who wrote *At Autumn Dusk*." It was long before she equalled it, though almost everything she did was far above a college standard; and one or two people will always think it her best poem, I have no doubt, in spite of more recent and perhaps more striking work.

For this poem was only the beginning, it may

as well be admitted now, of Susan's career as a genius. This degree is frequently conferred, no doubt, when unmerited; but the article is so susceptible of imitation, the recipe for producing the traditional effect so comparatively simple, that it is to be wondered at, on the whole, that the aspirants for the title should be, among so many clever young women, so relatively few. To a frank and recently awakened interest in Shelley, Keats, Rossetti, and Co., it is only necessary to add a vacant abstraction, a forgetfulness of conventional meal hours — supper, for choice — a somewhat occult system of reply to ordinary remarks, and the courage of one's convictions in the matter of bursting out with the irrelevant results of previous and prolonged meditation irrespective of the conversation of the moment. Any one who will combine with these infallible signs of the fire from heaven as much carelessness in the matter of dress as her previous bringing up will allow — though this is naturally a variable quantity — and a certain unmistakable looseness of *coiffure* — was there ever a genius with taut hair? heaven avert it! — may be reasonably certain of recognition. It is understood, of course, that with the qualifications above mentioned a taste for verse and an ear for rhythm, in conjunction with the frank appreciation of the poetical firm also above mentioned, have produced their inevitable result.

The character of the output naturally has something to do with the extent of the reputation, and although Susan, the most promising candidate for the degree then in the field, had alarmingly few of the most obvious signs of her rank, this was indulgently passed over, and she was allowed her laurels.

But it was Sue Jackson on whom all the first congratulations were heaped : roses and violets, that blossom at the slightest excuse in Northampton, covered the hall table in the Hubbard House, where she spent her first two years ; affectionate and mock-reverential notes crowded the bulletin board for her ; a spread was actually got up and the guests invited before the mistake was known. To do her justice she would have promptly despatched the notes and flowers to her defrauded namesake, but the donors, whom she consulted, would have none of it.

"Why, Sue ! Why, the idea ! *Did n't* you write it ? Oh, girls, what a joke ! How perfectly funny !—Send 'em to her ? Not at all. Why on earth should Neal and I send that girl flowers ? For that matter, she cut us dead day before yesterday, on Round Hill, did n't she, Pat? And she 's in our Greek, too. We 'll have the stuff to eat, anyhow. You 're a nice old thing, Sue, if you can't write 'this extraordinary poem'!"

Susan, who heard next to nothing of college news, heard about this. She heard how Sue had gayly responded to toasts: "The Poem I did not write," "My Feelings on failing to compose my Masterpiece"—this was Neal Burt's, and she was very clever over it—and others. The only thing she did not hear about was Sue's half-serious response to "My gifted God-child," suggested by an upper-class friend. She made a little graceful fun and then added quite earnestly, "And really, girls, I *do* think she ought to be here! After all, the Class, you know—Let 's take down the flowers and all the fudge—come on! She can't do more than squelch us!"

The very girls who had scoffed at the idea before were naturally the ones to take it up immediately, and they were hastily gathering the things together, when the bell rang. They could not hope to get there and back before ten, and most of them were already deep in the matron's black list for reported lights; so they gave it up, and put the flowers in the tub, where a sudden frost over night struck them and they perished miserably.

To Susan it was the bitterest thing of all; it took the sweetness from her success; it dulled the piquancy of her sudden position. She could not possibly know how little it meant to Sue; that it was only one of many spreads, and by no means the triumphal feast she imagined; that after the first they forgot why they had planned it, almost. To her it was her chance at life, her long-delayed birthright, and Sue had taken it, too, along with everything else. "She might have left me that!"—it was her thought for more than one unhappy night.

Before she went home in June she had written a Chaucer paper that became vaguely confounded in the matter of literary rank with the works of its famous subject, in her classmates' simple minds, so great was the commendation of Another High Authority in regard to its matter and style. It came out in the May *Monthly*, in which were some pretty little verses of Sue's. They were paraphrased from the French—Sue had taken any amount of French before she came up—and Susan spent her time at chapel in looking harder than ever at her namesake as she laughed and chattered and took her part in the somewhat crudely conceived jokes that seem to amuse girls so perennially. Less flexible, as she afterwards considered, less hypocritical, as she irritably felt then, she marvelled at the mental make-up of a girl capable of appreciating the force and pathos of De Musset's best work and expressing it so accurately, and able at the same time to find content in such tiresome, half-grown nonsense.

When the *Monthly* came out, she was amazed to receive a dozen copies with a hasty note:

D*EAR Miss Jackson: Here are the copies you wanted — never mind the money. There are always a lot left over since we enlarged the edition. If you want more, after we've sent out the Alumnæ list, we'll give them to you.*

H. STUART.

It was only one of the many notes intended for Sue that had been coming to her since the beginning. But none of the invitations to dinner, to Alpha and Phi Kappa, to walk, to ride, to wheel, to eat a box from home, had the effect of this one. For Sue came after her *Monthlies* and in a ten minutes' conversation wrought more ruin than she would have believed possible.

"Did you get all mine and your own, too?"

she asked laughingly. "I should send away a hundred, more or less, if *I* did 'absolutely satisfactory' Chaucer papers! I should be that proud. . . .

"You see, Papa has to have the *Monthly*, if there's anything of mine in it, *tout de suite* — directly — now. He was wild with rage at me because he learned about that little fool story I had in, once before, from Cousin Con, 'long afterwards,' he said — it was only a week! And then, other people, you know. . . .

"Did you get any of these off, before I came? Because it's all right if you did — I don't need a dozen. Isn't it funny I don't get any of your things? You must be somewhat cloyed with my notes and stuff — I should think you'd be bored to death. It's very wearing on me, Miss Jackson, explaining all the time, 'No, I'm not the one! I assure you I didn't write it.' You've no idea. . . .

"My cousin is on the *Harvard Monthly* board, you know — he telegraphed congratulations to me. He was that set up over it! It was really very funny. . . .

"I'm afraid I'm keeping you — were you going out? Shall I tell Helen Stuart to send yours down? She may think we've both got all we want. Do you know what Alpha's going to be to-night? Somebody said it was going to be Dr. Winthrop—he's my uncle, you know, and I thought if it was I'd go down to the station. . . ."

She had not the slightest idea that her thoughtless and, to tell the truth, somewhat embarrassed chatter was one succession of little galling pinpricks to the other. Her father, who expected his daughter's little triumphs to be his own, as a matter of course; her cousin at Harvard; her uncle who lectured to the Alpha; her notes and flowers—she must know that there was the best of reasons for her not getting her namesake's!—her light implication that everybody went to Alpha; her very expression: "No, I'm not the one!" seemed to the girl's angry sensitiveness a studied insult. Not the one! As if there were any one else! She did not know how unbearably formal and curt she seemed to the other, nor how strongly she gave the impression of wanting to be let alone.

Sue went away to mail her *Monthlies*, and Susan locked her door and considered at length and in detail the humor of her visitor's light remarks as applied to herself. She fancied *At Autumn Dusk* and *A Study of Chaucer* demanded by an enraged father, and smiled—

a very unpleasant and ungirlish smile. More-
over, it is possible that she did her father an
injustice here. While it is improbable that he
would have persisted in lending them about
among his friends, to his wife's open amusement, as did Mr. Jackson of Boston, and notwithstanding the fact that he would doubtless
have failed to appreciate them fully, he might
have liked to see them. Later, much later, Susan
was to find a number of her poems and stories
clipped with care from the magazines and pasted
into an old scrapbook, with the glowing notices
of her first really well-known work; the book
hidden under a pile of old newspapers in her
father's closet. She cried over them for days
—he was dead then—and published *Blind
Hearts* shortly afterward. None of her class-
mates, most of whom gave or received that
exquisite sonnet-cycle for Christmas that year,
could have known that the roots of it struck
back to her freshman year at college.

After a stupid, hot vacation, in which she
lost touch more than ever with her people,
from whom she was to draw slowly apart, it
seemed, forever, she came back with a little,
unowned hope for other things: a vague idea
that she could start fresh. She told somebody, afterwards, that just as she got to un-

derstand girls a little she lost all connection
with them; she did not lose connection with
them just then, so it must be that she did not
then understand them.

Indeed, what was, perhaps, her greatest
mistake was made at this time, and colored the
year for her. It happened in this way. The
Alpha had the first chance at the sophomores
that year, and for a wonder, the sophomores
were not only clever but possessed that in-
tangible quality, "the Alpha spirit," in a
gratifying degree. The ticket for the first drawing included the two Jacksons, Cornelia Burt,
Elizabeth Twitchell, and to fulfil that tradition that inevitably elects one perfectly un-
explainable girl, Kate Ackley, a young person
of many and judiciously selected friends. At
the very night of the election it was suddenly
rumored that Sue Jackson had openly declared her intention of refusing Alpha in favor
of the rival society, on the ground that she
liked Phi Kappa better and had more friends
there.

Now aside from the fact that this report
was utterly baseless, for Sue would have preferred the Alpha, if only to go in among the
first five of all, it was aside from the point.
As some irritated seniors afterwards explained

with much temper and reiteration to the chidden society, Alpha was sufficiently honorable in the sight of the college to endure very calmly rejection at the hands of any freshman whatsoever, whether or not they had any certainty of the truth of the rumor. But the girls were struck with the solemn necessity of immediate and drastic action, and with a gratifying thrill of excitement they struck off Sue's name and put in Margaret Pattison's, the sixth in order, whereat Phi Kappa greatly rejoiced and promptly elected Sue the next week.

Now it is very sad that the only person who seriously misunderstood this whole affair was Susan Jackson of Troy. Sue very quickly learned the whole matter; what her feelings may have been is not certain. Phi Kappa made a jubilee over her, and she became, as is well known, a great light in that society. Miss Pattison, by some mysterious free masonry—the girls who are "in everything" seem to absorb all such matters through their pores—soon found out her luck, and was frankly grateful for it. Alpha retained the courage of her convictions and assumed a distinctly here-I-stand-I-can-no-otherwise attitude. Phi Kappa chuckled privately and looked puzzled in public. But Susan had made a great mistake, and what is worse, never knew it. A little gossiping freshman in the boarding-house she had moved into, who had been injudiciously petted by the seniors and imagined herself in everybody's confidence, told Miss Jackson, with many vows of secrecy, that there had never been such a time in Alpha in the history of the college: they had meant to have Sue—oh, of course!—but there had been a terrible mistake at the balloting and names had been confused, and though etiquette forbade any expression of their real feeling, they were nearly wild at their clumsiness.

It is hardly to be wondered at that Susan jumped to her conclusion. She had got so many things intended for Sue—why not this? She knew that cleverness and even college fame are not the only calls to a society, and she had no real friends in either of the two organizations. She could not believe that the Alpha would purposely omit Sue: if they had chosen both, it would have been different, but as it was . . .

So she received their very earnest congratulations with a constraint that chilled them. They reasoned that she was perfectly certain of the election and took no pains to hide it, and though they could not blame her for this, they thought her more conceited than ever, and regarded her accordingly. The poor child was suffering from actual humility, however, not conceit. She could not know that her mark on both society lists was the highest ever given; that Alpha would cheerfully have sacrificed any two, or even three, of the others for her; that much as they regretted Sue, they wasted less sorrow over her now that they were sure of the leading girl in Ninety-red. For that was what they called her—the girls that she thought patronized her. They took her after-successes almost as a matter of course. "Oh, yes! she was far and away the most brilliant girl in the college!" they said. But she never heard them.

The house she had moved into with an un-acknowledged hope of getting more in touch with them was the last house she should have chosen. It was filled from cellar to roof with freshmen, and not only are they notoriously clannish under such conditions, but there were at least eight or ten of them from the same prominent preparatory school, and among them was their class president. It was not possible for Susan to join herself to this little circle of satellites, and they controlled the entire house in a very short time. So she took to visiting the head of the house, a faded, placid soul with a nominal authority and a gentleness that moved even her worst freshmen—and a bad freshman combines the brutality of a boy with the finesse of a woman of the world—to a little shamed consideration during their periodic fits of social reform. Sitting by her fire in the dusk, with the smell of hot cooked chocolate drifting in from the hall, and the din of the assembled tribes in the president's room overhead, Susan passed long, bored, miserable hours. Half listening to the older woman's talk, half sunk in her thoughts, she alternately chafed with rage at the idea of her college life drifting out in solitary walks and tired women's confidences, or took a sad kind of comfort in one fire where she was always welcome, one friend that loved to talk to her.

For Mrs. Hudson grew very fond of her, and something in the girl's own baffled, unsatisfied soul must have helped her to understand the stress and pathos of the tired little woman's life. Few of the girls who afterwards read *Barbara: A Study in Discipline*, would have believed that the high-hearted, wonderful

heroine was based on Miss Jackson's study of
their freshman landlady. But most of Susan's
knowledge was gained from such unscheduled
courses.

In her junior year she let her work go, to
a great extent, and spent much time in the
town libraries, reading omnivorously. As a
matter of fact, her class work deteriorated not
a little, as much by reason of dangerously extended cuts as anything else. But it all failed
to interest her, somehow: the detailed cam-
paigns, the actual value of money, the soul-
less translations, the necessarily primary character of the beginnings of any study of modern
language. She felt with growing irritation that
she should have learned genders and verbs
earlier in life, and she surprised her expectant
teachers with poorer and poorer recitations.
Mademoiselle had no means of knowing that
though Miss Jackson stammered through the
subjunctive she was reading dozens of novels
and plays with a very fair ease; Fräulein could
not tell from her imperfect handling of the
modal auxiliaries that she had written a better
paper on *Faust* than many a six years' student
of German, and already knew most of Heine
by heart.

This year she made a few friends, chiefly

in Phi Kappa, for some reason or other, which irritated the Alpha girls a little. To do her justice, she was utterly ignorant of this result of her connection with Bertha Kitts and Alida Fosdick, nor would it have resulted in the case of an ordinary girl. But Susan was more prominent than she ever realized, and her whole connection with the others being official and logical rather than social and actual, her conduct and opinions were very sharply criticised from a rather exacting standpoint. Nor was this wholly unfair, for she was herself an unsparing critic. More than one of the Faculty smarted under her too successful epigrams; various aspirants for popularity and power in the Alpha or the class learned to dread her comments; her few friends themselves were never quite sure of her attitude toward them. But she was not, for her part, sure of them : it is hard to make friends in one's junior year. And though she saw quite a little of Biscuits and Dick and Neal Burt —always her constant admirer—she never for a moment lost the consciousness that she was no friend of their friends, that she had no place in those groups long since formed and shaken into place. They were a little jealous of her, too, and resented her selection of this girl

and that from among them, though they could
not but admit that her judgment was good.

Her sources of irritation were the same always. Their very flexibility, the ease with which
those she had chosen out slipped from her to
their other friends (they laughed with her at
them, even, after the manner of girls — did they
laugh with them at her?), filled her with a
hopeless jealousy. It was not their nice clothes
and their good times she grudged them, though
she wanted both: it was their connections, their
environments, their very disciplines. When
Biscuits with loud lamentations elected Philosophy at the decree of her father; when
Neal took up two courses of Economics in
order to help her mother with "some footless
syllabi in mother's literary club;" when Betty
Twitchell endured the gibes of her friends every
rainy day because "Papa won't let me wear a
short skirt; he hates a woman in one — I think
it's perfectly horrid of him, too! Wait till I get
pneumonia! As if I'd 'get a carriage' to take
me from the Hatfield to College Hall!" Susan
would have given every rhyme in her head for
one year of their conventional, irresponsible
lives.

It was not money she longed for: Neal
Burt was poor enough, and made no secret

of "my cousin's boots, my dear, and my aunt's silk waist, and Patsy's gloves that don't fit her, that I have on this minute!" But Neal gave her one of her worst quarter-hours, at the time her mother came up. She was a pretty little woman with Neal's eyes; her simple clothes had, like Neal's, a distinct air of taste and selection about them; her interest in everything was so pleasant, her manner so cordial and charming, that she made an easy conquest of the girls and Neal's friends in the Faculty that came to meet her and drink tea in the quiet house where Neal lived almost alone, much petted by her landlady, an old family friend. Mrs. Burt was interested in Economics that year—"the dear thing has a new fad every time I go home!"—and a prominent professor of Economics from one of the universities happening to be in town just then, one of Neal's friends among the Powers invited mother and daughter to meet him. Mrs. Burt was equally charmed and charming; the distinguished professor begged to be allowed to send her a copy of his book, in which she had been much interested, "and she went home proud as Punch!" in the words of her daughter.

Every word the kindly little woman had with Susan—and she had a great many, for

Neal had interested her mother in her friend—
brought closer home to her what had steadily
grown to be the consuming trouble of her life.
She tried to imagine *her* mother drinking tea
with a roomful of strangers; finding the right
word for every one, talking with this girl about
her friends, with that about the last book, with
the other about college life in general. She
fancied her meeting the distinguished professor and discussing his book so brightly—and
saw the closet-shelves where Marie Corelli and
the Duchess jostled Edna Lyall: Mrs. Jackson said she liked some real heavy reading
now and then, and Edna Lyall had a good
many problems in her books. She had a sickening consciousness that her mother would inevitably defer to the girls, particularly to the
confident, well-dressed ones; and every time
that Neal patted Mrs. Burt's shoulder or
kissed the tip of her ear, she felt her heart
contract with a spasm of that terrible gnawing
envy that is surely reserved, with their equally
terrible capacity for loving, for a certain small
proportion of women, and women only. It is
a very sad thing for a girl to be ashamed of
her mother.

In her junior year occurred one of her greatest triumphs. The senior class had petitioned

vainly for the privilege of giving *Twel'th Night* as their Commencement play: the refusal, based on the obstacle presented by the part of Sir Toby, and couched in the undying phrases of the Greatest Authority—"he should be neither drunk, nor half drunk, nor bibulous, nor rioting"—impressed very deeply those more susceptible to the humorous. With a commendable intelligence the dramatics committee decided that under the limitations above quoted the play would lack in verisimilitude, and cast about for another, but that was not the end of it; for Susan, in whose hands the Alpha farewell-meeting had been unreservedly placed, wrote, staged, and directed the performance of an elaborate parody entitled *First Night*, from which "the objectionable element in the unfortunate William's comedy," to quote the preface, was successfully and unsparingly expurgated.

Not only were the most obvious situations cleverly treated; not only did Sir Toby, spare and ascetic, in a neat flannel wrapper, call decorously for "a stoup of thin gruel, Maria!" not only did he and his self-contained friends walk through a kind of posture dance with killing solemnity, chanting the while a staid canon in which the possibilities of "Why,

should I drink on *one* day ? " were interpreted
with a novel and gratifying morality; not only
did Malvolio utterly eschew an article of ap-
parel too likely to bring the blush of shame
to the cheek of the Young Person, but pains-
takingly assume, in the eyes of the delighted
audience, heavy woollen stockings, a constant
and effectual reminder of his hidden traditional garb: but a parody within a parody ran
cunningly through the piece. The trials of the
committee, the squabbles of the principal actors, open hits at the Faculty, sly comments
on the senior class, which had been active in
reforms and not wholly popular innovations
—all these were interwoven with the farce;
and this not in the clumsy harmless fashion
of most college grinds, but pointed by a keen
wit, a merciless satire, an easy, brilliant style
already well on to its now recognized maturity.

Most of the principal actors in the play finally selected by the seniors, with more than
half of the committee, were that year, as it happened, from Alpha, and their delight knew no
bounds. Susan did not act herself, but she was
a born manager; and the actors that cursed
her unsparing drill and absolute authority during the long rehearsal season that made it
the most finished affair of its kind, blessed her

vociferously on the great night of its production. It was the most perfect success of her life —though the girls who thought she scorned her college triumphs would have laughed had she told them so, later. Every point was eagerly caught and wildly applauded; the stage setting, the funny, clever costumes, the irresistible caricatures, the wit and humor of the thing, all acted with a *verve* and precision unusual in college dramatics, where criticism is too often forced to take the will for the deed, all called for a tremendous and well-earned appreciation. The author was frantically summoned again and again; the seniors exhausted a congratulatory vocabulary on her. Her classmates shook her hand many times apiece.

Nor did the triumph end with the night, for the juniors, unable to contain their pride, gave surreptitious bits of the play to chosen seniors in Phi Kappa, and it was even rumored that the other society was going to request a revival of the combination entertainment, now out of vogue, with a view to having it repeated. This was suppressed by the Powers, but it got about that one of the few type-written copies of the piece had fallen into the hands of an Influential Person—probably through Neal Burt, who admired it in

proportion to her own far from ordinary ability — and that the Person had assembled a select gathering of her Peers for the sole purpose
of reading it, with unmistakably appreciative
comments, to them. Some members of the
Faculty, old Alpha girls themselves, and present on the occasion of its production, expressed
their admiration in unstinted terms, and altogether the Alpha gained a tremendous prestige.

This and her appointment as editor-in-chief
of the *Monthly* for her senior year marked
the height of Susan's prosperity. She used to
think, afterwards, that the play was the only
pure pleasure she had ever had: it was certainly the only one that her namesake had left
to her unspoiled. Fate ordered it that she
should take off the bulletin-board with her
notice of editorial appointment a note hastily
addressed to S. Jackson, '9–. She opened it
mechanically.

D*EAR Old Sue: It's a miserable shame! You
ought to have had it! But it seems that it
makes no difference what we want, nor who would
work in best with the girls. Genius is n't everything, always — but you know what I wanted!*
Your disappointed
H. S. K.

The note was not sealed, and she folded it and put it back quietly. A moment later she received her congratulations, but to every one's "Of course you 're not surprised, Miss Jackson!" she smiled strangely. Sue used the phrase, fresh from her own congratulations as literary editor, and the concentrated bitterness of three years flashed out in the other's curt answer.

"Of course you 're not surprised—"

"*Are you?*"

Sue's startled flush was all the proof she needed, and crushing in her hand the note that had meant the highest college honor to more than one of the girls who had got its like, she went home to bear alone the sharpest disappointment she had yet known.

There was no one to tell her that the senior editor whose initials signed the note for Sue had been one of only two in Sue's favor; that the board, so far from acting unwillingly under the direction of the Rhetoric department, as she inferred from the note, had been practically unanimous for her, particularly as the two opposed held relatively unimportant positions and were far from popular. She did not know that the note itself was a gross breach of etiquette, anyway, and that both

officially and socially its writer had risked the
gravest censure; so much so that Sue, far
from being pleased, was heartily ashamed of
it and never told a soul about it till long afterwards. The person who could have explained
most effectively to her how perfectly her election met the favor of everybody, herself included—for Sue would have been as surprised
to find herself placed above her gifted namesake as to have found herself omitted entirely
from the board—was too chagrined at the
abrupt answer to her congratulations to dream
of mentioning the matter further.

So Susan got out her first two numbers of
the *Monthly* with none of the delighted importance of most editors. It was all spoiled
for her. She knew that she deserved it: it
was impossible for her not to realize that, so
far as originality and power went, nobody in
the class, or the college, for that matter, could
touch her work. It was not the position that
meant so much to her: she was perfectly competent to fill it easily and acceptably, and she
knew it. But she wanted them to think so,
too, and be glad to give it to her—and she
did not believe they were.

Shortly after her success of *First Night*,
she got one of her rare letters from home. She

had little correspondence with them, and had grown to regard their letters with dread, since each one had brought unpleasant news, from Doris', to announce her engagement to one of "the boys," a flashy, half-disreputable fellow, to her mother's, enclosing a cheque, with gloomy forebodings that it might be the last, and a disheartening chronicle of family affairs growing daily more sordid. The sight of her characterless, uncultivated handwriting always threw the girl into a gloomy, irritable mood, and as she opened this one the remorse that had begun to prick her more sharply of late at her inability to help them, if not in the way she would like, at least in the most obviously necessary manner, crept over her and saddened her even before she reached the crisis of the letter. It was very simple: she must come home. There was no more money; there had been none for some time, but her father was bent on her staying, and had put it off longer than he should have done. It had been a foolish expense, and she might have had a position long ago. There was car fare and a very little over, and it was hoped that she had no bills. They were going to move into an apartment over the store, and Veronica was going to keep her father's books. And that was all.

A FAMILY AFFAIR

Perhaps her mother felt sorrier than she knew how to say; perhaps it was only the constraint of years and lack of *savoir faire* that made the letter so cold and curt; but there it was, with nothing to break the shock: no regret for her, to lighten her sense of selfishness; no appeal to her, even, to help them. They could get along very well; to give up the house would be a great financial relief, and she would be more a hindrance than otherwise. She knew that: she knew that her presence would be a constant irritation, her criticism, impossible to conceal, a constant source of strife and estrangement. It was only that they had no more money for her—that was all.

She walked out to the long bridge, and sat down on a stone near the end of it. For perhaps the first time a complete consciousness of how bitterly she loved the place came to her. She, of whom many of the Faculty afterwards wondered that she stayed as long as she did, credited by all her acquaintances with infinite boredom at its restrictions and wearisome routine, dreaded to leave it as she herself could hardly endure to think. For three years she had taken a place, unchallenged, among people of a class she had never known before. Unknown, unhelped, she had by sheer personality and natural power made herself not only respected but respected to an unusual degree. She had patronized girls who would not have acknowledged her existence three years before; whether they loved her or not, her class was proud of her. Her going would be noticed—oh, yes indeed!

She rose to go home, and a little beyond the bridge turned to look back: something told her that she should not know that view soon again. Meadow and river and softly circling hills with the beautiful afternoon haze thick on them, she stamped it on her heart— and with it a sudden nearing figure. Down the long arch, slim and shapely against the blue background of the tunnel, Sue flew toward her on her wheel. Her hands swung by her sides—she had ridden from childhood —her feet were off the pedals, her perfectly fitting heavy skirt hung out in graceful fluted folds. Beneath her soft, trim hat her cheeks glowed rose-color, her eyes shone like stars. The sun caught her smooth, thick hair and framed her face in a glittering halo. She sat straight as a dart, her lips parted with the sheer physical delight of the swooping, effortless sensation—she was tremendously handsome. To the other girl she was victory incarnate; the essence of ease and triumph and perfect *bien-être;* her hopeless envy and despair. As she flew by she spread out her hands in a quick, significant gesture, half graceful and high-bred—half pert and of the music-hall: it typified her and her friends perfectly to Susan, who never forgot her as she saw her then, and whose *Mademoiselle Diana,* much admired by Sue and her family, is nobody more nor less than Sue herself.

She found a letter waiting for her at home, a letter that the maid explained had just been brought from the house where the other Miss Jackson lived—it had been kept there by mistake and neglected for two or three days. It was hoped it was not important. She opened it in the hall, read it hastily through, read it again, looked at the date, and asked for a time-table. The maid, suspecting bad news, was officious in assistance and eagerly agreed to pack her things and get a man to box the books when she had gone, which would be in the morning, she said, with a strange, absent-minded air. She gave the girl her last fifty cents, and while Maggie folded and packed, she wrote a letter home.

"*I*T *seems foolish for me to come to Troy; I should only have to go right back to Boston again,*" she said in it. "*They want me to begin to colle&t the stories right away and do some reading for them besides—so I must be there. There is a new magazine they have just bought, too, and I am to do some work on that. It is a very good position and will lead to a better, they say, and I am very fortunate to get it. They say very nice things about my work in the "Monthly"—the college paper that I was ele&ted editor of—they seem to have read them all. I must go on immediately. Their letter was delayed, and I shall try to get there to-morrow. I will let you know when I find a place to stay. I hope to be able to help you soon.*

"*Hastily,*   "SUSAN."

She wrote a note to the Registrar and one to Neal Burt, whom, in her letter of resignation, she recommended strongly to the board as her successor, overlooking the constitution, which provides for the literary editor's filling the first place when it falls vacant, and refusing supper, she walked out over the campus. The dining-rooms were opened to the soft air; the cheerful clatter of plates came out from every window; she could see the maids hurrying about. She sat for an hour in one of the

[198]

hammocks, and then walked about the larger buildings. The last dance of the season was on in the Gym; the violins rose above the tramping and the confused uproar inside. White-armed girls passed the windows and leaned out into the cool.

"How is it?" one called up from below.

"Mortal slow, dearie, but don't say I told you!" the other answered in a stage whisper from above, and the music dashed into a two-step.

"Be*hold* El *Cap*-i-*tan !* "

It haunted Susan's dreams for nights, that tune—it seemed impossible that the dancers' hearts should not ache as hers did. She lingered, fascinated, while the violins sang it over and over, and over again at the storm of clapping that followed it.

"Be*hold* El *Cap*-i-*tan !* "

It was a hideous, cruel tune, light and utterly careless, and yet with that little sadness in it that some sensitive ears find always in good dance music—is it because dancing must so obviously end so soon?—and Susan has loathed it all her life. Indeed, at a recent luncheon given in her honor by the alumnæ of New York, she requested that the orchestra stop playing it after the first few bars—these people of genius are so delightfully eccentric!

She left college as quietly as she had entered it; there is no doubt that they would have made her Ivy Orator, had she stayed. The mail that took the notice of her lodging-house to her family crossed one of Sue's to her Uncle Bradford, of the well-known Boston publishing firm. Among other things she said:

I'M glad you like her so well—I knew you would. She's really much better for the place than Con. And I'm sure it was better to write to her directly—she doesn't like any of us very well, except Neal and Biscuits, and I have an idea she really almost dislikes me. I knew that when you saw that essay on the French and English as short-story writers, you'd want to give her the chance. And she was the very girl to leave college, too—it isn't everybody would be so glad to go just before senior year. Not but what I would, fast enough, if I had her future before me—Mon dieu! she's the only girl I ever thought I'd rather be—you should see the poem she left with Neal for the "Monthly"! She turns them off over night, apparently. It's a loss to the class, of course, but everybody is very glad for her—she always seemed so out of place up here, somehow. If one does n't care for the little footless stunts, it must be a terrible bore, I should think. And when she's famous we can pat each other on the back and say we done it—partly. With a great deal of love for you and Aunt Julia,

SUE.

A FEW DIVERSIONS

A FEW DIVERSIONS

"I WISH you *would* ask her up, Nan," said Mrs. Harte, confidentially. "I want her to see the place. So far as I can judge, it's the best thing for her. There isn't any doubt that she's a very bright girl, but she's getting thoroughly spoiled here. You see, she does just as she pleases—she's the only young person in the family—and I know we spoil her terribly. Her mind is made up to come out in the winter, here in Chicago, and they'll refuse her nothing—her father and mother."

"They *don't* seem what you'd call oppressively strict with her," remarked Anne, twirling her racquet.

"Now what I want is for her to get somewhere where she isn't the only clever girl; to see that other girls can read and talk and play the guitar and wear nice clothes and order silly young men about. And judging from those of you that I've seen, you can!"

"We do our little best," said Anne, modestly.

"And I wanted her to see you all: that's one reason why I planned the house-party. I was so disappointed when she came so late. You see, her cousin Georgiana was—was un-

fortunate. She went to Yale and Columbia and
goodness knows where, and she had short hair
and was such a frump and she wore such hideous spectacles and talked about Socialism—or
was it Sociology?—all the time. I remember
she was always trying to persuade us to join
clubs and protest against something or other
—it was very wearisome. So Madge got to despise the whole thing: she has always thrown
Georgiana at me when I mentioned college.
It was perfectly useless to try to make her understand that every girl need n't be like Georgiana. She 's very obstinate. But she 's a nice
girl, too, and if she can only get out of her
present atmosphere for four years—"

"Pity she could n't have seen Ursula, if
she 's afraid we 're all frumps," Anne suggested.

"Yes, is n't it? But I think she stayed purposely. Now, you—she says you 're an ex-
ception; that there can't be many like you.
You see, Madge has a standard of her own; she
says she 'd be ashamed to go through college
the way some of the boys do, with just a good
time and as low marks as they can safely get.
She says she 'd want to be a student if she pre-
tended to, and yet she must have a good time,
and—"

A FEW DIVERSIONS

"And she thinks it can't be done? Dear me, what an error! Well, if she'll come up I'll be very glad to have her, I'm sure. I can trot out our little pastimes and er—omit the more *sociological* side," said Anne, with a grin.

Mrs. Harte leaned forward eagerly. "Yes, that's just what I mean! She got enough of that from Georgiana. I want her to watch you—"

"Sport about on the lawn? Gambol through the village? 'Make the picturesque little lake echo with sweet girlish gayety,' as the newspaper gentlemen say?"

"Yes, that's it," and Mrs. Harte patted Anne's broad shoulder. "That's what I mean, you silly child. Just let her see that there are a few diversions!"

Miss Marjory Cunningham, who was just then coming up from the lake, was a tall, well-grown young woman of seventeen, with a handsome, assured face and unexceptionable garments. She looked fully twenty, and was young enough to find satisfaction in this circumstance. She had been brought up, in the orthodox American fashion, to take a prominent part in the household, particularly in the entertainment of her mother's many guests, and this, added to the fact that she happened to be much cleverer than the young women with whom her social lot had hitherto been cast, inclined her to regard any one under thirty with a patronage somewhat offensive, if mild.

She dropped down beside Anne as her aunt left the broad piazza, and smiled politely.

"Aunt Frank says you're going to-morrow," she remarked, adding a little curiously, "Shall you be glad to get back?"

"East, you mean? Why, yes. You see I'm a week late. They've started up the show without me, so to speak, and naturally it's rather hard for them to worry along. They may have given me up and laid my new little single room at Lucilla Bradford's feet, which would more than trouble me."

"Do they allow you to come back whenever you want to?"

Miss Cunningham's tone was that of an indulgent aunt toward a pet nephew on his Christmas holidays, and Anne's reply was framed accordingly.

"Oh, easily! They only insist on our being back for the Glee Club concert. They're just bound up in that, you know. So we usually make a point of it. I must say," she changed her tone, "I'd like to hear Carol Sawyer's explanations to Miss Roberts! Carol has a fine imagination, but she's used it so much of late that she'll have to surpass herself this time to make much impression on Robbie. You see I have the great good fortune to possess an accommodating relative: the Amiable Parent is far from well, and asked me if I'd wait a week till he could go on, and cheer his last moments—smooth his pillow, as it were. So, since I've never gone away early once and only come back late twice before, and once with an excuse, I thought I was safe to stay. And I told him that, notwithstanding the fact that I was languishing among dirt courts and single-piece drivers and Saturday hops and—*and* your noble family, I'd stick it out a week longer. Said I to the Amiable Parent:

"My own convenience count as nil;
It is my duty, and I will!"

Next morning, when Nan came down to breakfast, pink under her tan and with that air that she always carried of having just come out of the tub, Marjory really regretted her going. She mentioned to her aunt that she would have liked to see more of her, and that if she *did* go to New York in the spring she should surely go up to Northampton. It was not only because Miss Gillatt danced and golfed and drove and played tennis so well that Marjory's interest was for the first time roused in a girl of her own age, nor because her clothes were nice and her ways amusing; what struck Miss Cunningham was her guest's entire absence of surprise at what she utterly failed to recognize as an unusual amount of interest on Marjory's part.

"This is Marjory—how do you do, Marjory?" she had said easily on their first meeting, and she had never cared to learn that Marjory intended her own "Miss Gillatt" for a lesson to forward schoolgirls. And she had taken Marjory's growing attentions quite as if she were accustomed to have handsome young women talk to her and row her about and give her their photographs. When she had herself mentioned looking Nan up in Northampton, her proposition had not evoked the grateful surprise that might have been expected.

"Glad to see you any time," the future hostess had returned. "Better come up in the spring; it's a lot prettier." And Madge had decided then and there to go, though her suggestion had been more or less perfunctory.

She would never have considered it for a moment had it not been perfectly obvious that the college girl did not regard herself at all in the light of a possible example. Georgiana's lectures on the Higher Education of Women and its Ultimate Effect on the Sex were not to be thought of in connection with this athletic damsel, whose quotations, though frequent, indicated a closer study of Lewis Carroll and W. S. Gilbert than her alma mater's official catalogue would suggest. She referred very little to the college and then only as the scene of incidents in which she and her "young friends," as she invariably called them, had taken amusing or amazing parts. Marjory's chief impression had been that of the jolliest possible crowd of girls, who seemed to derive great comfort and entertainment from one another's company, and it was a half-envious desire to see if they really did this to the extent that Anne implied, that drew her to Northampton one fine day in the late spring.

As she stood on the station platform looking in vain for a tall girl with broad shoulders and a persuasive grin, she heard her name called, and turned to meet the outstretched hand of a very different person. This person was small and slender, with a plain, distinguished little face, intelligent eyes, and a low and charming voice. From the very Parisian arrangement that topped her shining coils of hair to the tips of her tiny shoes, she was one of the most thoroughly well-dressed young women Marjory had ever seen. She reminded one vaguely, though not disagreeably, of Mr. Wenzell's pictures, and Marjory failed utterly in a dazed attempt to correlate her and Georgiana.

"You are Miss Cunningham, are you not? I am Ursula Wyckoff. Nan is so sorry, but Hodgkinson Davids or Davidson Hodgkins —I can't remember the way—has come up from New York to play over the course to-day, and of course all the golf people have to be out there. She and Caroline have been there all the afternoon, and I 'm to bring you out a little later, when they serve the tea. Is n't it dreadfully warm? Nan 's next to Caroline and Caroline holds the championship, so they 're naturally interested. I don't play at all. I was so sorry to miss you at the house-party: we all fell in love with your aunt. Oh, no, New York, but I 've lots of Western friends: you know I 've met your aunt before, in London. We bought some Liberty things, and we were staying at the same hotel, and they sent us each other's parcels, so we got acquainted picking them out. There was a lovely fan: she said it was for her niece. Was it you? I dream of that fan yet."

They walked slowly up the long street, Ursula chatting easily, and Marjory wondering how many of the girls they passed belonged to the college. They paused before a druggist's window, all Huyler's and violet soap, and Ursula walked by a long, shining soda fountain to a room in green and white, with little tables and a great palm in the centre. The tables were very nearly filled, and there was a cheerful clatter of tall spoons and a businesslike bustle of clerks with trays.

"This is Kingsley's," said Ursula, with a comprehensive gesture. "Will you have a chocolate ice?" While absorbing the inviting and pernicious mixture, Miss Cunningham looked about her with interest. In one corner four girls with rumpled shirt-waists and dusty golf stockings squabbled over scores, and illustrated with spoons preferred methods of driving and putting. Their voices rose above the level prescribed for drawing-room conversation, and they called each other strange names. In another corner a tall, dark girl with a grave expression talked steadily in a low voice to her companion, a clever-looking creature, whose bursts of laughter grew hysterical as the dignified one continued, with a perfectly impersonal manner, to reduce her to positive tears of mirth. To them Ursula bowed, and the narrator, politely recognizing her, went on with her remarks, to an accompaniment of gurgling protest from her friend. Near them a porcelain blonde, gowned in a wonderful pale blue stuff with a great hat covered with curly plumes, ate strawberry ices with a tailor-made person clothed in white piqué, mystic, wonderful. She was all stiffness and specklessness, and she looked with undisguised scorn at the clamoring athletes, a white leather card-case in her hand. Near one window a gypsy-faced child in a big pink sunbonnet imparted mighty confidences to her friend, who shook two magnificent auburn braids over her shoulders with every chuckle.

"And I heard a knock at the door and of course I thought it was Helen or some of the girls, and I called to come in and, my dear, *who* do you think it was? It was the *expressman!* 'Will you sign this book?' said he, and he brought the book right up to the bed and I leaned on my elbow and signed it! My dear, was n't that perfectly—"

"Oh, well, it 's awfully funny here, anyway. That beastly old laundry tore my lovely

lace nightgown to shreds and it was new, and
I put in an old dressing-sacque that was all
in rags and I was going to throw it away, and
they mended it carefully before they sent it
back!"

As they left the room and Ursula waited
while the clerk looked up her soda ticket, the
door flew open and an impish little creature,
with a large, deprecating, motherly girl in her
wake, slipped into the shop.

"Now don't make for the back room,
Bertie dear, for there is n't time. We 've got
lots of places to do yet!" she called, and catching sight of Ursula she dashed up to her.

"What do you think Alberta and I are doing? We 're *so* bored, and we 're going to stop
at every drug store on this side and have an
ice-cream soda, and the same going back on
the other side. Is n't that interesting? I tell
Alberta it 's bound to be—sooner or later!"

"Is that a freshman?" Marjory inquired
competently, and Ursula's eyes twinkled as
she replied gravely:

"No, that 's a senior. She has fits of idiocy,
but in her better moments she 's quite a person to know. She 's in the Lawrence with me.
Why on earth she should go and get Alberta
May and drag her into degradation and dys-

pepsia, nobody knows, but she always does."

They rested for a while in Ursula's room, which was "more than enormous," as Anne said—it was intended for a double room—and furnished very delightfully. There were some beautiful Copley prints and a cast or two and a long low shelf of books and fascinating wicker chairs with puffy cushions. There was the inevitable tea-table and chafing-dish paraphernalia and the inevitable couch with a great many Yale pillows; but there were not more than a dozen photographs of girls in any one place and only one Gibson girl, and she was very small. There was a beautiful desk all littered with papers and little photographs of Ursula's family and her horse at home, and a lot of the pretty little cluttering things one picks up abroad. Marjory saw no girl with such consistently fascinating clothes as Ursula's during her visit, nor did she sit in any room so charming as hers, the college girl being a generation behind her brother in this regard; but first impressions are strong, and Ursula's silver brushes, her beautiful etching, and the two wonderful rugs that nearly covered her shining floor formed the stage setting for all Marjory's subsequent imaginary dramas.

They went out to the links by trolley,

through the long quiet street, past pretty lawns and pleasant houses, into the real country of fields and scattered cottages. Marjory learned how "the crowd" had vacationed together more than once; how they were going up to Carol Sawyer's place in Maine next summer for "the time of their lives"; how, after their Commencement obsequies, they were going for two weeks to Nan at Sconset and live in a house all by themselves, and then four of them were going abroad together with Nan's father—"the dearest thing in the world"; how Caroline was going to study medicine in Germany and Lucilla Bradford was going to be married and continue to illumine Boston, and Ursula and her sister were going to stay indefinitely in France or Italy with various relatives.

They seemed to have a very intimate knowledge of one another's affairs, Marjory decided, as they got out at the links and strolled up to the tiny club-house. A straggling crowd was gradually melting away there: hot, dishevelled girls with heavy bags, cool and fluffy girls with tea-cups, men arguing in white flannels and men conversing in frock coats. Important small boys—professors' sons and their friends from the town—caddied for the great man and his followers, patronizing the urchins who ordinarily amassed wealth from this employment, and a crowd of interested golfers from the town trailed about the holes, admiring, criticising, and chattering. Here and there a crimson coat shone out, some of the ladies tilted gay parasols, white duck dotted the grass everywhere. It was all very jolly and interesting, and when Nan. came up with a white-flannelled youth and a cheerful if exhausted friend whom she introduced as "one of my little mates— Caroline Wilde," Marjory could have thought, as she sipped her tea and learned the score, that she was back on the links at home.

Caroline had learned much and Nan had held a reverent conversation with the champion and was basking in the recollection of it. Marjory met an ardent golfer in marvellous stockings, who was with difficulty restrained from illustrating, by means of his empty cup and the parasol his fellow-professor was guarding, the very latest method of effecting a tremendous drive from a bad spot in the course, and his friend turned out to be a classmate of her brother's; and so they started from Yale, which is a very good conversational starting-point, and their reminiscences attracted Ursula, who, with an adoring little freshman—

A FEW DIVERSIONS

Ursula was never without a freshman—and the Church and the Law wrangling pleasantly over a lost ball, was holding her court in a near corner. They drifted up, and the Church and the Law were so amusing and well set up that Marjory quite lost her heart to them and wished they would come "West," as they persisted in calling Chicago, remarking confidentially that nothing seemed to upset a person from Chicago so much as that!

They rode home with the Church and the Law, while the assistant in that great undertaking, the higher education of women, raced the trolley on a Columbia Chainless, to the wild delight of the passengers, who cheered his futile efforts and bribed the motorman to an exciting rate of speed.

"Do you have lessons with him, really?" Marjory demanded, as they left the rapidly churning golf stockings behind for the moment. Nan grinned. "Do you, Ursula?" she repeated. Ursula sighed but said nothing, and Nan explained that in the midst of his artless prattle last week he had mentioned a written lesson in the near future, based upon certain reference reading. "It comes off to-morrow," she added cheerfully, "and the young Lucilla is hastily sprinting through the volumes

and gathering information. She sought the
seclusion that a cabin grants last night, and
when I howled at her through the keyhole
that we were going to Boyden's for the evening meal, she said that if she got through two
hundred pages and her notes by then she'd
be along. Ursula does it bit by bit, and then
tells us to go to the ant, thou sluggard, but
little Lucy thinks she knows him better than
we do, and she said he would n't do it. I told
her, go to, he would; I saw it in his eye. So
Caroline started to fill her fountain pen—she
calls it that from force of habit—but what
she really does is to fill the room, and what
drips over—"

"There's Lucilla!" said somebody, and
they got off the car and teased Lucilla—a
small, tired person with a prim little face and
beautiful manners—all the way down to Boyden's. A striking, sulky-looking girl with a
stylish golf suit that made her look like the
costumers' plates of tailor-made athletic maid-
ens, was holding a table for them, and she
turned out to be Carol Sawyer. She was the
first girl of "the crowd" Marjory did not like.
Her voice was loud and her manner a little
overbearing; she wore too many rings and her
attitude toward the college was very different

from the harmless nonsense that in the case
of the other girls covered plenty of good work
and a real interest in it. She was evidently very
wealthy, and Marjory caught herself wondering if that was why the others put up with her.
When they had half finished their supper—
and a very good little supper it was—a large
girl, almost too tall for a girl, in a mussy short
skirt and badly fitting shirt-waist sauntered
into the room. From their own table and most
of the others a chorus of welcome went up.

"Hello, Teddy!" "Don't hurry, Dody!"
"Come over here, Dodo!" "Theodora, dear
child, your side-comb is nearly out!" "Have
some berries, Ted?"

She included them all in a cheerful
"Hello!" and strolled up to Nan's table.
"This is little Theodora Bent," said Nan,
kindly. "She is very shy and unused to company, but her heart—"

"Her heart," little Theodora interrupted,
dragging a chair from somewhere and quietly
appropriating Ursula's creamed chicken, "is
not here. It is with our friend, Mrs. Austin,
who sits at a lonely table wondering where her
loved ones are to-night. I met her at the door.
'Dorothea,' said she—and why she persists
in calling me Dorothea we shall know, per-

haps, when the mists have cleared away—
'Dorothea, there is hardly a Friday night that
you girls are in to supper. I'm sure I can't
see why!' I said that it *was* strange, but it
just happened so. Then she insisted on knowing why; so I suggested that perhaps you
found the noise in the dining-room trying—"

"Dodo! you did n't!"

"Certainly I did. I should suppose you
might. Anybody who sits near *you* certainly
does! And she said that some freshman or
other had been decorating the piazza all the
afternoon, lying in wait for me to tutor her,
and suggested that I ought to manage better.
And I told her I'd tutored three hours and
a half to-day and I had a written lesson and
Phi Kappa Farewell to-morrow night, and I
thought that if she did n't object to the freshman I'd leave her there till next week. So I
left her standing in the door—"

"*A thing she has never done before!*" sang
Nan, softly, and they laughed long and mer-
rily, as people laugh who are not very ancient,
and who have just had a good supper and are
the best of friends.

It was a little after that that the Glee Club
sang on the steps of Music Hall, while crowds
of girls streamed out and sat on the grass and

wandered up and down or listened on dormitory steps. They sang sweet songs and funny songs, and the audience sitting on the campus clapped and clapped again. Their repertoire amazed Miss Cunningham, who had been firmly impressed with the idea that *A Spanish Cavalier* and *Aunt Dinah's Quilting Party* were necessarily sung by the college girl to the exclusion of all other melodies. She was used to them now, used to pigtails and puffs, shirtwaists and evening dresses, Western rolled r's and Eastern broad a's, handsome matronly young women, and slim, saucy little chits, solitary walkers, devoted pairs, and rollicking bands. The light faded imperceptibly, turning the ugly brick to a soft pink, bringing out the pale mingling of colors that spread over the smooth, green campus, with here and there a girl vivid in crimson or violet. The leader raised her hand and they started a medley, with queer changes and funny little turns.

> Three blind mice!
> See how they run!
> They all ran after the farmer's wife—
> For she was the jewel of Asia,
>> Of Asia,
>> Of Asia—

How happy they seemed, how well able to amuse each other!

Then, as the faces on the steps grew indistinct and the little night noises grew plainer, just as the Club turned to go in somebody called, "*Mandalay!*" The crowd took it up and "*Mandalay!*" sounded from all the groups. Three or four girls with guitars turned up from somewhere, and a mandolin was produced from the Hubbard; a tall, slender girl stepped out a little from the rest and turned upon the waiting audience the kind of soft, rich voice that sounds rough and strained indoors, but only a little thrilled and anxious in the open air.

By the old Moulmein Pagoda, lookin' eastward to
    the sea,
There's a Burma girl a-settin' an' I know she thinks
    o' me!

Some of the girls perched on balcony railings; some leaned on each other's shoulders; the strolling pairs and groups stopped, interlocked, and listened as attentively as if they did not already know it by heart; their white dresses glimmered among the shrubbery. Ursula and Theodora Bent, a strange pair, Marjory thought, had dropped down on a bench, the little graceful figure balanced on the back of the seat with one arm over the broad shoulders of her big, careless friend. Nan's merry face took on the almost wistful look that music always brought there, and Marjory wondered if the silent, waiting group knew how soft their eyes grew and how much alike they all looked suddenly.

An' the dawn comes up like thunder out er China
  'crost the Bay!

A moment of silence, a burst of applause, and the crowd was scurrying away as if a bell had struck. The chatter rose again, the faces changed, and to crown the transformation a tall, dark girl with a handsome face—the girl they had seen at Kingsley's—rose languidly from the top step of the Washburn and sang with a startling imitation of the first singer, to a group of girls about her:

  Oh, that Road to Mandalay!
  Must we hear it night and day?
For the author 'd swear like thunder if he heard it
  sung that way!

Wild applause and a cry of, "Second verse, Neal! second verse!" followed, and as they walked past the Hatfield by a group of girls audibly disapproving of the parody and its singer, they caught the second verse:

For they sing it ev'ry evening, and they sing it ev'ry
    morn;
They will sing it at my fun'ral—was it sung when
    I was born?
Just as soon as I reach heaven, and they teach me
    how to play,
Oh, I know the tune I learn on will be Road to
    Mandalay!

The juniors chuckled, and as Nan commended the abilities of the cynical senior,
Marjory remembered her face as it had been
a few minutes before, and wondered.

They took her to her boarding-house and
left her to get to bed, for she was tired. And
in the morning she went, by previous arrangement, to the Lawrence, whence Dody Bent took
her down to Boyden's to eggs and toast, and
coffee in a shining silvery pot, and said that in
consequence of the apparently unchanged intentions of Dr. Robbins she should necessarily be much engaged from ten until eleven
and the few scant minutes preceding those
hours, and that Misses Gillatt, Bradford, and
Wyckoff expected to be similarly occupied.
Caroline Wilde, however, who apparently did
little but work in the laboratory and keep
out-of-doors, would be charmed to row her
about Paradise.

A FEW DIVERSIONS

Accordingly, at a few minutes after nine, Marjory stood at the foot of the main staircase, swaying backward and forward in the chapel rush, and picked out Caroline, sauntering down with a cheerful "Hello!" for everybody on the stairs and that air of leisure that was the despair and admiration of the perpetually rushed; for she was one of the notoriously busy people in the college—always "at everything," distressingly competent in several of the stiffest courses offered, the first aid to the injured in any capacity, and the prop of more committees than she had fingers. She was always perfectly well and always wore a shirt-waist, and she was one of the exceedingly few people who are equally popular with students, Faculty, and ladies-in-charge.

She pulled Marjory about in the most scientific manner over a somewhat restricted body of water boasting a great deal of scenery for its size, conversing at length on basketball, in which she had been twice defeated, and not at all on golf and tennis, in which she held the college championship. In the course of her remarks it became apparent that Ursula and Dodo formed one third of "their crowd," she and Nan another third, and Lucilla and Carol Sawyer one sixth each.

Of Lucilla there seemed to be little to say: she was of extensive ancestry and made the best fudge in the place. She was also a good person to tell things to and was always quiet and polite. Dodo spoke—very literally—for herself. She was one of the best actresses in the college; she had some very bad quarter-hours back of her continual nonsense; she was poor, and there was something the matter all the time at home. Ursula was one of the all 'round girls of the college; she did beautiful work, and wrote very well and knew a lot—and her clothes! She dressed for the crowd. Nan was, of course, the best girl in the world, as might be seen by anybody with an eye in its head.

And Carol? Oh, Carol was all right. You had to come to know her, that was all. People did n't understand Carol. Her mother died when she was a baby, and she did n't like her Eastern aunt, who took care of her part of the time. They were really ridiculously wealthy, and her father was—well, her father was n't very attractive. She had lived a great deal in San Francisco, and in the West girls do very much more as they please, you know. There was n't a more generous girl on the face of the earth. She was a mighty good friend to her friends. People said she was being tutored

through college. It was n't so. And what if she
was? Look at the men! Her bark was worse
than her bite: she said more than she did. If
all the things she had done for people up here
were known — but she would be horribly angry
if they were.

It occurred to Marjory during that morning and afterwards, as she was handed impartially from one to the other of the six juniors
who constituted her entertainment committee, that it was well to have five friends to
take care of your character with the world.

In the evening she went, by favor of Ursula
and Dodo, in the character of a distant relative, to the entertainment proper of the Phi
Kappa Farewell, a play given to the seniors
of that honorable body by the juniors. Nothing but a detailed account of the drama could
worthily treat of it, and that cannot be given.
It was a melodrama based on the Spanish
War, adapted from a blood-and-thunder novel
into a play of five acts with three and four
scenes to the act. A large cast presented it, com-
prising revolutionists, Cubans, spies, U. S.
Army and Navy, native population, planters,
New York belles, and English nobility, and
there were slow deaths, ghastly conspiracies,
horribly pathetic separations, magnificent pa-

triotic tableaux, and a final and startling adjustment that exceeded in scenic display the wildest expectation of the enraptured audience.

From the first act, in a Fifth Avenue parlor, furnished with a toy piano perched on a card-table and a Vision of Elegance accompanying, with much execution and one finger, a rival Vision who rendered *My bonnie lies over the ocean* with dramatic fervor and a sob that recalled Bernhardt, while Dodo, in irreproachable evening dress and a curly mustache, devotedly turned the half-inch sheet music, one elbow ostentatiously leaned on the twelve-inch piano; to the ecstatic *finale* in the Havana Cathedral, where two marvellous brides in window-curtain-trained wedding dresses, orange blossoms, and indefinite yards of white mosquito netting were led to the altar by a noble naval officer and a haughty peer of the realm, the entire cast in the character of bridal party performing an elaborate ballet to the Lohengrin March, the procession preceded by a priest two-stepping solemnly at the head, it was the most astonishingly, cleverly, unspeakably idiotic performance Marjory had ever seen. Revolvers went off, victims shrieked, dons and doñas sneered, terrible shell-trimmed, tawny-skinned natives leaped and brandished and gabbled, virtue pleaded, and villainy cried "Ha, ha!" and everybody called upon Heaven except the peer of the realm, who very properly called upon England. They rolled their r's and smote their chests and spoke in a vibrating contralto, while at the proper places the audience groaned and clapped and hissed and at the end fairly thundered its applause.

Nobody who had seen the two heroines under a trusty Spanish escort travelling through a mountain gorge, half of the escort placidly dragging a ramping, double-breasted rocking-horse cart, and the other half cavorting gracefully about with a small mounted horse under his arm, could ever forget the sight; nor the languishing ladies in glorious Spanish costumes tossing their trains behind and coquetting with enormous fans as they conspired in dramatic and deep-chested asides to the audience.

Ursula, Dodo, and another genius had adapted this never-sufficiently-to-be-praised work, and they appeared flushed and panting from the wedding scene, to receive the ovation prepared for them. Ursula said that to have seen Martha Williams in undisguised hysteria and B. S. Kitts and Susan Jackson collapsed in their chairs was honor enough for her, and that she would willingly have worked twice as hard as she did for it. Then they went over, costumes and all, to the Dewey, to eat ices and go home, for the play had occupied two hours or more and such a strain was naturally somewhat enervating, as Biscuits said.

They took breakfast next morning in Ursula's room: strawberries and rich chocolate and rolls and scrambled eggs. Lucilla cooked it in two chafing-dishes, and Carol and Caroline came over from the Morris to share it, Carol in a magnificent fluffy party-cloak with a gorgeous crêpe kimono under it, Dodo in a hideous house-jacket, and Caroline in the inevitable shirt-waist. Then Ursula went to church in a heavenly lavender bâtiste and white-rabbit gloves, as Nan called them; Lucilla accompanied her in a demure little checked silk, and Carol sulked in her room, wrapped in the kimono.

Dodo wrote some difficult letters home, and took a walk to get over them; Caroline tramped out to Florence, where she conducted a funny little Sunday-school—in a shirt-waist; Marjory and Nan strolled out to Paradise and talked. They dined in state with the house and its guests on the traditional Sunday turkey,

Nan speculating solemnly on the exhaustless energy of Providence, except for whose ceaseless intervention the race of turkeys must long since have become extinct. Later they retired to the parlor and sat on sofas while the after-dinner Sunday music was performed — an apparently mechanical process where the same girls offered the same things to the same audience with the same expression that they had presented the Sunday before. The *Marche Funèbre* received the usual sighs of pleasure, an optimistic young lady rendered the love song from *Samson et Dalila*, and at unmistakable evidences of approaching *Mandalay* the occupants of the sofa nearest the door murmured something about letters and melted away.

To vespers, referred to by the devout as "the sweetest of the college services," entitled by the profane "the Sunday strut," owing to the toilets of the carefully selected ushers and the general prevalence of millinery, Marjory did not go, for returning from a walk with Lucilla, they found Miss Gillatt pinching the ears of a gentleman upon whose lap she sat, whose not too abundant hair she had arranged in peculiarly foolish spirals that bobbed over his ears as he responded to the introduction, "*Voilà le père aimable! Il est arrivé avec un* box *énorme—c'est un enfant bien gentil, n'est-ce pas? Nous en mangerons* to-morrow night, *mon Dieu*, and for once *nous aurons quelqu'chose* fit to eat—*hein? A moi, Lucille—il y aura une chaleur excessive dans la ville ancienne ce soir!*"

Le père aimable greeted Marjory with an unfeigned interest, and when to his inquiring "Cunningham? Cunningham? I don't remember Cunningham, do I, Nannie?" Nan replied easily, "Oh, no, she's not a regular inmate!" Marjory felt suddenly left out and undeserving, somehow, of all the joy in store.

It was worth being away from home to be one of the four girls who hung upon the Amiable Parent the next day as he wandered happily through the campus, distributing Allegretti and admiration as he went. He beamed upon them all, annexing the pretty ones regardless of expense, as his irreverent daughter put it. He chartered a tally-ho, and they tooted off to Chesterfield and broke the horn beyond repair, convulsing him with laughter all the way. Caroline cut her laboratory for it and enjoyed it "with a serene and sickly suavity known only to the truly virtuous," to use her friends' quotation; Dodo was a continuous performance all the way; and at Chesterfield they ate till there was little left in the village, as it had not been sufficiently forewarned of their invasion.

They got back in time to dress, and here Marjory's ideas sustained a distinct shock. She had always perfectly understood from the fiction devoted to such descriptions that it was the custom of young ladies at boarding-schools and colleges, when they wished to be peculiarly uproarious and sinful, to gather in carefully darkened apartments, robed in blanket-wrappers and nightgowns, with braided or dishevelled hair, in order to eat olives and pickles with hat-pins from the bottles, toasting marshmallows at intervals, and discussing the suitability of cribs and the essential qualities of really earnest friendships. But the consumption of the "box *énorme*" was differently organized. If she had n't brought any evening dress it did n't matter, Nan assured her, but they considered the event more than worthy of it, though it was n't an occasion for a Prom costume by any means.

All the way down the corridor she smelled it, that night at seven. It was necessarily far from private—envious upper-class girls not invited sniffed it from afar, and the three little freshmen who waited on them glowed with

pride and anticipation. It was in Ursula's
room, for Nan's was too small and the guests
used it for a cloak-room. Mrs. Austin greeted
her cordially at the door, and Marjory, who
had always supposed that those in authority
were constitutionally opposed to spreads, could
not realize that her wreathèd smiles were gen-
uine. She did not know that the Amiable
Parent had dutifully called upon Mrs. Austin
in all good form, openly discussed the spread,
and cannily presented the lady with a fascinating box of Canton ginger-buds — ginger
being the Amiable Parent's professional interest.

When they were assembled, a baker's dozen
of them, the Amiable Parent grinning, as his
dutiful daughter expressed it, like a Cheshire
cat over his capacious shirt-front, Marjory
made their acquaintance over again from the
evening-dress standpoint. Against the dark
furniture and bookbindings their shoulders
shone soft and white; their hair was piled high;
they looked two or three years older. Ursula
in pink taffeta, with coral in her glossy dark
coils, was a veritable *marquise*; Nan in white
with lavender ribbons, and a pale amethyst
against her throat, was transformed from a
jolly, active girl to a handsome young woman

with charmingly correct shoulders; Caroline
was almost pretty; Lucilla's small prim head
was set on the most beautiful tapering little
neck in the world. Only Dodo in an organdie
many times laundered was the same as ever,
bony, awkward, and the greatest fun possible;
while Carol's strange half-sullen face looked
more impassive than ever under her heavy
turquoise fillet.

The freshmen, shy but delighted, passed
them "food after food," as Dodo called it: cold
roast chicken, lobster salad on crisp, curly
lettuce, delicious thin, little bread-and-butter
sandwiches with the crusts off, devilled eggs,
stuffed olives, almonds and ginger. There was
a great sheet of fudge-cake, which is a two-
storied arrangement of solid chocolate cake
with a thick fudge filling and a half-inch icing,
a compound possible of safe consumption to
girls and ostriches only. There were dozens and
dozens of a fascinating kind of thin wafer filled
with nuts, and there were plates of chocolate
peppermints. Also there were many bottles of
imported ginger ale, which the freshmen presented in graceful, curved glasses after the Amiable Parent had with much chuckling pulled
the corks, the freshmen pitching these last
cheerfully down the corridor at their friends

who came to scoff but went away to pray. That immediate amalgamation with the class of her hostesses which always occurs to guests made Marjory regard the pretty waitresses with upper-class patronage, till it occurred to her that they might be older than she, and that after all. . . .

One in especial, whom the Amiable Parent insisted on feeding from his own plate, was very pretty and apparently very popular. But why the brown-eyed, red-cheeked adorer of Ursula should be *Theo* Root, while Miss Bent was always *Dodo*; why Alida Fosdick was *Dick*, but Serena Burdick was Serena; why Elizabeth Twitchell was *Twitchie*, but Elizabeth Mitchell was *Betty*; why Ursula was always Ursula, and Nan was often *Jack* and sometimes *Pip* (it was because *Captain Gadsby* was one of her famous parts) Marjory could not tell.

When they were through and not another of all those two pounds of almonds could be eaten, and the freshmen had carried off the remains to dispose of them in the most obvious and economical manner, they proceeded to "do stunts," to the boundless joy of the Amiable Parent. Dick Fosdick, a plain, heavy-eyed senior, arose, draped in a black cashmere shawl, and delivered a lecture on the suffrage

in a manner to cause one to pinch oneself to
make sure it was not a dream and she was not
forty-five and horrible. The Amiable Parent
choked to suffocation, vowed she was the
cleverest actress this side the water, and called
for the next. Dodo, with lifted skirts and utterly unmoved features, jumping up heavily
and landing on both feet with turned-in toes
—she followed the good old custom of tan
walking-boots with evening dress—droned in
a monotonous nasal chant, to which her thudding feet kept time, an unholy song of no tune
whatever:

> Oh, it's *dance* like a *fairy* and *sing* like a *bird*,
>> And *sing* like a *bird*,
>> And *sing* like a *bird*,
> It's *dance* like a *fairy* and *sing* like a *bird*,
>> *Sing* like a *bird* in *June!*

Anybody who has not seen this done by a
solemn-looking girl of five feet seven or so,
who divests a naturally humorous mouth of
any expression whatever, and lands on the
floor like an inspired steam-roller, is not in a
position to judge of the comic quality of the
performance.

Nan, with much coy reluctance and very
Gallic gestures, rendered what was pessimisti-
cally called her "naughty little French song."

Its burden was not discoverably pernicious, however, consisting of the question, "*O Jean Baptiste, pourquoi?*" occasionally varied by the rapturous answer, "*O Jean Baptiste, voilà!*" But there was accent enough to make anything naughty, and she looked so pretty they made her do it again.

Lucilla resisted many appeals, but succumbed finally to the Amiable Parent, who could wheedle the gate off its hinges, according to his daughter, and delivered her "one and only stunt." She had performed it steadily since freshman year, always with the same wild success, never with a hint of its palling. Marjory wondered why they laughed so—they all knew it by heart—and asked if anybody else never did it; their amazed negative impressed her greatly. She stood before them slim and straight, this daughter of a hundred Bostonians, a little cold, a little bored, a little displeased, apparently, and with an utterly emotionless voice and a quite impersonal manner delivered the most senseless doggerel in the most delicately precise enunciation:

> Baby sat on the window ledge,
> Mary pushed her over the edge.
> Baby broke into bits so airy—
> Mother shook her finger at Mary.

A FEW DIVERSIONS

Sarah poisoned mother's tea,
Mother died in agonee.
Father looked quite sad and vexed —
"*Sarah, my child,*" he said, "*what next?*"

Any one to whom this seems a futile and non-humorous piece of verse needs only to hear Lucilla's delivery of it, and catch the almost imperceptible shade of displeasure and surprise that touched her slender eyebrows at the last line, to realize that all similar exhibitions must seem forever crude beside it.

They begged Marjory to sing and got her a guitar. As it had slowly dawned on her that most of the girls in the room played something, and that at least one third of them belonged to one or another of the musical clubs besides the many other organizations they carried, and thought nothing whatever of it — or concealed it if they did — her estimate of a hitherto much prized accomplishment had steadily decreased. She sang a little serenade for them, however, more tremulously than she had been wont to sing for a crowd of young people, and took an unreasoning and disproportionate amount of pleasure in their hearty applause. She sang again, and when Miss Cornelia Burt, who turned out to be the dark girl she had watched at Kingsley's and recognized,

thanked her particularly and told her with a
smile that she should "come up" and sing
that with the Glee Club, Marjory remembered
that she was a prominent senior, and found
her heart beating a little faster when her friend
Miss Twitchell, also prominent, repeated the
suggestion. It could not be, she asked herself
a moment afterwards, that *she* was proud to
have them notice her?

There were more stunts, for the Amiable
Parent could not have enough of what Nan
called Dodo's Anglo-Saxon attitudes. Only
the bell brought a stop to the proceedings,
which had grown more and more hilarious,
ending with a toast in ginger ale, to the delighted hero of the feast:

Oh, *here's* to Nannie's *Dad*, drink him *down!*
Oh, *here's* to Nannie's *Dad*, drink him *down!*
  Oh, *here's* to Nannie's *Dad*,
  He's the *best* she could have *had*,
Drink him *down*, drink him *down*, drink him *down*,
  down, *down!*

Nan and he and Marjory went out into the
cool, dark campus, and they marched to "Balm
of Gilead" all the way to Marjory's boarding-
house. She watched them from her window,
tramping arm-in-arm down to the hotel, where
Nan was to stay the night with him. Nan had

explained that while of course it would be a trial to her to be obliged to select her own breakfast, still her relative had desired it, and she had as usual bidden him "her own convenience count as nil."

Marjory undressed slowly, humming the tune they had marched to and surveying the plain boarding-house bed-room. It seemed lonely after the Lawrence, and there was no dashing about in the halls, nor glimpses of fudge-parties and rarebits and laughing, busy people through half-shut doors.

"Still, that Miss Burt was off the campus," she murmured as she braided her hair; and as she set the alarm-clock somebody had loaned her—for she took an early train— and climbed into bed, she explained to an imaginary aunt that people on the temporary list with no campus application whatever often "got on" miraculously—Lucilla had done that, and Caroline!

THE EVOLUTION of EVANGELINE

VIII

THE EVOLUTION OF EVANGELINE

TO those who knew her afterward it may seem an impossible condition of affairs, but it is nevertheless quite true that until the night of the sophomore reception she was utterly unheard of. Indeed, when her name was read to the chairman of the committee that looks up stray freshmen, yet uninvited, and compels them to come in, the chairman refused to believe that she existed.

"I don't believe there's any such person," she growled, "and if there is, there's nobody to take her. I can't *make* sophomores! Evangeline Potts, forsooth! What a perfectly idiotic name! Who's to take her? Where does she live? Where's the catalogue?"

"She lives on West Street," somebody volunteered, "and Bertha Kitts' freshman is sick, or her uncle is sick, or something, and Bertha says that lets *her* out—she never wanted to go, anyhow—and now she's not going. Couldn't she take her?"

"Not going!" the chairman complained bitterly. "If that's not like B. Kitts! Go get her, somebody, and send her after Evangeline, and tell her to hurry, too! Don't stop to argue

with her, there is n't time. She 'll prove that
there is n't any reception, if you let her. Just
get her started and then come right back. I
promised to send three Bagdads over, and I
can't get but two."

The messenger paused at Miss Kitts' door,
sniffed scornfully at the sign which read:
"Asleep! Please do not disturb under any circumstances whatever!" and entered the room
abruptly. Miss Kitts was curled comfortably
on the window-seat, with *Plain Tales from the
Hills* in one hand, and *The Works of Christopher Marlowe* in the other. From these volumes she read alternately, and the pile of cores
and seeds on the sill indicated a due regard for
other than mental nutriment. At intervals she
lifted her eyes from her book to watch the file
of girls loaded down with the pillows, screens,
and palms whose transportation forms so con-
siderable a portion of the higher education of
women. Just as the door opened Biscuits was
chuckling gently at the collision of a rubber-
plant with a Japanese screen and the consequent collapse of their respective bearers, who,
even in their downfall, poured forth the apologies and regrets that take the place of their
brothers' less considerate remarks upon similar occasions.

But her mirth was rudely checked by the messenger, who closed the Marlowe and put the Kipling under a pillow.

"Hurry up," she remarked briefly, "and find Evangeline Potts and tell her that you can't sleep at night till you take her to the sophomore reception. Nobody urged her to attend and yours is sick."

"She's not, either," returned B. Kitts, calmly. "She's quite well, and—"

"Oh, don't possum, Biscuits, but get along. Sue's nearly wild. It's her uncle, then; we know you were n't going, so we know you can take her. Can I take this couch cover along? She's on West Street, and I can't stop to discuss it, but we depend on you. Now *do* hurry up; it's three already."

Biscuits freed her mind to the heap of pillows in the middle of the floor, for there was no one else to hear her. Then, still grumbling, she put on her golf cape and walked over to West Street. In a pessimistic frame of mind she selected the most unattractive house, and on inquiring if Miss Evangeline Potts lived there and ascertaining that she did, she astonished the slatternly maid by a heartfelt ejaculation of "Sherlock Holmes!"—adding, with resignation, "Is she in?" She was in, and her guest climbed two flights of stairs and knocked at her door.

Although Evangeline Potts was not fully dressed and her room in consequent disorder, she did not appear at all embarrassed, but finished buttoning her shirt-waist and attached her collar with calm deliberation. She was a large, tall girl, with masses of auburn hair strained back unbecomingly from a very freckled face and heaped in tight coils on the top of her head. Her eyes were a rich red-brown; they struck you as lovely at first, till after a while you discovered that they were like glass or running water, always the same and absolutely expressionless. She had large hands and feet and a wide, slow smile, and she was dressed in unmitigatedly bad taste, with sleeves two years behind the style and a skirt that could have had nothing to do with it at any date.

"I came to—to see if you had been—if you were going to the sophomore reception," said Biscuits. "I'm Miss Kitts, Ninety-red, and—and I've nobody to go with me and—and I shall be glad—"

Biscuits was frankly embarrassed. She was a clever girl, and clever girls of her age are invariably conscious and more or less sensitive. She knew how she would have felt if she had been a freshman and a "left over": she would have resented such an eleventh-hour invitation and shown it, possibly. But if Evangeline Potts bore any resentment it was not apparent.

"No," she said quietly, "I have n't been asked and I 'd just as lieve go with you."

"Oh, that 's very nice!" returned Biscuits, cheerfully, "then that 's settled. And what color is your gown? I should like to send you some flowers."

"I 'm not sure what I *will* wear," said Evangeline; "what will you?"

"My dress is pink," and Biscuits carefully kept her surprise out of the answer. Miss Potts did not look like the kind of girl to possess more than one evening gown.

"How is it made?" Evangeline pursued. She was not curious, and yet she was not talking vaguely to cover any embarrassment: she merely desired information.

"Oh, it 's quite plain," and Biscuits rose to go; she was a little bored and there was nothing in Miss Potts' room to give any clew to her apparently pointless character. Biscuits prided herself on her ability to get at people through their belongings, and graded her friends as possessors of Baby Stuart, the Barye

Lion, a Botticelli Madonna, or the imp of Lincoln Cathedral.

But Evangeline did not rise. "I mean, is it low neck and short sleeves?" she insisted; and as Biscuits nodded, she added, "Does everybody wear them?"

"Why, yes," said Biscuits, hastily; and then, "That is, a great many do. It's not at all necessary, though: you'll see plenty of girls without. Any light organdie will do perfectly."

"I don't think I'll go, then," remarked Evangeline, calmly; "my dress would n't do."

She was not in the least apologetic or pathetic or vexed: she merely stated a fact, and it occurred to Biscuits, who was somewhat susceptible to personality, that she meant precisely what she said. Although absence from the reception was just what Biscuits had previously planned, she did not care to please herself at this price, and though Evangeline Potts was the last person she would have selected for her companion, and visions of the pretty little freshman she had had in mind on filling out her programme flashed before her with irritating clearness, she smiled encouragement and remonstrated cheerfully.

"Oh, nonsense! Why, anything will do, I tell you! You don't need evening dress! One of my friends last year had all her clothes ruined by a pipe or something that burst in the closet and she went in white duck. And she was one of the best-dressed girls in the class, really——"

"Yes, but I'm not," interrupted Evangeline, "and that's different. I'm just as much obliged to you for asking me, Miss Kitts, but I haven't any evening dress and I shouldn't go without one."

It was characteristic of Biscuits that she attempted no further argument. She knew that Evangeline Potts would not go unless she had an evening dress, and it seemed, somehow, imperative that she should go. She realized, too, that borrowing was out of the question.

"Why don't you cut one of your dresses out?" she suggested after a moment. "Suzanne Endicott did that once when she was unexpectedly asked to a dance and hadn't any low waist with her."

"I can't sew," Evangeline replied, "and I shouldn't know how to cut it."

In proportion as she seemed convinced of the impossibility of going, Biscuits waxed more eager to change her determination.

"See here," she said suddenly, "if I get Suzanne over here, will you let *her* cut one of your dresses out? I think she would; she's awfully clever about that sort of thing and she's very obliging, sometimes."

She was prepared for any answer but the one forthcoming.

"Why, I don't care," said Evangeline, indifferently, "only she'd better hurry, had n't she?"

Biscuits was by now so impressed with the vital necessity of getting Suzanne that she had hardly time to wonder at her haste or her nervous fear that the young lady might not be at home. She trudged up the two flights and sighed with relief at the sound of Suzanne's mandolin. Miss Endicott was not fond of the mandolin and played it solely for the purpose of annoying the senior next door, who had a nasty habit of rising early to study, and making her bed violently, driving it into the wall just opposite Suzanne's pillow. When remonstrated with she returned with calmness that she had not been accustomed, when herself a sophomore, to object to the habits of seniors, and that excitable young people who came to college for heaven knew what, had better acquaint themselves with habits of study in others, since that was their only probable source of knowledge of such habits.

THE EVOLUTION OF EVANGELINE

Henceforth it became at once Suzanne's duty and pleasure to give what she modestly called "little recitals from time to time," accompanied by her mandolin, which instrument maddened her neighbor beyond endurance. As Biscuits entered she was giving a very dramatic rendering of the Jewel Song from Faust, and to her guest's opening remarks she replied only by a melodious burst of laughter and the arch assurance:

> "*Non, non! Ce n'est plus toi!*
> *Ce n'est plus ton visage!*"

Biscuits obeyed an imperative gesture and held her peace till the song was over, when the performer, with an inimitable grin at the wall, laid down her mandolin and pointed to a chair.

"*Que voulez-vous, ma plus chère? Vous avez l'air —*"

"Oh, for heaven's sake talk English, Suzanne! I want you to come over and cut out Evangeline Potts' evening dress. Will you? She 's freckled and big, and she won't go unless you do. She 's got to go, too. We can't leave anybody out. Will you come?"

"*Mais qu'avez-vous donc, ma chère Berthe? Est-ce que j'suis couturière, moi?*"

"Yes," said Biscuits, obstinately, "you are, and you know it. You might be able to make

[255]

her look like something. She's a perfect stick now."

Suzanne shot one of her elfish glances at her visitor. It was impossible to know what she would do.

"*Mais certainement vous avez assez de joue, vous!*" she suggested. Biscuits did not reply, but watched the clock on the desk.

Suzanne shrugged her shoulders.

"*Eh bien!*" she said cheerfully, "*me voilà sage, Petits-pains, sage et bien aimable! Où demeure-t-elle donc, votre amie?*"

"Bless you, Suzanne, her name's Evangeline Potts! and she—"

"*Mon Dieu!* Evangeline Potts! *Mais quelle horreur! Est-ce que je saurais prononcer ce nom affreux?*" babbled Suzanne, while Biscuits found her golf cape and hustled her out of the door. Those who relied too long or too securely on Miss Endicott's moods were frequently disappointed in the end.

She had been born in San Francisco and brought up, alternately, in Paris and New York, by her brother, a rising young artist, whose views were as broad as his handling, and whose regret at parting with her was equalled only by his firm determination to fulfil the promise he had made their mother, long dead, to educate her properly. Only his solemn assurance that she should come back every summer if she would behave, and finally conduct their joint establishment in Paris with the Angora for chaperon and the silky Skye for butler, kept her from taking the first steamer back from the seaport nearest the town she had hated consistently since she left that scene of delicious little suppers and jolly painter-people and nights at the play and ecstatic exhibitions when Brother was "on the line."

Now a wealthy young woman from San Francisco who chooses to spend from two to four years at an Eastern college is a sufficiently complicated type in herself; when she has grown up in studios and done very much as she pleases all her life, she affords even more food for thought to the student of character.

People who disliked Suzanne called her unprincipled and shallow and lazy; people who admired her called her brilliant and irresponsible and lazy; people who loved her called her fascinating and spoiled and lazy. She could dance like a leaf in the wind; she could make herself the most bewitching garments out of nothing to speak of; she could create a Japanese tea-room with one parasol and two fans, and make a Persian interior from a rug, an inlaid table, and a jewelled lantern; she could learn anything perfectly in half the time it would take anybody else to get a fair idea of it, and she could, if so minded, carry insolence to the point of a fine art. She was far from pretty, but her clever little brown face, with its strange gray eyes, compelled attention, and her hair had that rare silvery tinge that is an individuality in itself. She was never without two or three devoted admirers, but her class disliked her, and it took all their self-control to bear with her to the extent that was necessary in order to profit by her special abilities. She was no more to be depended upon than a kitten, and her periodical bursts of rage rendered her unendurable to that large majority which objects to flaming eyes and torrents of assorted abuse, to say nothing of the occasional destruction of bric-a-brac.

And yet, to the wonder of these righteous critics, Suzanne kept her warm friends. There was always some amiable Philistine to watch her erratic movements with delighted awe, to run on her errands, to listen to her amazing confidences, and to stand up for her through thick and thin. Though Biscuits and her little circle were, even in their sophomore year, be-

ginning to draw away from her, vaguely conscious of a necessary parting of the ways,
frankly puzzled at the vagaries of this girl who
was half a spoiled baby, half a woman of the
world, at intervals the fascination of her personality drew them back for a while, and they
wondered that they could have thought her
irresponsible and selfish at heart.

To-day, as Biscuits walked beside her, con-
vulsed by her narration of a recent tussle with
the lady-in-charge—"I was only putting an
accordion-pleated crêpe-paper frieze above the
moulding, with thumb tacks, and if she had
kept out of the way—pig! 'What do you
think you came to college for, Suzanne? Certainly not work of this sort!' 'Oh, no, Mrs.
Wylie, of course not. I have long realized that
our real object in coming here was to save the
maids trouble!'"—she almost forgave her that
curt refusal to have anything to do with the
reception decorations: "You'd far better save
me for the Prom—I'll manage that, but I
won't do both, *vous savez, c'est un peu trop
fort!*" she had remarked royally, and the committee had smothered their wrath and agreed,
and cursed her afterwards in detail, after the
manner of practical young women who are far
from the short-sightedness of allowing their

[259]

emotions to interfere with their intentions.
Also, they do not enjoy giving needless pain
—on the spot. This is one of the sweetest at-
tributes of woman.

They knocked at Evangeline's door, and
omitting preliminary ceremonies, demanded
the dress. Evangeline produced a dark red
cashmere: Suzanne shook her head. A much
washed white lawn with what appeared to be
blue palm-leaf fans scattered over it was next
offered for consideration: Suzanne gasped,
" *Mon Dieu!* " A gray gingham decorated with
yellow spirals met her demand for "a summer
thing," and caused the artist to sink upon the
floor with a tragic groan.

" *Mais, Evangéline, vous me serrez le cœur!
C'est horrible! C'est effrayant!* "

Evangeline smiled politely but offered no
further suggestion.

Suzanne looked at her searchingly through
half-closed eyes. "Have you anything black?"
she demanded.

"I have a black silk," said Evangeline, and
she brought out a heavy, corded, ribbon-
trimmed affair with a pointed vest that would
have been highly suitable for a maiden aunt
who had, as Suzanne remarked, seen misfortune. Biscuits sighed, but Suzanne rose rapidly

to her feet and clutched the scissors she had brought with her.

"*Enfin! Ça y est!*" she cried. "Put it on her, Biscuits!"

She persisted in utterly ignoring Evangeline, or, more exactly, in treating her as if she had been a doll, talking to her in a pitying tone that required no answer and commenting upon her deficiencies in a manner that made Biscuits squirm visibly and glance apologetically at the object of such impersonal criticism.

"Perhaps Miss Potts does n't care to have such a—such a nice dress cut," she suggested, as Suzanne, with what seemed a perfectly careless gesture, slashed at the sleeves.

"*Quel malheur!*" replied the artist, indifferently, and Evangeline added, "I 'd just as lieve."

With pursed lips Suzanne snipped and pinched, while Biscuits followed her every motion and Evangeline silently adjusted herself to each new position as Suzanne pulled and pushed her arms and neck about. At length with a sudden motion Suzanne stripped off the detached sleeves as if they had been gloves, and snatched away the top of the scant middle-aged waist with a quick movement.

"*Voilà!* " she said, and Biscuits gasped: for Evangeline Potts was a transformed creature. Her arms and neck were ivory white and as soft and smooth as satin; the lovely curves of her throat and shoulders could never have been guessed at under the stiff black seams of the waist.

Suzanne patted her arms appreciatively. "I might have known it, with that hair and those freckles!" she murmured. Then, calmly, to Evangeline: "The trouble with your kind is, you never have any eyebrows and your eyelids get red, *n'est-ce pas?*"

She went a few steps back from the motionless figure and stood silent.

"You could twist a black scarf," suggested Biscuits, hastily. Suzanne waved her hand.

"*Tu me dégoûtes, à la fin!*" she said coldly; "Get your cape on!" Then, to Evangeline: "Undo your hair!" As the thick coil tumbled over her shoulders, the directress of ceremonies deliberately selected a light inner tress and snipped it off.

"Take it down town and match it—in velvet if you can, in silk if you can't," she commanded. "And get enough, get two, three yards!"

"But will Miss Potts want to spend—"

THE EVOLUTION OF EVANGELINE

Biscuits looked doubtfully at the white-armed goddess who contemplated herself quietly in the glass. It was impossible to know what she was thinking; she was apparently quite accustomed to strangers who dressed her in low-cut evening dresses and snipped her hair and spent her money.

Suzanne stamped her foot. "*Va-t-en!*" she cried, and then, with an irresistible mimicry of Evangeline, "*She'd* just as lieve!"

When Biscuits returned with a great strip of tawny velvet, it was taken from her at the door, and she was instructed to get from Suzanne's room her make-up box and the gold powder that had so unaccountably disappeared after the play last week.

"They borrowed the eyebrow pencil and that, the night of the dress rehearsal, and they *swore* to bring them back—beasts! What have I to call my own? *Rien!* Never, never, never will I lend anything again! *Il faut faire un fin, vraiment!*"

It was a long hunt for Biscuits, and more than once it occurred to her that she had refused to go on the decorating committee with a view to escaping just such wearisome trotting about. When she handed the box to Suzanne and suggested that the result should be extremely pleasing to justify such toil, the red spot in the artist's either cheek and her wide-opened eyes indicated the happy absorption to which no effort seems worthy of mention. Biscuits, not allowed to enter the room, sat wearily on the stairs, longing to go home but unwilling to abandon Suzanne. It was very nearly six, and she was not dressed; she had left the necessary perusal of *The Works of Christopher Marlowe* till late in the day, thinking to devote the evening to it; she took little interest in Evangeline Potts, and she did not care much for dancing.

But for the moment her resentment vanished when Suzanne called her in and she beheld the object of her labors under the gaslight in a carefully darkened room. Her milk-white shoulders rose magnificently from folds of auburn velvet that her wonderful hair repeated in loose waves about her face and a great mass low on her neck. Her long, round arms gleamed against the black of her skirt and melted into the glow of her velvet girdle. In the white light her freckles paled and her eyes turned wholly brown, and said mysterious things that could never by any possibility have occurred to her.

"*Tiens! J'ai eu la main heureuse, n'est-ce*

pas? Vous la trouvez charmante?" said Suzanne, turning her about as if she had been a dummy and indicating her opinion that the back view was, if anything, more satisfying than the front.

"You 're a genius, Suzanne! She 's simply stunning! How did you do it?"

Suzanne smiled. "*C'est pas grand' chose,*" she said modestly. But she looked contentedly at Evangeline and loosened her hair a little. "Now remember, don't put on those hideous rings," she commanded, "and don't wear anything on your head. Do you dance well?" she added.

Evangeline hesitated. "I dance a little," she replied, "pretty well, I guess."

Suzanne promptly encircled her waist and whistled a waltz. After a few turns she stopped.

"You dance very badly," she said encouragingly. "If I were you, I 'd sit out most of them. You can say it bores you—they 'll be glad enough. Besides, you might get red and then you 'd not be pretty. Now don't move about much, and when Miss Kitts brings you the white roses put them just where I told you."

"Very well," said Evangeline, and as the other two prepared to go she gave them one of her long, slow smiles. "I'm much obliged to you both, I'm sure," she said; "you've been very kind."

"*Adieu, mon enfant—à plus tard!*" and Suzanne seized the door knob. She turned in the door and threw a quick, piercing look at her handiwork. "If you take my advice, you'll never put on that dreadful shirt-waist again, *très chère*," she said lightly. "You'll spoil all this splendor, if you do. Give it away—or, no, don't! you'd corrupt the taste of the poor—burn it up, and the others with it, and get a black suit and a black silk waist and wear a big white tie, if you like. And a white tam—one of those pussy ones. Wear one color—*c'est plus distingué*—and if you want a big black hat with plumes, I'll make it for you. *Et maintenant, regarde-toi dans la glace!*"

With this invocation they left her, and Biscuits, learning that Suzanne had exhausted her energy and proposed to inform her freshman that she was ill and unable to attend the reception, became possessed by the idea that she was responsible for this particular illustration of the artistic temperament, and went without her dinner to hunt up a substitute. She wasted no time in argument with Suzanne,

She was one of the successes of the evening

who lay luxuriously on her couch pillows with her hands under her head, and planned costumes for Evangeline Potts all the evening, but tramped angrily over the campus till quarter of seven to find an unattached sophomore, forgetting that Evangeline's flowers were yet to be purchased. Coming up with them in her hand, a little later, she was forced to stop and explain to the substitute the intricacies of Suzanne's programme, breaking off abruptly to beat her breast like the wedding guest, for she heard the loud bassoon and fled to her room, tearing her evening dress hopelessly and completing her toilette on the stairs. The substitute suffered from a violent headache as the result of her unexpected exertions, and the little freshman cried herself to sleep, for she had dreamed for nights of going with Suzanne, whom she admired to stupefaction.

But of all this Evangeline Potts knew little, and, it may be, cared less. She was one of the successes of the evening, and her few remarks were quoted diligently. She could have danced dozens of extras, had so many been possible, and Biscuits was considered to have displayed more than her ordinary cleverness in procuring a creature so picturesque and distinguished.

This did not surprise her, nor did she particularly resent being pointed out by more than one freshman as "the sophomore that took that stunning Miss Potts"; but her amazement was undisguised, the next morning but one, at the sight of Evangeline walking out from chapel with a prominent junior, the glamor of the evening gone, it is true, her face somewhat heavy and undeniably freckled, but nevertheless an Evangeline transformed. From her fluffy white cap to the hem of her dignified black skirt she was the realization of Suzanne's parting suggestions, and the distinct intention of her costume had its full effect. She was far more impressive than the jolly little short-skirted junior, whose curly yellow hair paled beside the dark richness of Evangeline's massive coils, and Biscuits, remembering that she had called her "a perfect stick," marvelled inwardly.

She went to call on her a little later, but Evangeline was not in; and feeling that her duty was done, Miss Kitts gave no further thought to what she considered an essentially uninteresting person, but devoted herself to a study of the campus house into which she had moved only that year.

She saw Evangeline very rarely after that,

except at the dances and plays, where her white shoulders framed in auburn velvet appeared very regularly. Once, happening to sit beside her, she began a conversation, but she could not remember afterward that Miss Potts said anything but, "Yes, indeed," or, "Yes, I think so, too." Her surprise was therefore great when, on hearing the result of the sophomore elections the next fall, and audibly commenting on the oddity of Miss Evangeline Potts in the position of sophomore president, she was indignantly assured by a loyal member of that class that the vote was almost unanimous and that she was one of the ablest girls in the class.

Even this she did not consider long, for the sophomore presidency is the least important of the four; but when among the first five sophomores to be triumphantly ushered into Phi Kappa Psi she was asked to consider the name of Evangeline Potts, she remonstrated.

"But she's not clever! She's not half so bright as lots we haven't got!" she objected. "Why do we want her?"

"She's no prod, of course, but she's a prominent girl and class president," was the answer, "and she's really very strong, I think —they say she does fair work, and everybody but you wants her. Do you really disapprove of her?"

"Oh, no!" said Biscuits, and watched Miss Potts with interest. She received her congratulations quietly, with a manner that made one wonder if they had been quite in good taste, and acted altogether as if she had fully expected to enter the society with Ursula Wyckoff and Dodo Bent. The senior class president took her out of chapel at the head of the file, with a bunch of violets as big as her two fists pinned to her belt, and Biscuits was asked to a supper in her honor in the campus house she had recently entered.

One of the other guests was the little freshman Biscuits had first asked to the sophomore reception, herself a sophomore now, and one of Phi Kappa's first five.

"Was your class surprised at the elections?" asked Biscuits, glancing half unconsciously at Evangeline. The sophomore smiled gently, with a hardly perceptible recognition of Biscuits' look.

"Oh, no," she replied; "we expected them —except, perhaps, one or two." Her polite little blush showed her traditional surprise at her own success, and the junior gave the equally traditional deprecating smile.

"Who's the other?" she inquired bluntly. The sophomore was taken off her guard and glanced again at Evangeline.

"Why, some of us did n't exactly see—we think Alison Greer's terribly bright—we did n't expect—and yet, I don't know! After all, I think perhaps we were n't so awfully surprised!"

"Now, I wonder if you really were n't, or if you're lying?" thought Biscuits, and then, remembering suddenly, "but that's just the way *we* all talked last year about Evelyn Lyon!"

That summer Evangeline spent in France with Suzanne, who informed Biscuits before they sailed that though she could n't find out anything about Miss Potts' parents, she had learned of the existence of a well-to-do uncle in New Hampshire who intended leaving quite a little money to his uncommunicative niece —he had given her the money to go abroad.

"She planned it all out, and asked to go with me, and I could n't well refuse," said Suzanne, "though Brother will be wild with rage—he hates women who are not clever: *il est un peu exigéant, mon frère.*"

By senior year Biscuits had very nearly lost track of Suzanne, who left the campus and spent most of her time sketching. Brother had shown some pen-and-ink portraits of hers to a great critic, who had declared that Brother had by no means exhausted the family genius, and Suzanne, heavily bribed, had returned to her last year of durance. The day of the Junior Prom Biscuits received a very French little note inviting her to "*une première vue*," and with the full expectation of a pen-and-ink collection, she confronted Evangeline, glorious in white satin and gold passementerie, with an amber chain and a great amber comb in her hair.

"*Vous rappelez-vous cette première fois, hein?*" Suzanne asked, with a grin. "*Ça date de loin, n'est-ce pas?*" Adding cheerfully, "*L'oncle est mort et nous avons une jolie dot!*"

Biscuits was not surprised to learn that Ursula Wyckoff had moved heaven and earth to get her cousin from Columbia for Evangeline's escort; she had heard how Nan Gillatt actually took her own brother to the Glee Club concert because Evangeline preferred the youth selected by Nan for herself, and she remembered how *she* had hunted from shop to shop for the velvet that matched that auburn hair. It was not that Evangeline insisted: she did not beg favors. But her habit of receiving a proposition in silence filled one with an irresistible desire to better one's offer, and even the improvement seemed poor in the calm scrutiny of those red-brown eyes.

"What I can't see is, who pushes her!" mused Biscuits.

"Who? who?" repeated Suzanne. "*Par exemple!* Why, she herself, of course! Who else?"

"But how?" Biscuits persisted. "Now Evelyn made up to everybody so—she earned her way, heaven knows! And Kate Ackley was a sort of legacy—her sister's reputation started her and she was rushed so freshman year that you could n't blame her for failing to realize what a fool she really is. And the Underhills' coming in with the crowd they did, explains them. But nobody rushes Evangeline particularly—"

"*C'est bien dommage!*" Suzanne interrupted with mock sympathy. "*Seule au monde!* Don't be an idiot, Biscuits, we *all* rush her, and we shall—till she begins to see what a bluff she's making! The beauty of Evangeline is, that she fools herself—*mais parfaitement!* She really thinks she's somebody—*voilà tout!*"

"I suppose that's it," assented Biscuits, thoughtfully.

"Ursula," Suzanne remarked oracularly, "is so anxious to please that sometimes she does n't, and even Susan the Great has her little plans—*mais oui!* But Mlle. Potts does n't care a *sou.* It's all one to her, *vous savez,* she agrees with all; and what's the result? *Tout le monde l'admire! C'est toujours comme ça!*"

For some reason or other her large and shapely figure was the most prominent feature of Biscuits' Commencement. She was a junior usher, of course, and in aisles or under lanterns, at Phi Kappa Farewell or Glee Club promenade, her calm, heavy face and deliberate movements attracted Biscuits' eye.

The mob had not appealed to Miss Kitts as a desirable method of dramatic début, and she was, consequently, one of the few seniors in the audience on the night of her class dramatics. Between the acts she wandered down to the door, and caught a bit of conversation among a group of ushers.

"And all Ursula's friends were in the middle aisle, and she begged Evangeline to change, but she would n't. Ursula could have had a seat then, with Dick Fosdick's people, and she was frightfully tired, but Evangeline would n't."

"Pooh! did you expect she would?"

[274]

THE EVOLUTION OF EVANGELINE

"Oh, no! She's terribly selfish, of course, but you'd think, considering how nice Ursula's been to her—"

"Oh, my dear! As if *that* made any difference to Evange—sh, here she is!—What stunning violets, Evangeline! That's your Prom dress, is n't it? It's terribly sweet!"

Evangeline smiled and sank into the seat a little freshman promptly and adoringly vacated for her, and Biscuits went back to her place.

Suzanne stopped in America that summer, and with the promise of five subsequent years in Paris, prolonged her stay till the following June. She went so far as to come up to Northampton to her class reunion, assuring her friends that she had forgotten a few opprobrious epithets in her final anathema and had returned to deliver them in person.

As they stood in the crowd on Ivy Day, watching the snowy procession, the cameras suddenly snapped rapidly all about them and an excited voice murmured: "There she is! Is n't she grand? My dear, she had eleven invitations for the junior entertainment! Martha Sutton took her—" Evangeline Potts walked slowly by.

"And you ought to have seen her Com-

mencement flowers! She had a bathtub full
—literally! She would n't take 'em out and
the tub could n't be used—"

"She's president of Phi Kapp, I hear,"
said Biscuits.

"Oh, yes," replied Suzanne, "and on the
dramatics committee, you know. She has lots
of friends."

"I wonder why," said Biscuits, absently.

"'*Sais pas!* They're clever girls, too. She
knows the pick of the class—but then, she
always did, you know."

"I suppose she'll marry money," mused
Biscuits, the student of human nature.

"*Du tout!*" Suzanne returned, "she won't
care about that. It's clever people she wants
—she always went with the clever ones: *elle
aime les gens d'esprit*. She's got money enough;
she'll marry some clever man who knows the
best people and will make her one of them—
vous l' verrez!"

And the prophecy was fulfilled, for Evangeline very shortly married Walter Endicott,
the well-known artist, whose portrait of her
in white and gold attracted so much attention
at a very recent *Salon*.

AT COMMENCEMENT

IX
AT COMMENCEMENT

I

DRAMATICS

IT is the Saturday night performance of the senior play. The curtain is about to rise. The aisles and back of the house are packed with people struggling for seats; alumnæ and under-class girls who have admission tickets only, are preparing to sit on all the steps; the junior ushers are hopelessly trying to keep back the press. It is to be supposed that the orchestra is playing, judging from the motion of arms and instruments. The lights are suddenly lowered and the curtain rises. The struggle for seats at the back, the expostulations of the ushers, and the comments of the alumnæ and students, who have seen the play twice before and consequently do not feel the need of close attention, completely drown the first words of the scene.

Back of house. Large and fussy mother, looking daggers at the sophomores squatting beside her, giggling at the useless efforts of a small worried usher to prevent a determined woman, escorted by her apologetic husband, from prancing down into the orchestra circle; and unimportant senior.

Mother. What? What? Who is this, Emma? Where are we?

Emma. That's Viola, Mother. She's just been shipwrecked, you know.

Mother. Oh, she's the heroine. She's the best actor, then?

Emma. Dear me, no. Malvolio's 'way by the best. And then Sir Toby and Maria— they're awfully good—you'll see them pretty soon now. I don't care for Viola much. She tries to imitate Ada Rehan—.

Curtain drops on First Scene.

¶ *Orchestra Circle. Handsome, portly father, exceptionally well set up, his wife, and head of department.*

Father, with enthusiasm. By Jove! Is that a girl, really? You don't say so! Well, well! Sir Toby, eh? Well, well! And who's the little girl? Maria? Did you ever see anything much prettier than she is, Alice?

His Wife. She's very charming, certainly.

Head of Department. She's about the best of them. A very clever girl. But you ought to see Malvolio! I don't care for Sir Andrew—

Father. Alice, look at him! Did you ever see anything so odd? Now I call that clever —I must say I call that clever! To think

[280]

that's a girl—well, well! See him shiver, Alice! Capital, capital! Do they do this themselves—costumes and acting and ideas and all?

Head of Department. They make the costumes, I believe, most of them. Then they have a trainer at the last. It's amazing to me, but as a matter of fact their men's parts are as a rule, considering the proportionate difficulty, you know, much better than their women's. Comedy parts, at that. I've never seen but one woman's part really well done.

Father. Really? Now why do you suppose, sir, that is so?

Head of Department. I can't say. But they're very artificial women, as a rule. Overtrained, perhaps.

¶ *A group of last year's graduates and two ushers on the platform of the fire-escape upstairs.*

First Graduate. I suppose you're nearly dead, poor child?

First Usher. Heavens! I never slaved so in my life! Did you see Ethel Williams' mother *insist* on going down into her seat? I don't see how people can be so rude.

First Graduate. Going better, to-night, isn't it?

First Usher. Goodness, yes! I think it's fine. Don't you? Is n't Dick *simply fine!* There she is! (*A burst of applause as Malvolio and Olivia enter.*)

Second Usher. Do you know, they say that Kate Ackley thinks it's half for her!

Second Graduate. Not really?

Second Usher. Yes, really. She is stunning, there's no doubt.

Second Graduate. Oh, yes, she's stunning. Is that her own dress?

Second Usher. Yes. Her aunt gave it to her. It's liberty satin. But she's a stick, just the same. Do you like Viola?

Second Graduate, parrying. She looks very well. I was rather surprised she got it, though.

Second Usher. You know Mr. Clark wanted her for Sir Andrew, and she would n't. He was very angry, and so was the class. They don't care for Ethel at all. But it was Viola or nothing. She's seen it four times and she thinks she knows it all, they say. I *do* think she does some parts very well indeed.

First Usher. Oh, Miss Underhill, is n't Viola grand? Don't you think she's fine?

Second Graduate, sweetly. Yes, indeed. She looks so cunning in that short skirt!

Curtain falls on First Act.

AT COMMENCEMENT

¶ *Two fathers standing at back.*

First Father, smiling affably. A great sight,
I assure you, sir! All these young girls, and
parents, and friends—a proud moment for
them! And how well they do! That one
that takes the part of Malvolio, now, that
Miss Fosdick—pretty smart girl, now, is n't
she?

Second Father. That 's my daughter, sir.

First Father. Well, well! I expect you 're
pretty pleased. You ought to be.

Second Father, confidentially. I tell you, sir, I
never believed she had it in her, never! Her
mother and I were perfectly dumfounded—
perfectly. I don't know where she got it from;
certainly not from me. And her mother
could n't take part in tableaux, even, she got
so nervous.

First Father. Just so, just so! Now, I want
to tell you something, Mr.—Mr. Fosdick.
These colleges for women are a great thing,
sir, a great thing! You take my daughter.
When she came up here, she was as shy and
bashful and helpless as a girl that 's an only
child could possibly be. Could n't trust herself an inch alone. Never went away from
home alone in her life. Look at her now!
She 's head of this whole committee: you may

have noticed their names on the back of the programme. Costumes, scenery, music, lights, stage properties, scene shifting—all in her hands, as you might say! I slipped up to the stage door, and I begged the young woman there to let me step in and see her a moment. Girls do it all, you know! She was on police-man duty there. But she let me in and I just peeked at Mary, bossing the whole job, as you might say! It was "put this here" and "put that there" and taking hold of the end and dragging it herself, and answering this one's questions and giving that one orders—I tell you, I couldn't believe it! Short skirt and shirt-waist, note-book in her hand—Lord! I wished I had her up at the office with me!

Second Father. Then you're Miss Mollie Vanderveer's father?

First Father. Yes, sir, James L. Vander-veer.

Second Father. Pleased to meet you. 'Lida often speaks of her. She said to her mother and me to-night just as she went down to "be made up," as they call it, that Mollie was a brick and no mistake. It seems she's doing two girls' work to-night.

First Father. Yes, one of the committee is sick. After all, it's a pretty hard strain, it seems to me. Mary's pretty strong, but she said to me yesterday that if there had been another performance—

Curtain rises on Second Act.

¶ *Lobby. College physician and junior usher.*

Physician. Will you just step over to the drug store across the street and get me some brandy—quickly, please?

Usher. Oh, certainly, Dr. Leach!

Physician. Here, child, stop! Put on a cloak —are you crazy?

Usher. But I'm quite warm, Dr. Leach!

Physician. Put on a cloak! With your neck and arms bare! It's damp as a well outside. *(Usher runs out.)*

A ubiquitous member of the faculty suddenly appears. What's the matter? Anybody sick?

Physician. Oh, no! Not much. Miss Jackson was resting in her dressing-room and somebody leaned over the sill and spoke to her—you know she's on the ground floor. She's quite nervous, and she got a little hysterical—slight chill. My brandy was all out, so I—Oh, thank you! *(Usher disappears breathless.)*

Ubiquitous Member of Faculty, gloomily. I've always said there should be understudies—

[285]

always. What will they do without their Viola?
It's a ridiculous risk—

Physician, hastily. But Miss Jackson is all
right, or will be as soon as I get—yes, I'm
coming! Oh, nonsense!—She's all right:
there's no need for an understudy, I assure
you!—No, keep them all out! No, she has
enough flowers in there now! Yes, keep people away from the window!

¶ *Curtain rises on Third Scene.*
Group of ushers collapsed on stairs leading to
gallery.

Nan. (*White organdie over rose pink silk;*
rose ribbons.) Oh, girls, I'm nearly dead!

Ursula. (*Black net over electric blue satin;*
silver belt and high silver comb; black gloves.)
There's one good thing, we're downstairs
to-night. Last night I got so dizzy hopping
up and down those steps—

Leonora. (*Yellow liberty silk cut very low;*
gold fillet; somewhat striking Greek effect.) Oh,
what do you think I just did? I was so tired I
stumbled just behind the orchestra circle (after I'd shooed that funny woman out of three
seats) and I fell almost flat! And the nicest
man helped me up and made me take his seat,
and who do you think it was? It was Mr. Fos-

dick. He went and stood back, and I sat a long time then. Was n't he ducky?

Sally. (White dimity with green ribbons; a yard or more of red-gold hair; babyish face.) Where's your own seat, dear?

Esther. (Pale blue silk with long rope of mock pearls.) Oh, Piggy's given it to her little friend, as usual! It's a great thing to have— *(The door swings open, and the actors' voices are heard: "There dwelt a man in Babylon, lady, lady!" Another usher comes out.)*

Nan. How'd the song go? Better?

Usher. Oh, grand! They made her do the second verse again. Miss Selbourne says that she's the best all 'round clown they've ever had.

Sally. Oh, does she? I heard her tell Dr. Lyman that the plays deteriorated every year— *(Enter another usher.)*

Second Usher. Girls, you *must* be quiet! That woman at the back says she can't hear a word—

¶ *Curtain rises on Fourth Scene; applause, as audience takes in stage setting. Row of enthusiastic alumnæ in upper box.*

First Alumna. (Happy mother of three; head of sewing circle; leader of the most advanced set

[287]

*in her college days; president of the Anti-En
gagement League, junior year.)* Oh, girls, did
you ever see anything so lovely? How *do* they
manage it? We never imagined anything like
it, I'm perfectly willing to admit. Are n't those
lords and ladies fine? Why, look at them —
there must be forty or fifty! And are n't the
costumes beautiful? How handsome Orsino
is!

*Second Alumna. (Rising journalist; very well
dressed; knows all the people of note in the audience; affects a society manner; was known as the
Gloomy Genius in her college days, and never
talked with any one who did n't read Browning.)*
Quite professional, really! How that Miss
Jackson reminds one of Rehan! I wonder if
Daly sends the trainer? That little Maria,
now — she's quite unusual. Lovely figure,
has n't she? Elizabeth Quentin Twitchell.
Dr. Twitchell of Cambridge, I wonder? Do
they set that stage alone?

*Third Alumna. (Blonde and gushing; sister
in the cast.)* You know, that Miss Twitchell
was the best Viola, too, they say. Peggy tells
me Mr. Clark says he wished she could play
them both. She's very popular with the class.
But Miss Jackson does everything. Writes,
acts, plays basket-ball, beautiful class work —

AT COMMENCEMENT

Oh, isn't that sweet! (*Clown and chorus of ladies with mandolins and guitars sing to wild applause.*)

Fourth Alumna. (*Tall, thin, dark, and dowdy; very humble in manner; high-principled; worth two millions in her own right; slaved throughout her entire college course.*) I don't see how anybody can say that girls can't do anything in the world they set out to. Isn't it wonderful? You can say what you please, but it's just as Ella says—they do ten times what we did and do it better too. I think they're prettier than they used to be, don't you? And they're just like real actors—I'm sure it's prettier than any play I ever saw! They make such wonderful men! Would you ever know that Sir Toby was a girl? And Malvolio—he's just too good for anything!

Curtain falls on Fourth Scene.

¶ *There is a long wait in total darkness. The audience smiles, then settles down to be amused. Somebody faints and is restored with shuffling, apologies, and salts.*

Slender, dark-eyed, gray-haired man, with non-committal expression, uncle of one of the Mob; with his wife, who grows more frankly puzzled as the play advances.

[289]

Uncle. I suppose they've outdone themselves in this garden scene.

Aunt. Yes, Bertha says they've worked tremendously over it. Henry, what *do* you think of it?

Uncle. Very ingenious, my dear.

Aunt. But Henry, their voices—

Uncle. They *are* a little destructive to the illusion, but you hear the gentleman behind me. He assures us that he thinks they are men!

Aunt. Oh, *Henry!*

Uncle. It's a pity they haven't more like Maria. Viola could take a few points from her.

Aunt. But Bertha says that they adore Viola. She writes, and plays basket-ball, and stands high in her classes, and—

Uncle. But she isn't an actress, that's all. She shouldn't grasp all the arts! She's too melodramatic—she rants.

Aunt. Bertha says the trainer admires her very much—he wants her to go on the stage.

Uncle. Oh! does he?

Aunt. Did you know that even the mobs are trained very carefully? Bertha says she goes to rehearsals all the time. And the principal parts —Malvolio worked six hours with Mr. Clark one day and eight the next. And Viola had to do more. And the stage committee *slave*,

Henry, they simply slave. Little Esther Brookes is worn to a shadow—not but what they love to do it.

Uncle. And when did Malvolio and Viola and the stage committee do their studying?

Aunt. Oh, they keep up with their work. It's a point of honor with them, Bertha says. Of course they can't do *quite* so much, I suppose—

Uncle. I suppose not.

Aunt. But Bertha says that they would give up anything in college sooner than that. Viola and Malvolio, both of them, say that they regard it as the most valuable training they've gotten up here. They say it's quite the equal of any of their courses.

Uncle. Ah! do they?

¶ *Curtain rises on a very elaborate garden scene of arbors and flowers; frantic applause, doubled at the entrance of Sir Toby and Sir Andrew.*

Group of cynical alumnæ on fire-escape.

First Alumna. As for that Sir Toby—

Second Alumna. Hush, my dear, that may be the bosom of her family forninst us!

First Alumna, lowering her voice. I think he's indecent and ridiculous.

Second Alumna. He'll be the pride of the class,

my little cousin says. They're raving over him.

First Alumna. Then they're idiots. My dear, we may have had our faults, but we were seldom vulgar, if we weren't remarkable!

Third Alumna. What I mind so much is that all the papers are filled with that trash about gracefulness and womanliness and girlish delicacy and the great gulf between us and the coarse professionals, and as far as I can see, we are filling in that gulf as fast as possible. We seem to be striving after the very thing—

First Alumna. Precisely. In a word, it's Daly, not Shakespeare. And they don't see that Dalyism takes money—we haven't the scenery and costumes for it.

Second Alumna. That horrible Sir Andrew!

Fourth Alumna. But Malvolio—

First Alumna. Oh, Malvolio's all right. As far as a girl can do it. The question is, *can* a girl do it? I think she can't.

Third Alumna. And as for allowing that Miss Jackson to imitate all Ada Rehan's bad points, when she naturally fails of her good ones—

Fourth Alumna. But, my dear, the men like it. They're all pleased to death. They think it's the cleverest thing they ever saw. They say Viola's magnetic—

Third Alumna. Hgh! She's coarse, if that's

what you mean! The whole tone of the thing is lowered. I think that way she acted the duel scene last night was simply vulgar. But the girls all howled with laughter.

Fourth Alumna. Well, if they 're pleased—

First Alumna. They should n't be pleased!

Fourth Alumna. Surely, Annie, you think this garden scene is funny!

First Alumna. Why, I laughed. It 's a good acting play. But I wish the Literature department had more to do with it and the trainer confined himself to—

Usher interrupts. If you please, I must ask you to make less noise. You are disturbing the people near the door!

¶ *The curtain has fallen on the Fourth Act. A group of last year's graduates standing at the back in party-cloaks, with a few of the Mob in shirt-waists and make-up.*

Recent Court Lady, tentatively. Did you like the dance?

First Graduate. Oh, it was fine! It was terribly pretty, Ellen, the whole thing!

Recent Court Lady, relieved. I 'm so glad you liked it. Was n't Sue grand!

First Graduate. Yes, indeed, but I liked Malvolio so much!

Court Gentleman. Good old Dick! My, don't we love her! Orsino's going to do him at class supper, you know. And Olivia's going to be Sir Toby.

Second Graduate. How noble! Sir Toby is about the best I ever saw, May.

Court Gentleman. Isn't she that? She's going to be Viola. She squirms and twists just like her—

Court Lady. Oh, come on, May Lucy, and get to bed! *(They go out whistling airs from the play and are violently suppressed by a group of ushers, whose excited remonstrances are loudly criticised by a large and nervous lady in the rear, greatly delighting the contingent from the Mob.)*

First Graduate. Now, Katharine, just tell me, perfectly impartially of course, how you think it compares with ours.

Second Graduate. Well, girls, frankly I must say I'm a little disappointed. *(Nods from the others.)*

Third Graduate. It's not that it's not well done, for it is, but it's such a fine play it ought to have been well done by anybody. And for all that Sue Jackson's such a wonder, I must say—

Fourth Graduate. Yes, exactly. She's too heavy for the part, I think.

[294]

AT COMMENCEMENT

Second Graduate. Of course Toby was fine and Malvolio and Maria—

Fifth Graduate. Well, then, with three fine ones I should think—

Second Graduate. But Olivia and Sebastian and Orsino were such sticks—

Fourth Graduate. Still, those third and fourth and fifth scenes in the second act were beautiful.

Second Graduate. But the others were so plain. They just stacked on the good ones. Still, I suppose they did the best they could. Mary Vanderveer has just *slaved* over it.

Fifth Graduate. We know what *that* is!

Second Graduate. Well, honestly, I think this is a *prettier* play than ours, but I do feel that ours was a little *better done!* Here, let's see Sue in this. I think she's pretty good.

¶ *The curtain has fallen on the Fifth Act. Malvolio and Viola come out of their dressing-room to the street, and slip out of a crowd of ushers and under-class girls. A general flutter of congratulation and sympathy follows them.*

Oh, Miss Jackson, it was great! Simply fine! Susy, my child, say what you'd like and it's yours!—Where's Lida Fosdick?—Lida! Dick! She's gone long ago. Where's Toby?

Gone, too. Somebody has some flowers for her. Oh, take 'em up to the Wallace!—Well, good-night! Was n't it grand!—Grand! There 's Betty! Hi, Betty! Oh, Miss Twitchell, it was so—

Miss Twitchell, mechanically. So glad, so glad you liked it—we loved to do it! Oh, yes! Oh, dear, no! Just a little, yes. The making-up was so long. Mother—thank you, *thank* you—Mother, where *is* the carriage? Oh, thank you *so* much!

Mrs. Twitchell, nervously. Yes, indeed, she 's tired to death. I 'm very glad, I 'm sure, if you liked it. Oh, how do you do, Mrs. Waite? Yes, here she is. Bessie, here is Mrs. Waite. You see she sat in the Opera House since five o'clock to be made up, and only sandwiches and all the strain—yes, indeed. Fanny looked very pretty, I thought. In the dance, was n't she? Yes, so pretty. I 'm sure I wish Bessie had only been in the dance—Oh, here 's the carriage, dear!

¶ *Malvolio and Viola, slipping quietly past the crowd; make-up not off; arms on each other's shoulders.*

Malvolio. I suppose Dad 's holding that carriage somewhere.

AT COMMENCEMENT

Viola. Well, I can't help it. I simply can't talk to everybody.

Malvolio. Do you know your speech?

Viola. I think so. It's so short, you know. I hate to have the president's speech long. *(A pause.)*

Malvolio. Well, it's over, Susy Revere! No more glory for little Lide and Sue!

Viola. All over! Well, we've had the time of our lives, Dick! I'd—I'd give anything to do it over again, three nights!

Malvolio. Me too. It's a pleasant little spot up here. *(They walk to the campus in silence.)*

¶ *Recent court lady and two young gentlemen, brothers of her friend, the stage manager. Her eyes are underlined heavily, and she has not gotten the rouge quite off her cheeks.*

Recent Court Lady. Oh, *thank* you, it would be *such* a help! Mollie is nearly wild, and these things must be got out to-night. If you would take this and this and this, and oh, Father, would you please carry this tankard and the cups? And could you take those two swords? I'll take the distaff and the mandolin. Jack, have you room for the moon? Will, here are more poppies, and I promised Ada that I'd put that rubber-plant in her room to-

[297]

night. You're so good! You're sure you
don't mind carrying them? Now don't get
laughing, Father, and drop the cups.

A Recent Court Gentleman. Good-night, dear!
I knew you'd like it. Oh, I think everybody
seems to feel it's the best yet. Of course, last
year they had so much better opportunity, so
much easier scenery. But with four such stars
—yes, indeed. It was so much harder to find
people to take—oh, she *did!* She thinks that
just because it does n't all depend on one or
two people, it's easier? Well, just find your
extra people, that's all!—Did you like it? Most
people seemed to think it *was* a pretty dance.
Well, we rehearsed enough, heaven knows.
Did you know Orsino's fiancé was there? She
said she felt like such an idiot. Too bad Sue
got scared, was n't it? Well, good-night.

¶ *Steps of the Dewey House. Three ushers
propped against the pillars. The night watchman
approaches with lantern.*

Watchman. Well, well, well! Want to get
in? *Hi'll* bet yer do! (*First usher nods her
head.*) Are yer h'ushers? Fine play, wa'n't
it? (*Second usher nods her head.*) Well, you
do look tired! 'You pretty tired, Miss Slater?
(*Third usher murmurs something about sleeping*

[298]

till noon, and second usher chuckles feebly and mentions Baccalaureate. They stumble into the Dewey, and the watchman shuts the door.)

II

IVY DAY

THE sun is glaring down on the campus. *A crowd of parents and other relatives is surging toward an awning near the steps of College Hall; a stream of white-dressed seniors continually flows toward the Hatfield House, where a procession is forming. Forty junior ushers struggle with a rope wound with laurel, which is to encompass the column of seniors. A few scattered members of the Faculty and a crowd of alumnæ wander aimlessly about, obstructing traffic generally.*

Small imperious mother, dragging large good-humored father toward the awning. Hurry up, Father, hurry up!

Father. But Mother, I want to see 'em!

Mother. Well, you 've got to take your choice of seeing 'em and not hearing a word of the speech or—

Father. You go right along, Mother, and I 'll get there on time. I want to see Hattie marching.

¶ *A crowd of girls with cameras rushes up and*

[299]

lines both sides of the walk. Two ushers sail up the path, clearing a way with white-ribboned sticks. The crowd becomes unmanageable, torn by the desire to watch the progress of the march and at the same time to secure a good place at the exercises. People summon each other wildly from various points of the campus.

A group of strolling sophomores, dodging some ushers and wheedling programmes from others, screws its way in a body to the best possible position in the front, smiling at the efforts of the displaced to reinstate themselves.

First Sophomore. There they come! There's Sue and Betty Twitchell! My, what roses!

Second Sophomore. Roses? Did the ushers—

Third Sophomore. Oh, goodness, Win, haven't you heard that yet?

Second Sophomore. No—tell me!

Third Sophomore. Why, Miss Tomlinson's fiancé sent her fifteen dozen American Beauties, and there wasn't any room for them in the house, and she asked if the class would like to carry them, and first they voted no and then they voted yes, and some of the girls don't like it, but they are doing it just the same— Oh, isn't Helen Estabrook's gown stunning! There's Wilhelmina—Hello, Will! Sue looks well, don't you think?

[300]

AT COMMENCEMENT

Second Sophomore. Fifteen dozen American Beauties! Great heavens!

First Sophomore. I think it's perfectly absurd and bad taste, too. The idea!

Third Sophomore. Well, she's not to blame, is she? They're certainly lots prettier than laurel or daisies or odd flowers — Oh, girls, *I* think Louise Hunter is too silly for anything! She feels too big to live, leading the way! I'd try to look a little less like a poker if I *was* an usher!

¶ *The Ivy Procession marches to the steps two and two, each girl with an enormous American Beauty in her hand. At every step the girls with cameras snap and turn, so that the sound resembles a miniature volley of cannon. There is a comparative silence during their progress.*

Mother and daughter standing on their seats under awning, clutching at the heads of those near them for support.

Mother. Who is that with Susy, dear?

Daughter. That's the vice-president — I don't know her name. Sue looks pale, does n't she?

Mother. And that's Bess Twitchell next — with the tucks. She's Ivy Orator, you know. I think Sue's dress drops too much in the back—Ah, Miss Fosdick has stepped on it! Good heavens—right on that Valenciennes! *(She sits down abruptly.)*

¶ *The procession winds slowly up and groups itself on the steps. The last third stands a long while before the awning and exchanges somewhat conscious remarks with its friends outside the rope, which the ushers endeavor to carry without straining or dropping: this attempt puckers their foreheads and tilts their hats.*

A group of last year's graduates standing close to the enclosure.

First Graduate. Stunning gowns, are n't they?

Second Graduate. Awfully. Prettiest I ever saw. And so different, too! And yet they 're all alike—organdie over silk or satin, mostly. Is n't Sue Jackson's lovely?

Third Graduate. I like Esther Brookes'; it's so plain, but there 's not a more artistic—

Fourth Graduate. How do you like Lena Bergstein's?

Fifth Graduate. What 's that?

Fourth Graduate. My dear, have n't you seen that? It 's solid Valenciennes as far as I can see. I think it's altogether too elaborate. But I tell you, it's stunning, all the same!

AT COMMENCEMENT

Fifth Graduate. Ah, I see it! Poor taste, I think.

Fourth Graduate. I know it. Betty Twitchell's is so simple—

First Graduate. Simple, yes! It's imported, I happen to know!

Fourth Graduate. Really! It *does* hang beautifully! Oh, they're moving: there's Sir Toby. You know nobody ever heard of her before, girls. Isn't that funny? Wasn't she great, though?

Second Graduate. Well, they won't forget her in a hurry. I think it's a mighty good thing that Dramatics brings out that kind of girl and gives her a place in the class. It keeps two or three girls like Sue Jackson and Twitchie and Mollie Van from running everything. Well, going to stay here?

¶ *A Ubiquitous member of the Faculty suddenly dashes from her seat and pushes through the crowd, which lets her out, under the impression that she is faint.*

Ubiquitous Member of Faculty, to a scared usher. Where is Dr. Twitchell? Is he back there?

Usher. I—I don't know! Is he big?

Ubiquitous Member of Faculty. Big? Big?

[303]

What do you mean? A pretty thing—to have the father of the Ivy Orator have no seat! He must be found!

Usher. I—I 'll go see—

Ubiquitous Member of Faculty. Do you know him?

Usher, helpless but optimistic. No, but I 'll—

Ubiquitous Member of Faculty, suddenly dashing through the crowd into a lilac clump and producing, to every one's amazement, a large and amiable gentleman from its centre. Well, well! Are you going to remain here long, Dr. Twitchell? Why are n't you in your seat?

Dr. Twitchell, somewhat embarrassed at his prominent position, but beaming on every one. Why, no—that is, yes, indeed! Certainly. I only wanted to see Bessie march along with the rest. A very pretty sight—remarkably so! All in white—I counted ninety couples, I think. Has—has she begun? Is her mother—

Ubiquitous Member of Faculty. We 're all in the front row, and they 've not begun. The class president will be making her speech in a moment—there is plenty of time, but we were a little anxious—*(They enter the enclosure.)*

¶ *The class is crowded upon the steps and over-flows before and behind them. The sun is in their eyes, and they look strained and pale. Under the awning a few hundred relatives fan themselves, and smile expectantly.*

The class president makes an indistinguishable address, in which the phrases "more glad than I can say," "unusual opportunity," "women's education," "extends a hearty welcome," rise above the rest, and sinks back into the crowd.

The leader of the Glee Club frowns at her mates and leans forward: the class sings "Fair Smith," with a great deal of contralto. The Ivy Orator steps back and upward instinctively, with an idea of escaping from the heads and shoulders that are packed like herring about her, realizes that the audience is entirely out of her reach, steps down to meet them, becomes lost to view, and with a despairing consciousness that nothing can better the most futile position she has ever occupied, steps back to her first place and shrieks out her opening phrases.

Two mothers sitting on a bench just behind the enclosure, looking over the campus.

First Mother. So you did n't get a seat?

Second Mother. Well, I did n't try, to tell the truth. I 'm interested in the speech, but my daughter tells me that I can see it in the *Monthly* next fall, and as I got here so late, I could n't possibly hear it from the back.

First Mother. I was sorry to leave, for Kate wanted me to hear Bessie so much; but after Miss Jackson's speech I had to go — the heat made me rather faint. And as you say, one can read it.

Second Mother. That's what every one seems to think — see them all walking up and down here. One of the old graduates — a friend of my daughter's — told me that this was the chance for them to talk with the professors!

First Mother. Well, I suppose if they *will* have it outdoors, very many people can't expect to hear. It's very hard to speak in the open air.

Second Mother. Yes, indeed. What a fine-looking girl that Miss Ackley is — the dark one — did you notice her?

First Mother. That is my daughter, so I've noticed her quite a little!

Second Mother. Oh, indeed! I'm sure I didn't know —

First Mother. It isn't necessary to be told that *you* have a daughter here, Mrs. Fosdick!

Second Mother. No, everybody seems to think that the resemblance is very strong indeed. Isn't it pleasant to meet people so strangely, and without any ceremony, like this? It's a very pleasant place, anyway, isn't it?

AT COMMENCEMENT

First Mother. Yes, indeed. It's beautiful all the spring, but particularly beautiful now, I think, with all the girls in their pretty dresses and the general holiday effect.

Second Mother. What I like so much is the spirit of the place. When we found out from things in my daughter's letters and stories she would tell us in the vacations that all her little set of friends were very much richer than she and could afford luxuries and enjoyments that she could n't, Mr. Fosdick and I were quite worried for fear that she would feel hurt, you know, or want to get into a style of living that she could not possibly keep up. But, dear me, we need n't have worried! It never made the least difference, just as she assured us. We were very glad to find that she was the friend of some of the leading girls in the class, when we saw that she went right along as she had to, tutoring and selling blue prints and going about just as contentedly as if her shirt-waists had been their organdies. Not that that sort of thing *ought* to make any difference, but sometimes it *does*, you know. She was telling me about Bess Twitchell's Commencement dress, and Sue Jackson's, and I grew quite alarmed, for I thought that perhaps that was expected, and we could n't possibly afford anything like it. But, dear me, it was all the same to her! She was perfectly satisfied with muslin, and when I asked her if she was sure she'd prefer to walk with Bess, she actually made me feel ashamed! Bess herself said that it wasn't every one who could have the honor of walking with Malvolio, and she'd like to see herself lose it!

First Mother. Oh, of course! Why, I have always understood, both from Kate and her cousin who graduated three years ago, that some of the leading girls in every class were poor. The girls seemed prouder of them, if anything. As you say, it's the spirit of the place. Now Kate herself—well, it's a little thing, I suppose, but her father and I—well, I suppose any one would think us silly, but we actually cried, we were so touched. Her father gave her her dress—it was really lovely. Not elaborate, but it was made over beautiful silk, and he gave her a handsome string of those mock pearls they wear so much now, you know. It was very becoming to her indeed, and she was delighted with it.

Well, just three weeks ago I got a long letter from her saying that Eleanor Hunt's father had lost every cent he had in the world and that they were in a dreadful condition. Eleanor's mother had sold her Commencement gown and Eleanor was going to wear an old white organdie that she'd worn all the year to dances and plays. She said that Eleanor was feeling very bad indeed about it and especially about Commencement time. They had planned to walk together in all the processions—they are great friends. So she asked me if I thought Papa would mind if she wore her old organdie, too, to all the things, because Eleanor seemed to feel it so. Her father offered to give Eleanor one for a Commencement present from her, but she wouldn't have that—she said Eleanor wouldn't like it—she was feeling very proud about gifts, just now.

Well, her father was more pleased than I've seen him for years. You see, Kate has always thought a great deal of her clothes, and she's always had a good allowance, besides lots of presents from us and her aunts. And being an only child, you know—well, I wouldn't say she was *spoiled* at all, but she certainly was a little thoughtless, perhaps selfish, when she came up here. Her father and I feel that it has done a great deal for her. He says that he'd call it a good investment if she'd never learned anything in all the four years but just how to do that one thing!

Second Mother. Yes, indeed! We feel, Mr. Fosdick and I, that my daughter's friends have been almost as good for her as what she learned, though that comes first, as she must teach, now. She was always so solitary and reserved and never cared for the girls at home, but here she has such good friends and loves them all so—she's grown more natural, more like other girls; and we lay it all to her having been thrown in from the beginning with such pleasant, nice girls as these. You know them, I suppose—Bessie and Sue and Bertha Kitts—

¶ *Two alumnæ strolling between the houses and the enclosure, chatting with friends and spying out acquaintances.*

First Alumna. Good gracious, isn't she through yet? I pity the poor girls, standing all this while!

Second Alumna. Yes, that's just it! Arrange the oration to suit the girls, do!—If they're tired, let them sit down! It's absurd to criticise the one really academic exercise of the whole affair entirely on the basis of the girls' comfort, I say!

First Alumna. But, my dear, the poor things have done so much and stood so much anyhow—and I should think Miss Maria would be tired herself.

Second Alumna. Then it's her own lookout. She should have dropped one or the other. They try to do too much. I can tell you that we were proud enough to stand twenty minutes when Ethel Richardson talked, and she didn't feel that it was beneath her notice to devote all her time and attention to that one thing, either. We didn't make so much of these universal geniuses then, but I doubt if we had poorer results from the less widely gifted.It's too much strain; one simply can't do everything.

First Alumna. No. They're 'way ahead of us in lots of things, but I'm glad I came when I did. Don't you remember what a good time we used to have spring term? Dear old last spring term! Do you know there isn't any, now? Don't you remember how we dropped ev—well, a good deal, and lay in the hammocks in the orchard and mooned about and took a long, comprehensive farewell to all our greatness? We'd made or lost our reputations by then, and we just took it all in and—oh, I suppose we did sentimentalize a little, but it all meant more to us apparently. . . . Well, it's all gone now. They

[311]

begin on the play so early, and it's all rehearsing, and then they can't let their work
drop, so they keep everything right up to the
pitch—according to their story. And there are
six societies to our one, you know. And all
the houses give receptions to them right in a
bunch, and every one is so bored at them—
at least Kitty says they are. But you can't
always tell by that, I suppose.

¶ *Applause from the enclosure and a general
scurry as the ushers crowd up to surround the
class, who begin their Ivy Song—a piece of musical composition something between a Gregorian
chant and a Strauss waltz, with a great deal of
modulation, in which the words "hopes and fears,"
"coming years," "plant our vine," and "still en-
twine" occur at suitable intervals. They wander
away in a bunch, frantically surrounded by the
ushers and the chain, to another side of College
Hall, where the Ivy is interred. A general break-
up then begins, the orator and the president join
their admiring families, and people begin to stroll
home, the prominent members of the class pausing
at every sentence to have their pictures taken.*

Two members of the class and one of the Faculty.

First Member of Class. It was the funniest
thing I 've heard this year, really! You know

A general break-up then begins

the girls simply *slave* for her—they *slave*. They can't help it, you know, for she thinks that's all there is in the world and if you don't have your note-book made out she looks at you in such a way—oh, well, it makes Mollie's spine cold, she says. Mollie's done splendid work for her—not that she does n't do it for everybody—but she was determined to make her see that she could be at all the rehearsals and take the observations, too. The only thing she did n't do was to go the last two or three nights, but gracious, she'd more than made that up! I thought I did pretty well when I put in five hours of Lab., but those girls have done eight and ten hours a week some weeks, note-books and observations and all. Just to satisfy her, you know—they love to work for her. And what do you think she said the last time they met? Do you know about Astronomy, Mr. Brooke? If you do, I shall spoil the story for you, for I don't know the first thing. But I think it was the parallax of the sun. "Now, I should think you could just step out between the acts," said she, calmly, "if you could n't get out for all the evening, and take your note-book with you, Miss Vanderveer, and just take it—it 's a beautiful observation! And you 've taken one, and it will be a great thing to tell your children that you 've gotten the parallaxes of the sun yourself!"

Second Member of Class. And when we thought of Mollie dancing about there with her collar undone, trying to make those idiotic men understand something and being everywhere at once—between the acts, you know, being a fairly occupied time for her—when we imagined her walking out of the garden scene or Orsino's house to take the what-do-you-call-it of the sun (though I don't see how she could take it of the sun at night—it must have been the moon, Ethel).

Member of Faculty. And what did Miss Vanderveer say?

First Member of Class. I 'm sure it was the sun, Teddie, Mollie said sun—why, she coughed and said, "I certainly will, if I get time, Miss Drake!"

Member of Faculty. Great presence of mind, I 'm sure.

¶ *Group of relatives and three members of the class.*

First Member. Mamma, this is Miss Twitchell and Miss Fosdick—Maria and Malvolio, you know.

Mother. I am pleased to meet you both. I want to tell you how much I enjoyed, *etc.*

[314]

Misses Twitchell and Fosdick. We're so glad if you did, *etc.*

Mother. I was not able to catch much of your speech, but Ellen tells me we can have the pleasure of reading it later.

Miss Twitchell, moving away. I'm afraid you will have the opportunity—but I tried to make it as short as I could!

Mother. And now I suppose you're going home to sleep all day? I should think you'd need it.

Miss Twitchell. Oh, dear, no! I'm going to the Alpha on the back campus this afternoon, and I want to look in at Colloquium, and then there's the Glee Club to-night, you know. I've no more worry now, nothing to do but enjoy myself.

Aunt. What is this, Ellen? The Glee Club—

Ellen. Why, Aunt Grace, the Glee Club promenade, don't you know? That's when the lanterns are all over, and they give a concert, and we all walk about, and it's so pretty —don't you remember I told you?

Aunt. Well, then, I'll go right home and take my nap, if I'm to go out to-night. Are you going to all these things, too, Ellen?

Ellen. Well, practically. Only I'm going to Phi Kapp and Biological instead. But I *am* going to lie down—I 'm so tired, I can't think straight, and you know I 'm on the Banjo Club, and we have to have a short rehearsal—

¶ *The crowd gradually disperses, and the campus is practically deserted; men begin to put up poles and wires for lanterns; others gather and arrange scattered chairs. Stray relatives hunt for each other and their boarding-places or inquire with interest which is the Science Building and the Dewey House. Belated members of the class wander homewards or patiently seek out their families, whose temporary guardians are thus relieved.*

Abstracted member of the class and large, domineering woman in black satin, before the Morris House gate.

Large Woman. This is the Hatfield, is it not?

Member of Class. Oh! I beg your pardon? No, it 's the Morris.

Large Woman. Ah! I was told it was the Hatfield.

Member of Class, simply. Well, it 's not.

Large Woman. And that over there *(pointing to the Observatory)*, that is the Lilly House?

Member of Class. No, that 's the Observatory. Lilly Hall is up farther. It 's just beyond the Dickinson—no, the Lawrence—I mean the *Hubbard House!*

AT COMMENCEMENT

Large Woman. And where is the Hubbard House?

Member of Class. Oh, dear! *(pulls herself together with an effort)* it's up in a line, the one, two, three, third from here.

Large Woman. Thank you. And I wish to see the Botanical Gardens, too. Where are they? *(Member of Class points out their position.)*

Large Woman. And where is the Landscape Garden?

Member of Class, vaguely. Why, I suppose it's over there, too. I don't exactly—it's all landscape garden, I suppose—it's not big—

Large Woman, severely. I was told there was a fine landscape and botanical garden—are you a member of the college?

Member of Class, leaning against the post. Why, yes, but it's all botanical garden, for that matter. *(Catches sight of a tree with a tin label tied to it and points luminously at it.)* That's botanical, you know—all the trees and shrubs!

Large Woman, with irritation. I am quite aware that it is—I—

Member of Class, despairingly. Oh, excuse me, I mean it's—it's—*I mean they all have labels! (Large Woman stalks majestically away; Member of Class makes a few incoherent gestures*

[317]

in the air, murmurs, "I am *such* a fool, but I 'm
so tired!" *Throws out her hands wearily and
trails into the Morris House.)*

THE END OF IT

X
THE END OF IT

THERE are two methods of conducting a class supper. The first is something like this: you pick out three utterly unrelated girls who never had anything to do with one another in their lives, and call them the supper committee; you pick out two clever, uninterested girls and call them the toast committee; you pick out an extremely busy girl who lives half a mile off the campus and call her the seating committee; ycu pick out a popular girl who is supposed to be humorous because she laughs at everybody's jokes and knows one comic song, and call her the toast-mistress.

And this is the result of it: The supper committee meets, wonders what under heaven induced the president to appoint the other two, finds out what caterer they had last year, and after a little perfunctory argument employs him again without further action, with the result that one end of the table has five kinds of ice cream and the other a horrifying recurrence of lukewarm croquettes; the toast committee spends a great deal of time in hunting out extremely subtle quotations from Shakespeare and Omar Khayyam, with the result that no one of the toasters gets the least idea of how she is expected to elaborate her theme; the seating committee is so harassed by everybody that she gives up her diagram in despair, and successive girls erase and sign and re-erase till nobody but the three or four leading sets in the class are satisfied, and they are displeased because the toasters are either put in a line at the head or scattered about the tables, and that separates them from their immediate cliques; the toast-mistress turns out to be more appreciative than constructive, and worries her friends and bores her enemies beyond previous conception. The main body of unimportant necessary people are crowded off by themselves and feel somewhat flat and heavy and irritated at the noisy groups beyond them; the toasts are apt to be a little sad and vague because the girls don't fit them and talk too much about enduring friendships, the larger life, four years of stimulating rivalry, and alma mater. Why they do all this at this season and this alone, only the Lord who made them knows.

But Ninety-yellow did not employ this method. It occurred to Theodora somewhat originally, perhaps, as she looked around her that last Tuesday evening, that a better class

supper was never arranged. It can hardly be
asserted that it was a really good supper, for
it is to be doubted if a hundred and seventy-
five women ever sat down to a really good supper; but there was almost enough of it, and it
was very nearly hot. Kathie Sewall had picked
the supper committee well, and they knew
one another thoroughly enough to give it all
to the chairman to do and to make fun of her
till she was spurred on to a really noble effort. She knew that it is always damp and cold
class supper night, and planned accordingly.
Kitty Louisa Hofstetter managed the toasts,
and though Kitty Louisa was uneven and a
little vulgar at times, she was clever in her
unexpected hail-fellow-well-met way and popular with the class for the most part. She had
a genius for puns of the kind that grow better
as they grow worse, and they were shamelessly
italicized in the toast-cards, which caused great
merriment before the toasts had begun. And
the seating was very well done, for the class
was nicely broken up and mixed about among
the tables till everybody was within four or
five of a reasonably important person.

As for the toast-mistress—well, you see,
Theodora's opinion of her might have been
a trifle exaggerated, for she was Theodora's

[323]

best friend. How little she had changed, Theo thought, as she watched her rumple her hair in the same funny, boyish way that she had freshman year. Theo had seen her first in the main hall, floating with the current of freshmen that pushed its way almost four hundred strong to meet its class officer and find out that O. G. meant Old Gymnasium. That far-off freshman year! Theo smelt again the clean, washed floor; saw again the worried shepherds herding their flocks into the scheduled stalls and praying that the parents might go soon and leave their darlings, if misunderstood, at least unencumbered; heard again the buzz and hum of a thousand chattering, scuffling girls, bubbling over with a hundred greetings for each other.

"Hello, Peggy! Peggy! I say, *hello Peggy!*"

"Oh, hello! Have a good time?"

"Grand! Did you?"

"Perfectly fine—I saw Ursula and Dodo and—Oh, Ursula! hello! Here I am!"

"Why, Peggy Putney, you dear old thing! When did you come? They say you're in the Hatfield—how did you get there?"

"Two ahead of me and they dropped out. Miss Roberts only just told me—"

THE END OF IT

Theodora had felt very lonesome and homesick just then—everybody but herself knew so many people! And then Virginia had happened along and jostled her and begged pardon, and they had fallen into a conversation on the relative merits of the Dewey and the Hatfield. Later they had studied Livy together and confided their difficulties to each other. Virginia's mother was a Unitarian and her father was an Ethical Culturist, and her room-mate was a High Church Episcopalian and never ate meat in Lent! She thought Virginia would very probably be damned, if not in the next life, certainly in this, and she intimated as much. Virginia thought it was very hard to live with somebody who disapproved of you so much.

Theodora had been brought up to be a neat, self-helpful little person, and her room-mate, Edith Bliss, had never even seen her bed made up and left her clothes in piles on the floor just as she stepped out of them. She was horribly homesick and wept quarts every Sunday afternoon, and confided to Theodora in moments of hysterical relaxation that she thought every girl owed it to herself to have soup and black coffee for dinner and that she was going to wire Papa to take her home immediately.

Theo looked at her now, eagerly devouring a doubtful lobster concoction and openly congratulating herself on the olives at her left. She was fond of Frankfurters now, was Edith, and had recently alarmed the authorities by her ingenuous scheme for annexing a night-lunch cart and keeping it on the campus: it would have been so nice, she said regretfully, to slip out and get a Frankfurter between hours!

How pretty the Gym looked! The juniors had decorated it as well as they could at odd minutes, and they had lingered in a bunch as the class came in to lean over the balcony and sing to them.

Theodora remembered how the Gym had looked the night of the sophomore reception: all light and music and girls and a wonder of excitement. She had never had an evening dress before, and her little square-necked organdie had been dearer to her than any other gown before or since. They played *Rastus on Parade*, and she had such nice partners and some of the girls were so lovely and had such white, beautiful shoulders—they seemed to count evening dress but a slight and ordinary thing. By junior year house-dances are wont to pall, and seniors have been known to make rabbits and read Kipling in preference; even among the freshmen Theodora had found some disillusioned souls who lamented the absence of men and found the sophomore reception slow!

Across the table an odd, distinguished-looking girl, with a clever face and dark, short-sighted eyes, smiled at her, and Theo's thoughts flashed back to that great day when she first really loved the class—the day of the Big Game. What a funny, snub-nosed little nobody Marietta Hinks had been then! But how she played! How she dodged and doubled and bounced the ball, and how they cheered her!

> Oh, *here's* to Marietta,
> For we *shall* not soon *forget* her—

Well, well, how they had grown up! Now she was " Miss Root " to the little, dark-eyed girl in the back seat in chapel, who smiled so shyly at her when the seniors led out down the middle aisle. Theo was wearing her roses to-night, and as she scratched off a little note to thank her she had seemed to see herself, another little dark-eyed girl, sending anonymous roses to Ursula Wyckoff. Dear me! would anybody ever again combine such graces of mind and body as that ornament

of Ninety-purple? She had gone on wheel-
rides with Theo, and once she had asked her
over to wait on the juniors at a spread—
Theo had sat up and got her light reported
in order to write home about it.

There are those, I understand, who disapprove strongly of this attitude of Theodora's
happy year: dogmatic young women who have
not learned much about life and soured, middle-aged women who have forgotten. I am
told that they would consider Theodora's
adoration morbid and use long words about
her—long words about a freshman! I have
always been sorry for these unfortunate people: their chances for reconstructing Human
Nature seem to me so relatively slight.

When Theo had gone home that summer
with hands almost as well cared for as Ursula's,
sleek, gathered-in locks, and a gratifying hold
on the irregular verbs (Ursula spoke beautiful
French), her mother had whimsically inquired
if Miss Wyckoff could not be induced to remain in Northampton indefinitely and continue her unscheduled courses! But perhaps
she was a morbid mother.

Her mother! The plates and flowers swam
before Theodora's misted eyes, and the sight
of Virginia—so kind that year—brought back

somehow those waves of desolation that would come over her again and again, in lecture rooms, in her own dear room, at meals—all that clouded sophomore year. It was just as her good fortune came through the mail to her—a room in the Nicest House—that her mother died, and rooms mattered little to Theo, then. There were kindly aunts and other children, and she was not needed at home; so it seemed best to go on, and she had come up the steps of the Nicest House, a little black-dressed figure, and into the arms of the Nicest Woman.

It seemed to her that there was never a room so cheerful, nor pictures so lovely, nor a fire so red, nor tea and bread and butter so good, nor a smile so comfortable as the Nicest Woman's. Mademoiselle and Fräulein and Miss Roberts were sweet and kind, and the girls did all they could, but it was to the Nicest Woman that one came when conditions and warnings were in the air or one's head ached or one had eaten too much fudge or been annoyed by somebody's banjo practice. When the seniors of the Nicest House were eating and laughing there at night, it was a gay room —the Nicest Woman's; but it was very dim and quiet in the dusk, when Theodora slipped in by herself with reddened lids, and sat on the couch, and they talked of things that started to be sad but somehow always turned out cheerful; for when it was about the children and Will at Yale little jokes were sure to come up, and when Theo wondered if perhaps she had n't been careless about writing home, and if Mother had gotten more letters in the spring, maybe—the conversation always changed, and she found herself feeling so glad and thankful that she 'd gone right home in June and not visited at Virginia's.

Virginia had gone into Phi Kappa that winter, and Theo had been so proud of her. She was in the first five, and as she really had n't expected it at all it was quite exciting. Adelaide Carew went in too, and though she went about with the seniors a great deal and called most of her class "Miss," she was much more generally liked than in her freshman year, and Virginia had got to know her better and better. Through her Theo had seen more of Adelaide, and she had been amazed to find out how really kind-hearted and human she was beneath her unapproachable ways.

But then, you never could tell—girls were so queer! Only last night, when they were walking about under the lanterns after the concert, she and Virginia and Adelaide, with two of the junior ushers, and the juniors, sophisticated young people, had cynically suggested that perhaps they'd better take themselves away in order that the three might seek out their Ivy and bedew it with their final tears, Adelaide had coughed a little huskily and suggested that perhaps when they'd planted their own Ivy they would n't be feeling so gay! They had stared at her blankly, hesitated, decided that coming from such a source it must have been an extraordinarily acute sarcasm, and gone away giggling, leaving Theo to wonder and Adelaide to flush and talk very hard about Bar Harbor and the comfort of a big room all to yourself once more.

Such a strange room-mate as Theo had had that year—she seemed fated to room with girls who had never made up their beds. This one had lived freshman year with friends in the town, and had had everything done for her, and when Theo asked her one day if campus life was wearing on her, she had turned two stormy gray eyes on her and burst out, "Oh, no, Theodora, but I am so *deadly* tired of picking up my night-gown every *single* morning, I think I shall *die!*"

On one historic occasion, early in the year,

[331]

Theo had happened to make up her bed for her, and upon her pleased recognition of the fresh linen it had come out that she had been for some weeks accustomed to change her upper sheet and leave the under one undisturbed on the bed—it had seemed more logical, she said, and how was she to know? They had teased her about it till the Nicest Woman interfered and fined every girl who mentioned it, and they bought *Sentimental Tommy* with the money, and read it evenings in the Nicest Woman's room after supper.

Well, well, they'd sit about her fire no more, as the poem said that somebody wrote to go with the silver tea-ball the seniors gave her when she served them their last tea. They'd come in no more after Alpha and Phi Kapp to tell her all about it—how nice she had been when Theo got into Alpha! That was junior year and they took her to Boyden's for supper, and her bowl and pitcher were full of violets for days. Everybody seemed so glad, and Martha Sutton had pinned her own pin on Theo's red blouse. Kathie Sewall had taken her over—nobody dreamed that Kathie would be senior president then—and what a hand-shaking there had been! And such a funny, clever play, with butlers and burglars and lady's-maids — it was illustrative of American literature, she learned later, but it was not a pedantic illustration.

Theodora loved plays, and she had delighted in her very humble part in the House play. She was a little house-maid, and said only, "Yes, madam," and "No, madam," and, "Oh, sir, how can you — a poor girl like me!" but she had a great American Beauty and two bunches of violets, and she sent the programme home. Next to its basket-ball decorations she remembered the Gym arranged for a play, with the running-track turned into boxes and the girls prettier than ever against the screens and pillows. She had been chairman of the stage-setting committee, and the *Monthly* had especially commended the boudoir scene.

Were they ready for the toasts so soon? Where had the time gone? she thought, as Virginia, with solemn pomp, called upon Miss Farwell to respond to "Our Team." Dear old Grace — she stammered a little when she was excited, and she was not the most fluent of speakers, but they cheered her to the echo. "Team! Team! Team!" they called, and the teams, freshman and sophomore, Regulars and Subs, had to stand on their chairs and be sung to. As Theo balanced on a tottering seat, she

caught sight of a crowd of girls moving toward the Gym, and as they sat down a shout
from below greeted them:

> Oh, *here's* to Ninety-*yellow*,
> And her *praise* we'll ever *tell—oh*,
> Drink her *down*, drink her *down*, drink her *down*,
> down, *down!*

A cheerful, aimless creature at the bottom
of one of the great tables, whose one faculty
was for improvised doggerel, instructed her
neighbors rapidly, and they sent back a tune-
ful courtesy:

> Oh, *here's* the Junior *Ushers*,
> And I *tell* you they are *rushers!*

Theodora had "ushed," in classical phrase,
in her day, and the bustle of last year, so much
more exciting somehow than this one, came
back to her. Her little, white-ribboned stick
was packed now—in fact, everything was
packed: she was going away for good! Some
one else would lounge on the window-seat in
her room in the Nicest House, and light the
cunning fire. . . .

Who was this? Oh, this was Sallie Wilkes
Emory, responding to "The Faculty." Kitty
Louisa, whose soul knew not reverence, had
attached to this toast the pregnant motto,

[334]

THE END OF IT

That we may go forward with Faculties unimpaired, an excerpt from one of the President's best-known chapel prayers, and Sallie was developing the theme in what she assured them was a very connotative manner. Theo saw them pass in review before her, those devoted educators, from her dazed freshman Livy to her despairing senior Philosophy—*that* was over, at least! Theodora was not of a technically philosophical temperament. Sallie was quoting liberally from a recent famous essay of her own: *The Moral Law, or the End-Aim of Human Action According to Kant*, apropos of which she had remarked to the commendatory professor that she was glad if *somebody* understood it! Sallie was a great girl—how grand she had been in the play! Theo had been in the mob herself, having first tried for every part, and had enjoyed every minute of it, from the first rehearsal to the last dab of make-up. She had been an attendant and had n't an idea how pretty she looked, nor how many people spoke of her and called her graceful.

It may have been because Theo had so few ideas about herself that she had so many friends. And how many she had! She took great pride in them, those fine, strong, good-looking girls that hailed her from all directions, and always wanted a dance or a row or a skating afternoon with her. She wondered if anybody so ordinary — for Theo knew she was n't clever — ever had so many jolly good friends. There was the Mandolin Club, now — all friends of hers. She got on late in junior year and played in the spring concert. Her father came up and said he 'd never seen such a pretty house in his life — packed from orchestra circle to balcony with fluffy girls alternated with dapper, black-coated youths. He gave Theo such a darling white gown for it, all ruffled with white ribbon, and she had her picture taken in it, holding the mandolin, and sent it to him in a big white vellum frame covered with yellow chrysanthemums, with "Smith" scrawled in yellow across one corner. He kept it on his desk and was tremendously proud when his friends asked about it.

Here were the class histories. Theodora thought she listened, but though she laughed with the rest and applauded the grinds, it was her own history that she was reading as face after face recalled to her some joke or mistake or good luck. Not that it was sad — oh, dear, no! If any member of the class of Ninety-yellow dared to be sad that night there was a fine, and more than that, the studied coldness of the class directed toward her: it was an orgy, not an obsequy, as Virginia elegantly put it. Just as the junior history, which is always the best for some unexplained reason—perhaps because of the Prom—was finished, there was a loud knock, and a big bunch of yellow roses from the class that was having a decennial supper somewhere was brought in by a useful sophomore. They clapped it and sent some one back to thank them—a point of etiquette that some self-centred classes have been known to omit—and then they remembered that Ninety-green was supping at its first reunion in the Old Gym, and sent over some of the table flowers to them. Virginia motioned to Theo, and proud of the mission and blushing a little at the eyes that turned to her as she went, she took them over. They clapped and sang to her:

> Oh, *here's* to *Theodora*,
> And we're *very* glad we *sor* her !

Martha Sutton waved to her and the toast-mistress thanked her for the class, and she went back—alone, because, being an older class, Ninety-green didn't need a delegate. On the way, two juniors met her, and they condoled with her cheerfully : " How do you feel, Theo dear? Is n't it kind of dreadful? Do you keep thinking it 's the last time? Goodness—I should!" One of them threw a sympathetic arm over her shoulder and looked at the moon, but Theo grinned a little and said that she was tired as a dog and that if there was one place in the world she wanted it was her room At Home. And as the juniors gaped at this matter-of-fact attitude, Theodora added, pausing at the Gym door, "Of course I 've had a perfectly grand time here, and all that, but I 've been here four years and that 's about long enough, you know. And they want me, of course, and—I want to come! I think it gets a little—well, toward the end, you know—"

But Theo was tired, and so are seniors all, and until three or four generations of them have learned how to do it easily, so will they be.

They were doing stunts upstairs: Clara Sheldon had seen Cissie Loftus who had seen Maggie Cline who sang *Just tell them that you saw me*, and Clara, who was the most tailor-made and conventional creature imaginable to the outward eye, was forced by those from whose farther-reaching scrutiny she was never free, to imitate the imitator at all social functions that admitted song. She used stiff, ab-

surd gestures and a breathy contralto that
never palled upon her friends. Cynthia Lov-
ering danced her graceful little Spanish dance
for them, and Leslie Guerineau told them her
best darkey story in her own delicious South-
ern drawl. And then there was a murmur that
grew to a voice that swelled into a shout as
they drummed on the table and called, "*We*
want *Dutton! We* want *Dutton! We* want *Dutton, Dutton, Dutton!*"

She said no; that she'd had a toast; that
they knew all her stunts by heart—but they
hammered on her name with the regularity of
a machine till she got up at last with a sigh
and, "Well, what do you want?" They wanted
a temperance lecture, and she drooped her head
to one side, and with an ineffably sickly smile
and a flat nasal drawl she told them " haow
she'd been a-driving 'raound your *graounds*,
and they're *reel* pleasantly situated, *too*, dears,
and your *President*, such a nice, *gentlemanly* man,
accompanied me, and pointed aout to me your
beeyutiful homes and I said to him, 'Oh, what
a *beeyutiful* thought it is that all these *hundreds*
of young souls are a-drinking *water*, nothing
but *water*, all the time and every day!'"

She was going to teach in a stuffy little
school in the wilds of Maine, and Ethel Eaton,

who had been taught in that school, was going to travel abroad for a year—it was a strange shuffle.

What, was it half-past eleven? Impossible! But somebody had started up their great song that had been their pet one since freshman year, and they were shouting it till the Gym rang:

Hurrah! hurrah! the *yellow* is on *top,*
Hurrah! hurrah! the *purple* cannot *drop;*
We are Ninety-*yellow* and our *fame* shall never *stop,*
    'Rah, 'rah, *'rah,* for the *seniors!*

They sang all the verses, and then the watchman and the superintendent of buildings, waiting like sleuth-hounds to prevent any demonstration from without, gritted their teeth and dashed furiously down the wrong stairs as Ninety-green, who had softly assembled at the back of the Gym, having come from different directions, burst into the traditional tribute:

    Oh, *here's* to Ninety-*yellow,*
    And her *fame* we'll ever *tell—oh!*

"'Ere, 'ere! stop that now! Miss Sutton, it ain't allowed—will you please to go 'ome quietly! No, they ain't a-comin' h'out till you go—'e says they ain't!"

[340]

THE END OF IT

"Oh, come now! We are n't students any more! We can do what we like——"

"Oh, come on, girls! Don't make a fuss; we don't want to stay, anyhow!"

They sang themselves away, and the class upstairs looked around the tables and thought things, for it was time to go. And here I am afraid I shall lose whatever friends I may have gained for Theodora, for it is necessary to state that none of those comprehensive, solemn moments of farewell, known to us all to be the property of departing seniors, came to her. She was conscious of a little vague excitement, but all the last days had been more or less exciting—generally less—and her mind was occupied with irrelevant details. Had Uncle Ed remembered to change at Hartford? Had Aunt Kate packed her black evening dress? Would the post-office forward that note to the little freshman? Could she get Virginia up in time for the 9.15? Had she lost the slip with the Nicest Woman's address on it? And had she given Marietta that senior picture yet?

There had been one moment when her throat had contracted and her eyelids had crinkled: it was that very evening, when Annie, the cook, had beckoned to her in the hall of the Nicest House, and said: "There's three o' them little cakes on a plate on your table, Miss The'dora. I shan't be bakin' 'em agin, an' I know you do be terrible fond of 'em!"

"Thank you, Annie," she had said, and shaken her hand warmly. Annie had cooked fifteen years in the Nicest House, and what she and her mistress did n't know about girls you could put in a salt-spoon. It was n't every girl that Annie liked, either.

Grace was getting up, and they stood a moment irresolutely by the chairs.

"Let's make a ring, girls, and sing once 'round, and say good-by till next year," she said; and then there was a little quick shuffling, and the carefully divided sets got together and stood as they had stood for the last two or three years. Theo took tight hold of Virginia and Adelaide, and they moved slowly around the tables, a great circle of girls, so quiet for a moment that Ninety-green, singing one another home around the campus, sounded as loud and clear as their own voices a moment ago. They listened with a common impulse as the rollicking *Tommy Atkins* song paused awhile under the Washburn windows; they had been very fond of Ninety-green.

THE END OF IT

Ninety-*green* she is a *winner*,
Ninety-*green* she is a *star*,
Is there *anything agin* her?
No, we *do* not think there *are!*
There have *been* some other *classes*,
Other *seniors* have been *seen*,
But they *cannot* match the *lasses*
That are *wearing* of the *green!*

They smiled a little and remembered the great mass of green flags and ribbons that had waved to that song in last year's Rally. But they did not answer with one of their own; a little of the first faint conviction that the college owns all her classes, the feeling that grows with the years, came to them, and as the circle pressed closer and closer and their steps fell into an even tramp, Grace called out, "Now, girls, here's to old Smith College!" and they sent it out over the campus, so strong and loud that the decennial people and the groups of Ninety-green and the juniors and the belated sophomores lurking about heard them and joined in:

Oh, *here's* to old Smith *College*, drink her *down!*
Oh, *here's* to old Smith *College*, drink her *down!*
    Oh, *here's* to old Smith *College*,
    For it's *where* we get our *knowledge*,
Drink her *down*, drink her *down*, drink her *down*,
    down, *down!*